THE GALTON CASE

'The name is Lew Archer . . . By the time I finished this case I was lucky it wasn't permanently engraved on a stone . . .'

The simple search for a missing heir brought Archer into contact with some pretty unsavoury characters. Like the rich, nice old lady; the handsome, eager-to-please young man; the dim-witted bodyguard; the lawyer with a nervous tic; and the blonde who lived quietly in a bottle. And behind one of these masks of innocence there lurked a brilliant and unscrupulous killer.

ROSS MACDONALD

The Galton Case

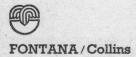

FONTANA / Collins

First published 1959
First issued in Fontana Books 1972
Second Impression July 1972
Third Impression May 1975

© John Ross Macdonald 1959

Made and printed in Great Britain by
William Collins Sons & Co Ltd Glasgow

For John E. Smith, bookman

CHAPTER ONE

The law offices of Wellesley and Sable were over a savings bank on the main street of Santa Teresa. Their private elevator lifted you from a bare little lobby into an atmosphere of elegant simplicity. It created the impression that after years of struggle you were rising effortlessly to your natural level, one of the chosen.

Facing the elevator, a woman with carefully dyed red hair was toying with the keyboard of an electric typewriter. A bowl full of floating begonias sat on the desk in front of her. Audubon prints picked up the colours and tossed them discreetly around the oak walls. A Harvard chair stood casually in one corner.

I sat down on it, in the interests of self-improvement, and picked up a fresh copy of the *Wall Street Journal*. Apparently this was the right thing to do. The red-headed secretary stopped typing and condescended to notice me.

'Do you wish to see anyone?'

'I have an appointment with Mr. Sable.'

'Would you be Mr. Archer?'

'Yes.'

She relaxed her formal manner: I wasn't one of the chosen after all. 'I'm Mrs. Haines. Mr. Sable didn't come into the office today, but he asked me to give you a message when you got here. Would you mind going out to his house?'

'I guess not.' I got up out of the Harvard chair. It was like being expelled.

'I realize it's a nuisance,' she said sympathetically. 'Do you know how to reach his place?'

'Is he still in his beach cottage?'

'No, he gave that up when he got married. They built a house in the country.'

'I didn't know he was married.'

'Mr. Sable's been married for nearly two years now. Very much so.'

The feline note in her voice made me wonder if she was married. Though she called herself Mrs. Haines, she had the air of a woman who had lost her husband to death or divorce and was looking for a successor. She leaned toward me in sudden intimacy:

'You're the detective, aren't you?'

I acknowledged that I was.

'Is Mr. Sable hiring you personally, on his own hook? I mean, the reason I asked, he didn't say anything to me about it.'

The reason for that was obvious. 'Me, either,' I said. 'How do I get to his house?'

'It's out in Arroyo Park. Maybe I better show you on the map.'

We had a brief session of map-reading. 'You turn off the highway just before you get to the wye,' she said, 'and then you turn right here at the Arroyo County Day School. You curve around the lake for about a half a mile, and you'll see the Sables' mailbox.'

I found the mailbox twenty minutes later. It stood under an oak tree at the foot of a private road. The road climbed a wooded hill and ended at a house with many windows set under the overhang of a flat green gravel roof.

The front door opened before I got to it. A man with streaked grey hair growing low on his forehead came across the lawn to meet me. He wore the white jacket of domestic service, but even with this protective coloration he didn't fit into the expensive suburb. He carried his heavy shoulders jauntily, as if he was taking his body for a well-deserved walk.

'Looking for somebody, mister?'

'Mr. Sable sent for me.'

'What for?'

'If he didn't tell you,' I said, 'the chances are that he doesn't want you to know.'

The houseman came up closer to me and smiled. His smile was wide and raw, like a dog's grin, and meaningless, except that it meant trouble. His face was seamed with the marks of the trouble-prone. He invited violence, as certain other people invite friendship.

Gordon Sable called from the doorway: 'It's all right, Peter. I'm expecting this chap.' He trotted down the flagstone path and gave me his hand. 'Good to see you, Lew. It's been several years, hasn't it?'

'Four.'

Sable didn't look any older. The contrast of his tanned face with his wavy white hair somehow supported an illusion of youth. He had on a Madras shirt cinched in by form-fitting English flannels which called attention to his tennis-player's waistline.

'I hear you got married,' I said.

'Yes. I took the plunge.' His happy expression seemed a little forced. He turned to the houseman, who was standing there listening: 'You'd better see if Mrs. Sable needs anything. And then come out to my study. Mr. Archer's had a long drive, and he'll be wanting a drink.'

'Yaas, massuh,' the houseman said broadly.

Sable pretended not to notice. He led me into the house, along a black-and-white terrazzo corridor, across an enclosed court crowded with tropical plants whose massed colours were broken up and reflected by an oval pool in the centre. Our destination was a sun-filled room remote from the rest of the house and further insulated by the hundreds of books lining its walls.

Sable offered me a leather chair facing the desk and the windows. He adjusted the drapes to shut off some of the light.

'Peter should be along in a minute. I'm afraid I must apologize for his manners, or lack of them. It's hard to get the right sort of help these days.'

'I have the same trouble. The squares want security, and the hipsters want a chance to push people around at fifty dollars a day. Neither of which I can give them. So I still do most of my own work.'

'I'm glad to hear that.' Sable sat on the edge of the desk and leaned toward me confidentially: 'The matter that I'm thinking of entrusting to you is a rather delicate one. It's essential, for reasons that will emerge, that there should be no publicity. Anything you find out, if you do find anything out, you report to me. Orally. I don't want anything in writing. Is that understood?'

'You make it very clear. Is this your personal business, or for a client?'

'For a client, of course. Didn't I say so on the telephone? She's saddled me with a rather difficult assignment. Frankly, I see very little chance of satisfying her hopes.'

'What does she hope for?'

Sable lifted his eyes to the bleached beams of the ceiling. 'The impossible, I'm afraid. When a man's dropped out of sight for over twenty years, we have to assume that he's dead and buried. Or, at the very least, that he doesn't want to be found.'

'This is a missing-persons case, then?'

'A rather hopeless one, as I've tried to tell my client. On the other hand, I can't refuse to make an attempt to carry out her wishes. She's old, and ill, and used to having her own way.'

'And rich?'

Sable frowned at my levity. He specialized in estate work, and moved in circles where money was seen but not heard.

'The lady's husband left her excellently provided for.' He added, to put me in my place: 'You'll be well paid for your work, no matter how it turns out.'

The houseman came in behind me. I knew he was there by the change in the lighting. He wore old yachting sneakers, and moved without sound.

'You took your time,' Sable said.

'Martinis take time to mix.'

'I didn't order Martinis.'

'The Mrs. did.'

'You shouldn't be serving her Martinis before lunch, or any other time.'

'Tell her that.'

'I intend to. At the moment I'm telling you.'

'Yaas, massuh.'

Sable reddened under his tan. 'That dialect bit isn't funny, you know.'

The houseman made no reply. His green eyes were bold and restless. He looked down at me, as if for applause.

'Quite a servant problem you have,' I said, by way of supporting Sable.

'Oh, Peter means well, don't you, old boy?' As if to fore-close an answer, he looked at me with a grin pasted on over his embarrassment. 'What will you drink, Lew? I'm going to have a tonic.'

'That will do for me.'

The houseman retreated.

'What about this disappearance?' I said.

'Perhaps disappearance isn't exactly the right word. My client's son walked out on his family deliberately. They made no attempt to follow him or bring him back, at least not for many years.'

'Why not?'

'I gather they were just as dissatisfied with him as he was with them. They disapproved of the girl he'd married. "Disapproved" is putting it mildly, and there were other bones of contention. You can see how serious the rift was from the fact that he sacrificed his right to inherit a large estate.'

'Does he have a name, or do we call him Mr. X?'

Sable looked pained. It hurt him physically to divulge information. 'The family's name is Galton. The son's name is, or was, Anthony Galton. He dropped out of sight in 1936. He was twenty-two at the time, just out of Stanford.'

'That's a long time ago.' From where I sat, it was like a previous century.

'I told you this thing was very nearly hopeless. However, Mrs. Galton wants her son looked for. She's going to die any day herself, and she feels the need for some sort of reconciliation with the past.'

'Who says she's going to die?'

'Her doctor. Dr. Howell says it could happen at any time.'

The houseman loped into the room with a clinking tray. He made a show of serviceability as he passed us our gin-and-tonics. I noticed the blue anchor tattoo on the back of his hand, and wondered if he was a sailor. Nobody would mistake him for a trained servant. A half-moon of old lipstick clung to the rim of the glass he handed me.

When he went away again, I said:

'Young Galton got married before he left?'

'Indeed he did. His wife was the immediate cause of the trouble in the family. She was going to have a child.'

'And all three of them dropped out of sight?'

'As if the earth had opened and swallowed them,' Sable said dramatically.

'Were there any indications of foul play?'

'Not so far as I know. I wasn't associated with the Galton family at the time. I'm going to ask Mrs. Galton herself to tell you about the circumstances of her son's departure. I don't know exactly how much of it she wants aired.'

'Is there more to it?'

'I believe so. Well, cheers,' he said cheerlessly. He gulped his drink standing. 'Before I take you to see her, I'd like some assurance that you can give us your full time for as long as necessary.'

'I have no commitments. How much of an effort does she want?'

'The best you can give, naturally.'

'You might do better with one of the big organizations.'

'I think not. I know you, and I trust you to handle this affair with some degree of urbanity. I can't have Mrs. Galton's last days darkened by scandal. My overriding concern in this affair is the protection of the family name.'

Sable's voice throbbed with emotion, but I doubted that it was related to any deep feeling he had for the Galton family. He kept looking past me or through me, anxiously, as if his real concerns lay somewhere else.

I got some hint of what they were when we were on our way out. A pretty blonde woman about half his age emerged from behind a banana tree in the court. She was wearing jeans and an open-necked white shirt. She moved with a kind of clumsy stealth, like somebody stepping out of ambush.

'Hello, Gordon,' she said in a brittle voice. 'Fancy meeting you here.'

'I live here, don't I?'

'That was supposed to be the theory.'

Sable spoke carefully to her, as if he was editing his sentences in his head: 'Alice, this is no time to go into all of it again. Why do you think I stayed home this morning?'

'A lot of good it did me. Where do you think you're going now?'

'Out.'

'Out where?'

'You have no right to cross-examine me, you know.'

'Oh yes I have a right.'

She stood squarely in front of him in a deliberately ugly posture, one hip out, her breasts thrust forward under the white shirt, and at the same time sharp and tender. She didn't seem to be drunk, but there was a hot moist glitter in her eyes. Her eyes were large and violet, and should have been beautiful. With dark circles under them, and heavy eyeshadow on the upper lids, they were like two spreading bruises.

'Where are you taking my husband?' she said to me.

'Mr. Sable is doing the taking. It's a business matter.'

'What sort of business, eh? Whose business?'

'Certainly not yours, dear.' Sable put his arm around her. 'Come to your room now. Mr. Archer is a private detective working on a case for me—nothing to do with you.'

'I bet not.' She jerked away from him, and swung back

to me. 'What do you want from me? There's nothing to find out. I sit in this morgue of a house, with nobody to talk to, nothing to do. I wish I was back in Chicago. People in Chicago *like* me.'

'People here like you, too.' Sable was watching her patiently, waiting for her bout of emotion to wear itself out.

'People here hate me. I can't even order drinks in my own house.'

'Not in the morning, and this is why.'

'You don't love me at all.' Her anger was dissolving into self-pity. A shift of internal pressure forced tears from her eyes. 'You don't care a thing about me.'

'I care very much. Which is why I hate to see you fling yourself around the landscape. Come on, dear, let's go in.'

He touched her waist, and this time she didn't resist. With one arm holding her, he escorted her around the pool to a door which opened on the court. When he closed the door behind them, she was leaning heavily on him.

I found my own way out.

CHAPTER TWO

Sable kept me waiting for half an hour. From where I sat in my car, I could see Santa Teresa laid out like a contour map, distinct in the noon light. It was an old and settled city, as such things go in California. Its buildings seemed to belong to its hills, to lean with some security on the past. In contrast with them, Sable's house was a living-machine, so new it hardly existed.

When he came out, he was wearing a brown suit with a wicked little red pin stripe in it, and carrying a cordovan dispatch case. His manner had changed to match his change in costume. He was businesslike, brisk, and remote.

Following his instructions and his black Imperial, I drove into the city and across it to an older residential section. Massive traditional houses stood far back from the street, behind high masonry walls or topiary hedges.

Arroyo Park was an economic battleground where managers and professional people matched wits and incomes. The people on Mrs. Galton's street didn't know there had been a war. Their grandfathers or great-grandfathers had won it for them; death and taxes were all they had to cope with.

Sable made a signal for a left turn. I followed him between stone gateposts in which the name Galton was cut. The majestic iron gates gave a portcullis effect. A serf who was cutting the lawn with a power-mower paused to tug at his forelock as we went by. The lawn was the colour of the ink they use to print the serial numbers on banknotes, and it stretched in unbroken smoothness for a couple of hundred yards. The white façade of a pre-Mizener Spanish mansion glared in the green distance.

The driveway curved around to the side of the house, and through a porte-cochere. I parked behind a Chevrolet coupé displaying a doctor's caduceus. Farther back, in the shade of a great oak, two girls in shorts were playing badminton. The bird flew back and forth between them in flashing repartee. When the dark-headed girl with her back to us missed, she said:

'Oh, damn it!'

'Temper,' Gordon Sable said.

She pivoted like a dancer. I saw that she wasn't a girl, but a woman with a girl's body. A slow blush spread over her face. She covered her discomfiture with an exaggerated pout which made the most of her girlishness:

'I'm off my form. Sheila *never* beats me.'

'I do so!' cried the girl on the other side of the net. 'I beat you three times in the last week. Today is the fourth time.'

'The set isn't over yet.'

'No, but I'm going to beat you.' Sheila's voice had an intensity which didn't seem to go with her appearance. She was very young, no more than eighteen. She had a peaches-and-cream complexion and soft doe eyes.

The woman scooped up the bird and tossed it over the net. They went on playing, all out, as if a great deal depended on the game.

A Negro maid in a white cap let us into a reception room. Wrought-iron chandeliers hung like giant black bunches of withered grapes from the high ceiling. Ancient black furniture stood in museum arrangements around the walls under old dark pictures. The windows were narrow and deep in the thick walls, like the windows of a medieval castle.

'Is Dr. Howell with her?' Sable asked the maid.

'Yes, sir, but he ought to be leaving any time now. He's been here for quite a while.'

'She didn't have an attack?'

'No, sir. It's just the doctor's regular visit.'

'Would you tell him I'd like to see him before he leaves?'

'Yes, sir.'

She whisked away. Sable said in a neutral tone, without looking at me: 'I won't apologize for my wife. You know how women are.'

'Uh-huh.' I didn't really want his confidences.

If I had, he wouldn't have given them to me. 'There are certain South American tribes that segregate women one week out of the month. Shut them up in a hut by themselves and let them rip. There's quite a lot to be said for the system.'

'I can see that.'

'Are you married, Archer?'

'I have been.'

'Then you know what it's like. They want you with them all the time. I've given up yachting. I've given up golf. I've practically given up living. And still she isn't satisfied. What do you do with a woman like that?'

I'd given up offering advice. Even when people asked for it, they resented getting it. 'You're the lawyer.'

I strolled around the room and looked at the pictures on the walls. They were mostly ancestor-worship art: portraits of Spanish dons, ladies in hoop skirts with bare monolithic bosoms, a Civil War officer in blue, and several gentlemen in nineteenth-century suits with sour nineteenth-century pusses between their whiskers. The one I liked best depicted a group of top-hatted tycoons watching a bulldog-faced tycoon hammer a gold spike into a railroad tie. There was a buffalo in the background, looking sullen.

The maid returned with a man in Harris tweeds. Sable introduced him as Dr. Howell. He was a big man in his fifties, who carried himself with unconscious authority.

'Mr. Archer is a private investigator,' Sable said. 'Did Mrs. Galton mention what she has in mind?'

'Indeed she did.' The doctor ran his fingers through his grey crewcut. The lines in his forehead deepened. 'I thought that whole business of Tony was finished and forgotten years ago. Who persuaded her to drag it back into the light?'

'Nobody did, so far as I know. It was her own idea. How is she, Doctor?'

'As well as can be expected. Maria is in her seventies. She

has a heart. She has asthma. It's an unpredictable combination.'

'But there's no immediate danger?'

'I wouldn't think so. I can't say what will happen if she's subjected to shock or distress. Asthma is one of those things.'

'Psychosomatic, you mean?'

'Somatopsychic, whatever you want to call it. In any case it's a disease that's affected by the emotions. Which is why I hate to see Maria getting all stirred up again about that wretched son of hers. What does she hope to gain?'

'Emotional satisfaction, I suppose. She feels she treated him badly, and wants to make up for it.'

'But isn't he dead? I thought he was found to be legally dead.'

'He could have been. We had an official search made some years ago. He's already been missing for fourteen years, which is twice the time required by the law to establish presumption of death. Mrs. Galton wouldn't let me make the petition, however. I think she's always dreamed of Anthony coming back to claim his inheritance and all that. In the last few weeks it's become an obsession with her.'

'I wouldn't go that far,' the doctor said. 'I still think somebody put a bee in her bonnet, and I can't help wondering why.'

'Who do you have in mind?'

'Cassie Hildreth, perhaps. She has a lot of influence on Maria. And speaking of dreams, she had a few of her own when she was a kid. She used to follow Tony around as if he was the light of the world. Which he was far from being, as you know.' Howell's smile was one-sided and saturnine.

'This is news to me. I'll talk to Miss Hildreth.'

'It's pure speculation on my part, don't misunderstand me. I do think this business should be played down as much as possible.'

'I've been trying to play it down. On the other hand I can't downright refuse to lift a finger.'

'No, but it would be all to the good if you could just keep it going along, without any definite results, until she gets interested in something different.' The doctor included me in his shrewd glance. 'You understand me?'

'I understand you all right,' I said. 'Go through the motions but don't do any real investigating. Isn't that pretty expensive therapy?'

'She can afford it, if that's what worries you. Maria has more coming in every month than she spends every year.' He regarded me in silence for a moment, stroking his prow of a nose. 'I don't mean you shouldn't do your job. I wouldn't ask any man to lie down on a job he's paid to do. But if you find out anything that might upset Mrs. Galton—'

Sable put in quickly: 'I've already taken that up with Archer. He'll report to me. I think you know you can rely on my discretion.'

'I think I know I can.'

Sable's face changed subtly. His eyelids flickered as though he had been threatened with a blow, and remained heavy over his watchful eyes. For a man of his age and financial weight, he was very easily hurt.

I said to the doctor: 'Did you know Anthony Galton?'

'Somewhat.'

'What kind of person was he?'

Howell glanced toward the maid, who was still waiting in the doorway. She caught his look and withdrew out of sight. Howell lowered his voice:

'Tony was a sport. I mean that in the biological sense, as well as the sociological. He didn't inherit the Galton characteristics. He had utter contempt for business of any kind. Tony used to say he wanted to be a writer, but I never saw any evidence of talent. What he was really good at was boozing and fornicating. I gather he ran with a very rough crowd in San Francisco. I've always believed myself that one of them killed him for the money in his pockets and threw him in the Bay.'

'Was there any indication of that sort of thing?'

'Not to my certain knowledge. But San Francisco in the thirties was a dangerous place for a boy to play around in. He must have dredged pretty deep to turn up the girl he married.'

'You knew her, did you?' Sable said.

'I examined her. His mother sent her to me, and I examined her.'

'Was she here in town?' I said.

'Briefly. Tony brought her home the week he married her. I don't believe he had any notion the family would accept her. It was more a case of flinging her in their faces. If that was his idea, it succeeded very well.'

'What was the matter with the girl?'

'The obvious thing, and it was obvious—she was seven months' pregnant.'

'And you say they'd just been married?'

'That's correct. She hooked him. I talked with her a little, and I'd wager he picked her up, hot off the streets. She was a pretty enough little thing, in spite of her big belly, but she'd had a hard life. There were scars on her thighs and buttocks. She wouldn't explain them to me, but it was evident that she'd been beaten, more than once.' The cruel memory raised faint traces of scarlet on the doctor's cheekbones.

The doe-eyed girl from the badminton court appeared in the doorway behind him. Her body was like ripening fruit, only partly concealed by her sleeveless jersey and rolled shorts. She glowed with healthy beauty, but her mouth was impatient:

'Daddy? How much longer?'

The colour on his cheekbones heightened when he saw her. 'Roll down your pants, Sheila.'

'They're not pants.'

'Whatever they are, roll them down.'

'Why should I?'

'Because I'm telling you to.'

'You could at least tell me in private. How much longer do I have to wait?'

'I thought you were going to read to your Aunt Maria.'

'Well, I'm not.'

'You promised.'

'You were the one who promised for me. I played badminton with Cassie, and that's my good turn for the day.'

She moved away, deliberately exaggerating the swing of her hips. Howell glared at the chronometer on his wrist, as if it was the source of all his troubles. 'I must be getting along. I have other calls to make.'

'Can you give me the wife's description?' I said. 'Or her name?'

'I don't recall her name. As for appearance, she was a little blue-eyed brunette, rather thin in spite of her condition. Mrs. Galton—no, on second thought I wouldn't ask her about the girl unless she brings the matter up herself.'

The doctor turned to go, but Sable detained him: 'Is it all right for Mr. Archer to question her? I mean, it won't affect her heart or bring on an asthmatic attack?'

'I can't guarantee it. If Maria insists on having an attack, there's nothing I can do to prevent it. Seriously, though, if Tony's on her mind she might as well talk about him. It's better than sitting and brooding. Good-bye, Mr. Archer, nice to meet you. Good day, Sable.'

CHAPTER THREE

The maid took Sable and me to a sitting-room on the second floor where Mrs. Galton was waiting. The room smelled of medicine, and had a hushed hospital atmosphere. The heavy drapes were partly drawn over the windows. Mrs. Galton was resting in semi-twilight on a chaise longue, with a robe over her knees.

She was fully dressed, with something white and frilly at her withered throat; and she held her grey head ramrod straight. Her voice was reedy, but surprisingly resonant. It seemed to carry all the remaining force of her personality:

'You've kept me waiting, Gordon. It's nearly time for my lunch. I expected you before Dr. Howell came.'

'I'm awfully sorry, Mrs. Galton. I was delayed at home.'

'Don't apologize. I detest apologies, they're really just further demands on one's patience.' She cocked a bright eye at him. 'Has that wife of yours been giving you trouble again?'

'Oh, no, nothing of that sort.'

'Good. You know my thoughts on the subject of divorce. On the other hand, you should have taken my advice and not married her. A man who waits until he's nearly fifty to get married should give up the idea entirely. Mr. Galton was in his late forties when we were married. As a direct consequence, I've had to endure nearly twenty years of widowhood.'

'It's been hard, I know,' Sable said with unction.

The maid had started out of the room. Mrs. Galton called her back: 'Wait a minute. I want you to tell Miss Hildreth to bring me my lunch herself. She can bring up a sandwich and eat it with me if she likes. You tell Miss Hildreth that.'

'Yes, Mrs. Galton.'

The old lady waved us into chairs, one on each side of her, and turned her eye on me. It was bright and alert but somehow inhuman, like a bird's eye. It looked at me as if I belonged to an entirely different species:

'Is this the man who is going to find my prodigal son for me?'

'Yes, this is Mr. Archer.'

'I'm going to give it a try,' I said, remembering the doctor's advice. 'I can't promise any definite results. Your son has been missing for a very long time.'

'I'm better aware of that than you, young man. I last set eyes on Anthony on the eleventh day of October 1936. We parted in bitter anger and hatred. I've lived ever since with that anger and hatred corroding my heart. But I can't die with it inside of me. I want to see Anthony again, and talk to him. I want to forgive him. I want him to forgive me.'

Deep feeling sounded in her voice. I had no doubt that the feeling was partly sincere. Still, there was something unreal about it. I suspected that she'd been playing tricks with her emotions for a long time, until none of them was quite valid.

'Forgive you?' I said.

'For treating him as I did. He was a young fool, and he made some disastrous mistakes, but none of them really justified Mr. Galton's action, and mine, in casting him off. It was a shameful action, and if it's not too late I intend to rectify it. If he still has his little wife, I'm willing to accept her. I authorize you to tell him that. I want to see my grandchild before I die.'

I looked at Sable. He shook his head slightly, deprecatingly. His client was just a little out of context, but she had quick insight, at least into other people:

'I know what you're both thinking. You're thinking that Anthony is dead. If he were dead, I'd know it here.' Her hand strayed over the flat silk surface of her breast. 'He's my only son. He must be alive, and he must be somewhere. Nothing is lost in the universe.'

Except human beings, I thought. 'I'll do my best, Mrs. Galton. There are one or two things you can do to help me. Give me a list of his friends at the time of his disappearance.'

'I never knew his friends.'

'He must have had friends in college. Wasn't he attending Stanford?'

'He'd left there the previous spring. He didn't even wait to graduate. Anyway, none of his schoolmates knew what happened to him. His father canvassed them thoroughly at the time.'

'Where was your son living after he left college?'

'In a flat in the slums of San Francisco. With that woman.'

'Do you have the address?'

'I believe I may have it somewhere. I'll have Miss Hildreth look for it.'

'That will be a start, anyway. When he left here with his wife, did they plan to go back to San Francisco?'

'I haven't any idea. I didn't see them before they left.'

'I understood they came to visit you.'

'Yes, but they didn't even stay the night.'

'What might help most,' I said carefully, 'would be if you could tell me the exact circumstances of their visit, and their departure. Anything your son said about his plans, anything the girl said, anything you remember about her. Do you remember her name?'

'He called her Teddy. I have no idea if that was her name or not. We had very little conversation. I can't recall what was said. The atmosphere was unpleasant, and it left a bad taste in my mouth. *She* left a bad taste in my mouth. It was so evident that she was a cheap little gold-digger.'

'How do you know?'

'I have eyes. I have ears.' Anger had begun to whine in the undertones of her voice. 'She was dressed and painted like a woman of the streets, and when she opened her mouth—well, she spoke the language of the streets. She made coarse jokes about the child in her womb, and how'—her voice faded almost out—'it got there. She had no respect for herself as a woman, no moral standards. That girl destroyed my son.'

She'd forgotten all about her hope of reconciliation. The wheezing in the passages of her head sounded like a ghost in a ruined house. Sable was looking at her anxiously, but he held his tongue.

'Destroyed him?' I said.

'Morally, she destroyed him. She possessed him like an evil spirit. My son would never have taken the money if it hadn't been for the spell she cast on him. I know that with utter certitude.'

Sable leaned forward in his chair. 'What money are you referring to?'

'The money Anthony stole from his father. Haven't I told you about it, Gordon? No, I don't believe I have. I've told no one, I've always been so ashamed.' She lifted her hands and dropped them in her robed lap. 'But now I can forgive him for that, too.'

19

'How much money was involved?' I said.

'I don't know exactly how much, to the penny. Several thousand dollars, anyway. Ever since the day the banks closed, Mr. Galton had had a habit of keeping a certain amount of cash for current expenses.'

'Where did he keep it?'

'In his private safe, in the study. The combination was on a piece of paper pasted to the inside of his desk drawer. Anthony must have found it there, and used it to open the safe. He took everything in it, all the money, and even some of my jewels which I kept there.'

'Are you sure he took it?'

'Unfortunately, yes. It disappeared at the same time he did. It's why he hid himself away, and never came back to us.'

Sable's glum look deepened. Probably he was thinking the same thing I was: that several thousand dollars in cash, in the slums of San Francisco, in the depths of the depression, were a very likely passport to oblivion.

But we couldn't say it out loud. With her money, and her asthma, and her heart, Mrs. Galton was living at several removes from reality. Apparently that was how it had to be.

'Do you have a picture of your son, taken not too long before his disappearance?'

'I believe I have. I'll ask Cassie to have a look. She should be coming soon.'

'In the meantime, can you give me any other information? Particularly about where your son might have gone, who or where he might have visited.'

'I know nothing of his life after he left the university. He cut himself off from all decent society. He was perversely bound to sink in the social scale, to declass himself. I'm afraid my son had a *nostalgie de la boue*—a nostalgia for the gutter. He tried to cover it over with fancy talk about re-establishing contact with the earth, becoming a poet of the people, and such nonsense. His real interest was dirt for dirt's own sake. I brought him up to be pure in thought and desire, but somehow—somehow he became fascinated with the pitch that defileth. And the pitch defiled him.'

Her breathing was noisy. She had begun to shake, and scratch with waxy fingers at the robe that covered her knees.

Sable leaned towards her solicitously. 'You mustn't excite yourself, Mrs. Galton. It was all over long ago.'

'It's not all over. I want Anthony back. I have nobody. I

have nothing. He was stolen away from me.'

'We'll get him back if it's humanly possible.'

'Yes, I know you will, Gordon.' Her mood had changed like a fitful wind. Her head inclined toward Sable's shoulder as though to rest against it. She spoke like a little girl betrayed by time and loss, by fading hair and wrinkles and the fear of death: 'I'm a foolish angry old woman. You're always so good to me. Anthony will be good to me, too, won't he, when he comes? In spite of all I've said against him, he was a darling boy. He was always good to his poor mother, and he will be again.'

She was chanting in a ritual of hope. If she said it often enough, it would have to come true.

'I'm sure he will, Mrs. Galton.'

Sable rose and pressed her hand. I was always a little suspicious of men who put themselves out too much for rich old ladies, or even poor ones. But then it was part of his job.

'I'm hungry,' she said. 'I want my lunch. What's going on downstairs?'

She lunged half out of her long chair and got hold of a wired bellpush on the table beside it. She kept her finger pressed on the button until her lunch arrived. That was a tense five minutes.

CHAPTER FOUR

It came on a covered platter carried by the woman I'd seen on the badminton court. She had changed her shorts for a plain linen dress which managed to conceal her figure, if not her fine brown legs. Her blue eyes were watchful.

'You kept me waiting, Cassie,' the old woman said. 'What on earth were you doing?'

'Preparing your food. Before that I played some badminton with Sheila Howell.'

'I might have known you two would be enjoying yourselves while I sit up here starving.'

'Oh come, it's not as bad as all that.'

'It's not for you to say. You're not my doctor. Ask August Howell, and he'll tell you how important it is that I have my nourishment.'

'I'm sorry, Aunt Maria. I thought you wouldn't want to be disturbed while you were in conference.'

She stood just inside the doorway, still holding the tray like a shield in front of her. She wasn't young: close up, I could see the fortyish lines in her face and the knowledge in her blue eyes. But she held herself with adolescent awkwardness, immobilized by feelings she couldn't express.

'Well, you needn't stand there like a dummy.'

Cassie moved suddenly. She set the tray on the table and uncovered the food. There was a good deal of food. Mrs. Galton began to fork salad into her mouth. The movements of her hands and jaws were rapid and mechanical. She was oblivious to the three of us watching her.

Sable and I retreated into the hallway and along it to the head of the stairs which curved in a baronial sweep down to the entrance hall. He leaned on the iron balustrade and lit a cigarette.

'Well, Lew, what do you think?'

I lit a cigarette of my own before I replied. 'I think it's a waste of time and money.'

'I told you that.'

'But you want me to go ahead with it anyway?'

'I can't see any other way to handle it, or handle her. Mrs. Galton takes a good deal of handling.'

'Can you trust her memory? She seems to be reliving the past. Sometimes old people get mixed up about what actually happened. That story about the money he stole, for example. Do you believe it?'

'I've never known her to lie. And I really doubt that she's as confused as she sounds. She likes to dramatize herself. It's the only excitement she has left.'

'How old is she?'

'Seventy-three, I believe.'

'That isn't so old. What about her son?'

'He'll be about forty-four, if he's still extant.'

'She doesn't seem to realize that. She talks about him as if he was still a boy. How long has she been sitting in that room?'

'Ever since I've known her, anyway. Ten years. Occasionally, when she has a good day, she lets Miss Hildreth take her for a drive. It doesn't do much to bring her up to date, though. It's usually just a quick trip to the cemetery where her husband is buried. He died soon after Anthony took off. According to Mrs. Galton, that was what killed him. Miss Hildreth says he died of a coronary.'

'Is Miss Hildreth a relative?'

'A distant one, second or third cousin. Cassie's known the family all her life, and lived with Mrs. Galton since before the war. I'm hoping she can give you something more definite to go on.'

'I can use it.'

A telephone shrilled somewhere, like a cricket in the wall. Cassie Hildreth came out of Mrs. Galton's room and moved briskly toward us:

'You're wanted on the telephone. It's Mrs. Sable.'

'What does she want?'

'She didn't say, but she seems upset about something.'

'She always is.'

'You can take it downstairs if you like. There's an extension under the stairs.'

'I know. I'll do that.' Sable treated her brusquely, like a servant. 'This is Mr. Archer, by the way. He wants to ask you some questions.'

'Right now?'

'If you can spare the time,' I said. 'Mrs. Galton thought you could give me some pictures, perhaps some information.'

'Pictures of Tony?'

'If you have them.'

'I keep them for Mrs. Galton. She likes to look at them when the mood is on her.'

'You work for her, do you?'

'If you can call it work. I'm a paid companion.'

'I call it work.'

Our eyes met. Hers were dark ocean blue. Discontent flicked a fin in their depths, but she said dutifully: 'She isn't so bad. She's not at her best today. It's hard on her to rake up the past like this.'

'Why is she doing it?'

'She had a serious scare not long ago. Her heart almost failed. They had to put her in an oxygen tent. She wants to make amends to Tony before she dies. She treated him badly, you know.'

'Badly in what way?'

'She didn't want him to live his own life, as they say. She tried to keep him all to herself, like a—a belonging. But you'd better not get me started on that.'

Cassie Hildreth bit her lip. I recalled what the doctor had

said about her feeling for Tony. The whole household seemed to revolve around the missing man, as if he'd left only the day before.

Quick footsteps crossed the hallway below the stairs. I leaned over the balustrade and saw Sable wrench the front door open. It slammed behind him.

'Where's he off to?'

'Probably home. That wife of his—' She hesitated, editing the end of the sentence: 'She lives on emergencies. If you'd like to see those pictures, they're in my room.'

Her door was next to Mrs. Galton's sitting-room. She unlocked it with a Yale key. Apart from its size and shape, its lofty ceiling, the room bore no relation to the rest of the house. The furniture was modern. There were Paul Klee reproductions on the walls, new novels on the bookshelves. The ugly windows were masked with monks-cloth drapes. A narrow bed stood behind a woven wood screen in one corner.

Cassie Hildreth went in to the closet and emerged with a sheaf of photographs in her hand.

'Show me the best likeness first.'

She shuffled through them, her face intent and peaked, and handed me a posed studio portrait. Anthony Galton had been a handsome boy. I stood and let his features sink into my mind: light eyes set wide apart and arched over by intelligent brows, short straight nose, small mouth with rather full lips, a round girlish chin. The missing feature was character or personality, the meaning that should have held the features together. The only trace of this was in the one-sided smile. It seemed to say: to hell with you. Or maybe, to hell with me.

'This was his graduation picture,' Cassie Hildreth said softly.

'I thought he never graduated from college.'

'He didn't. This was made before he dropped out.'

'Why didn't he graduate?'

'He wouldn't give his father the satisfaction. Or his mother. They forced him to study mechanical engineering, which was the last thing Tony was interested in. He stuck it out for four years, but he finally refused to take his degree in it.'

'Did he flunk out?'

'Heavens, no. Tony was very bright. Some of his professors thought he was brilliant.'

'But not in engineering?'

'There wasn't anything he couldn't do, if he wanted to. His

real interests were literary. He wanted to be a writer.'

'I take it you knew him well.'

'Of course. I wasn't living with the Galtons then, but I used to visit her, often, when Tony was on vacation. He used to talk to me. He was a wonderful conversationalist.'

'Describe him, will you?'

'But you've just seen his picture. And here are others.'

'I'll look at them in a minute. Right now I want you to tell me about him.'

'If you insist, I'll try.' She closed her eyes. Her face smoothed out, as if years were being erased: 'He was a lovely man. His body was finely proportioned, lean and strong. His head was beautifully balanced on his neck, and he had close fair curls.' She opened her eyes. 'Did you ever see the Praxiteles Hermes?'

I felt a little embarrassed, not only because I hadn't. Her description of Tony had the force of a passionate avowal. I hadn't expected anything like it. Cassie's emotion was like spontaneous combustion in an old hope chest.

'No,' I said. 'What colour were his eyes?'

'Grey. A lovely soft grey. He had the eyes of a poet.'

'I see. Were you in love with him?'

She gave me a startled look. 'Surely you don't expect me to answer that.'

'You just did. You say he used to talk to you. Did he ever discuss his plans for the future?'

'Just in general terms. He wanted to go away and write.'

'Go away where?'

'Somewhere quiet and peaceful, I suppose.'

'Out of the country?'

'I doubt it. Tony disapproved of expatriates. He always said he wanted to get *closer* to America. This was in the depression, remember. He was very strong for the rights of the working class.'

'Radical?'

'I guess you'd call him that. But he wasn't a Communist, if that's what you mean. He did feel that having money cut him off from life. Tony hated social snobbery—which was one reason he was so unhappy at college. He often said he wanted to live like ordinary people, lose himself in the mass.'

'It looks as if he succeeded in doing just that. Did he ever talk to you about his wife?'

'Never. I didn't even know he was married, or intended to

get married.' She was very self-conscious. Not knowing what to do with her face, she tried to smile. The teeth between her parted lips were like white bone showing in a wound.

As if to divert my attention from her, she thrust the other pictures into my hands. Most of them were candid shots of Tony Galton doing various things: riding a horse, sitting on a rock in swimming trunks, holding a tennis racket with a winner's fixed grin on his face. From the pictures, and from what the people said, I got the impression of a boy going through the motions. He made the gestures of enjoyment but kept himself hidden, even from the camera. I began to have some glimmering of the psychology that made him want to lose himself.

'What did he like doing?'

'Writing. Reading and writing.'

'Besides that. Tennis? Swimming?'

'Not really. Tony despised sports. He used to jeer at me for going in for them.'

'What about wine and women? Dr. Howell said he was quite a playboy.'

'Dr. Howell never understood him,' she said. 'Tony did have relations with women, and I suppose he drank, but he did it on principle.'

'Is that what he told you?'

'Yes, and it's true. He was practising Rimbaud's theory of the violation of the senses. He thought that having all sorts of remarkable experiences would make him a good poet, like Rimbaud.' She saw my uncomprehending look, and added: 'Arthur Rimbaud was a French poet. He and Charles Baudelaire were Tony's great idols.'

'I see.' We were getting off the track into territory where I felt lost. 'Did you ever meet any of his women?'

'Oh, no.' She seemed shocked at the idea. 'He never brought any of them here.'

'He brought his wife home.'

'Yes, I know. I was away at school when it happened.'

'When what happened?'

'The big explosion,' she said. 'Mr Galton told him never to darken his door again. It was all very Victorian and heavy-father. And Tony never did darken his door again.'

'Let's see, that was in October 1936. Did you ever see Tony after that?'

'Never. I was at school in the east.'

'Ever hear from him?'

Her mouth started to shape the word 'no,' then tightened. 'I had a little note from him, some time in the course of the winter. It must have been before Christmas, because I got it at school, and I didn't go back after Christmas. I think it was in the early part of December that it came.'

'What did it say?'

'Nothing very definite. Simply that he was doing well, and had broken into print. He'd had a poem accepted by a little magazine in San Francisco. He sent it to me under separate cover. I've kept it, if you'd like to look at it.'

She kept it in a manila envelope on the top shelf of her bookcase. The magazine was a thin little publication smudgily printed on pulp paper; its name was *Chisel*. She opened it to a middle page, and handed it to me. I read:

'*LUNA*, by John Brown

'White her breast
As the white foam
Where the gulls rest
Yet find no home.

'Green her eyes
As the green deep
Where the tides rise
And the storms sleep.

'And fearful am I
As a mariner
When the sea and the sky
Begin to stir.

'For wild is her heart
As the sea's leaping:
She will rise and depart
While I lie sleeping.'

'Did Tony Galton write this? It's signed "John Brown." '

'It was the name he used. Tony wouldn't use the family name. "John Brown" had a special meaning for him, besides. He had a theory that the country was going through another civil war—a war between the rich people and the poor people.

He thought of the poor people as white Negroes, and he wanted to do for them what John Brown did for the slaves. Lead them out of bondage—in the spiritual sense, of course. Tony didn't believe in violence.'

'I see,' I said, though it all sounded strange to me. 'Where did he send this from?'

'The magazine was published in San Francisco, and Tony sent it from there.'

'This was the only time you ever heard from him?'

'The only time.'

'May I keep these pictures, and the magazine? I'll try to bring them back.'

'If they'll help you to find Tony.'

'I understand he went to live in San Francisco. Do you have his last address?'

'I had it, but there's no use going there.'

'Why not?'

'Because I did, the year after he went away. It was a wretched old tenement, and it had been condemned. They were tearing it down.'

'Did you make any further attempt to find him?'

'I wanted to, but I was afraid. I was only seventeen.'

'Why didn't you go back to school, Cassie?'

'I didn't especially want to. Mr. Galton wasn't well, and Aunt Maria asked me to stay with her. She was the one sending me to school, so that I couldn't very well refuse.'

'And you've been here ever since?'

'Yes.' The word came out with pressure behind it.

As if on cue, Mrs. Galton raised her voice on the other side of the wall: 'Cassie! Cassie? Are you in there? What are you doing in there?'

'I'd better go,' Cassie said.

She locked the door of her sanctuary, and went, with her head down.

After twenty-odd years of that, I'd have been crawling.

CHAPTER FIVE

I met the doctor's daughter on the stairs. She gave me a tentative smile. 'Are you the detective?'

'I'm the detective. My name is Archer.'

'Mine's Sheila Howell. Do you think you can find him for her?'

'I can try, Miss Howell.'

'That doesn't sound too hopeful.'

'It wasn't meant to.'

'But you will do your best, won't you?'

'Is it important to you? You're too young to have known Anthony Galton.'

'It's important to Aunt Maria.' She added in a rush of feeling: 'She needs somebody to love her. I try, honestly, but I just can't do it.'

'Is she a relative of yours?'

'Not exactly. She's my godmother. I call her aunt because she likes me to. But I've never succeeded in feeling like a niece to her.'

'I imagine she makes it hard.'

'She doesn't mean to, but she simply doesn't know how to treat *people*. She's had her own way for so long.' The girl coloured, and compressed her lips. 'I don't mean to be *critical*. You must think I'm an awful person, talking about her to a stranger like this. I really do wish her well, in spite of what Dad thinks. And if she wants me to read *Pendennis* to her, I will.'

'Good for you. I was on my way to make a phone call. Is there a telephone handy?'

She showed me the telephone under the stairs. It was an ancient wall telephone which nobody had ever bothered to change for a modern one. The Santa Teresa directory lay on a table under it. I looked up Sable's number.

He was a long time answering. Finally, I heard the receiver being lifted at the other end of the line. After another wait, I heard his voice. I hardly recognized it. It had a blurred quality, almost as if Sable had been crying:

'This is Gordon Sable.'

'Archer speaking. You took off before we could make defin-ite arrangements. On a case like this I need an advance, and expense money, at least three hundred.'

There was a click, and then a whirring on the wire. Some-one was dialling. A woman's voice said: 'Operator! I want the police.'

'Get off the line,' Sable said.

'I'm calling the police.' It was his wife's voice, shrill with hysteria.

'I've already called them. Now get off the line. It's in use.'

A receiver was fumbled into place. I said: 'You still there, Sable?'

'Yes. There's been an accident, as you must have gathered.' He paused. I could hear his breathing.

'To Mrs. Sable?'

'No, though she's badly upset. My houseman, Peter, has been stabbed. I'm afraid he's dead.'

'Who stabbed him?'

'It isn't clear. I can't get much out of my wife. Apparently some goon came to the door. When Peter opened it, he was knifed.'

'You want me to come out?'

'If you think it will do any good. Peter is past help.'

'I'll be there in a few minutes.'

But it took me longer than that. The Arroyo Park suburb was new to me. I took a wrong turning and got lost in its system of winding roads. The roads all looked alike, with flat-roofed houses, white and grey and adobe, scattered along the terraced hillsides.

I went around in circles for a while, and came out on top of the wrong hill. The road dwindled into a pair of ruts in a field where nothing stood but a water tower. I turned, and stopped to get my bearings.

On a hilltop a mile or more to my left, I could make out a flat pale green roof which looked like the Arizona gravel roof of Sable's house. On my right, far below, a narrow asphalt road ran like a dark stream along the floor of the valley. Be-tween the road and a clump of scrub oaks an orange rag of flame came and went. Black smoke trickled up from it into the still blue air. When I moved I caught a flash of sunlight on metal. It was a car, nose down in the ditch, and burning.

I drove down the long grade and turned right along the

asphalt road. A fire siren was ululating in the distance. The smoke above the burning car was twisting higher and spreading like a slow stain over the trees. Watching it, I almost ran down a man.

He was walking toward me with his head bent, as if in meditation, a thick young man with shoulders like a bull. I honked at him and applied the brakes. He came on doggedly. One of his arms swung slack, dripping red from the fingers. The other arm was cradled in the front of his sharp flannel jacket.

He came up to the door on my side and leaned against it. 'Can you gimme a lift?' Oily black curls tumbled over his hot black eyes. The bright blood on his mouth gave him an obscene look, like a painted girl.

'Smash up your car?'

He grunted.

'Come around to the other side if you can make it.'

'Negative. This side.'

I caught the glint of larceny in his eyes, and something worse. I reached for my car keys. He was ahead of me. The short blue gun in his right hand peered at the corner of the open window:

'Leave the keys where they are. Open the door and get out.'

Curlyhead talked and acted like a pro, or at least a gifted amateur with a vocation. I opened the door and got out.

He waved me away from the car. 'Start walking.'

I hesitated, weighing my chances of taking him.

He used his gun to a point toward the city. 'Get going, Bud. You don't want a calldown with me.'

I started walking. The engine of my car roared behind me. I got off the road. But Curlyhead turned in a driveway, and drove off in the other direction, away from the sirens.

The fire was out when I got to it. The county firemen were coiling their hose, replacing it on the side of the long red truck. I went up to the cab and asked the man at the wheel:

'Do you have two-way radio?'

'What's it to you?'

'My car was stolen. I think the character who took it was driving the one in the ditch there. The Highway Patrol should be notified.'

'Give me the details, I'll shoot them in.'

I gave him the licence number and description of my car,

and a thumbnail sketch of Curlyhead. He started feeding them into his mike. I climbed down the bank to look at the car I'd traded mine in on. It was a black Jaguar sedan, about five years old. It had slewed off the road, gouging deep tracks in the dirt, and crumpled its nose against a boulder. One of the front tyres had blown out. The windshield was starred, and the finish blistered by fire. Both doors were sprung.

I made a note of the licence number, and moved up closer to look at the steering-post. The registration was missing. I got in and opened the dash compartment. It was clean.

In the road above, another car shrieked to a halt. Two sheriff's men got out on opposite sides and came down the bank in a double cloud of dust. They had guns in their hands, no-nonsense looks on their brown faces.

'This your car?' the first one snapped at me.

'No.'

I started to tell him what had happened to mine, but he didn't want to hear about it:

'Out of there! Keep your hands in sight, shoulder-high.'

I got out, feeling that all this had happened before. The first deputy held his gun on me while the second deputy shook me down. He was very thorough. He even investigated the fuzz in my pockets. I commented on this.

'This is no joke. What's your name?'

The firemen had begun to gather around us. I was angry and sweating. I opened my mouth and put both feet in, all the way up to the knee.

'I'm Captain Nemo,' I said. 'I just came ashore from a hostile submarine. Curiously enough, we fuel our subs with seaweed. The hull itself is formed from highly compressed sea-weed. So take me to your wisest man. There is no time to be lost.'

'He's a hophead,' the first deputy said. 'I kind of figured the slasher was a hophead. You heard me say so, Barney.'

'Yeah.' Barney was reading the contents of my wallet. 'He's got a driver's licence made out to somebody name of Archer, West Hollywood. And a statewide private-eye ducat, same name. But it's probably a phony.'

'It's no phony.' Vaudeville had got me nowhere except into deeper trouble. 'My name is Archer. I'm a private investigator, employed by Mr. Sable, the lawyer.'

'Sable, he says.' The deputies exchanged significant looks. 'Give him his wallet, Barney.'

Barney held it out to me. I reached for it. The cuffs clinked snug on my wrist.

'Other wrist now,' he said in a soothing voice. I was a hop-head. 'Let's have the other wrist now.'

I hesitated. But rough stuff not only wouldn't work. It would put me in the wrong. I wanted them to be in the wrong, falling on their faces with foolishness.

I surrendered the other wrist without a struggle. Looking down at my trapped hands, I saw the dab of blood on one of my fingers.

'Let's go,' the first deputy said. He dropped my wallet in the side pocket of my jacket.

They herded me up the bank and into the back of their car. The driver of the fire truck leaned from his cab:

'Keep a close eye on him, fellows. He's a cool customer. He gave me a story about his car getting stolen, took me in completely.'

'Not us,' the first deputy said. 'We're trained to spot these phonies, the way you're trained to put out fires. Don't let anybody else near the Jag. Leave a guard on it, eh? I'll send a man as soon as we can spare one.'

'What did he do?'

'Knifed a man.'

'Jesus, and I thought he was a citizen.'

The first deputy climbed into the back seat beside me. 'I got to warn you anything you say can be used against you. Why did you do it?'

'Do what?'

'Cut Peter Culligan.'

'I didn't cut him.'

'You got blood on your hand. Where did it come from?'

'Probably the Jaguar.'

'Your car, you mean?'

'It isn't my car.'

'The hell it isn't. I got a witness saw you drive away from the scene of the crime.'

'I wasn't in it. The man who was in it just stole my car.'

'Don't give me that. You can fool a fireman with it. I'm a cop.'

'Was it woman trouble?' Barney said over his shoulder. 'If it was a woman, we can understand it. Crime of passion, and all. Shucks,' he added lightly, 'it wouldn't even be second-degree, probably. You could be out in two-three years.

Couldn't he, Conger?'

'Sure,' Conger said. 'You might as well tell us the truth now, get it over with.'

I was getting bored with the game. 'It wasn't a woman. It was seaweed. I'm a seaweed-fancier from way back. I like to sprinkle a little of it on my food.'

'What's that got to do with Culligan?'

Barney said from the front seat: 'He sounds to me like he's all hopped up.'

Conger leaned across me. 'Are you?'

'Am I what?'

'All hopped up?'

'Yeah. I chew seaweed, then I orbit. Take me to the nearest launching pad.'

Conger looked at me pityingly. I was a hophead. The pity was gradually displaced by doubt. He had begun to grasp that he was being ragged. Very suddenly, his face turned dusky red under the tan. He balled his right fist on his knee. I could see the packed muscles tighten under the shoulder of his blouse. I pulled in my chin and got ready to roll with the punch. But he didn't hit me.

Under the circumstances, this made him a good cop. I almost began to like him, in spite of the handcuffs. I said:

'As I told you before, my name is Archer. I'm a licensed private detective, retired sergeant from the Long Beach P.D. The California Penal Code has a section on false arrest. Do you think you better take the jewellery off?'

Barney said from the front seat: 'A poolroom lawyer, eh?'

Conger didn't say anything. He sat in pained silence for what seemed a long time. The effort of thought did unexpected things to his heavy face. It seemed to alarm him, like a loud noise in the night.

The car left the country road and climbed Sable's hill. A second sheriff's car stood in front of the glass house. Sable climbed out, followed by a heavy-set man in mufti.

Sable looked pale and shaken. 'You took your time about getting here.' Then he saw the handcuffs on my wrists. 'For heaven's sake!'

The heavy-set man stepped past him, and yanked the car door open. 'What's the trouble here?'

Conger's confusion deepened. 'No trouble, Sheriff. We picked up a suspect, claims he's a private cop working for Mr. Sable.'

The Sheriff turned to Sable. 'This your man?'

'Of course.'

Conger was already removing the handcuffs, unobtrusively, as if perhaps I wouldn't notice they'd ever been on my wrists. The back of Barney's neck reddened. He didn't turn around, even when I stepped out of the car.

The Sheriff gave me his hand. He had a calm and weathered face in which quick bright eyes moved with restless energy. 'I'm Trask. I won't apologize. We all make mistakes. Some of us more than others, eh, Conger?'

Conger didn't reply. I said: 'Now that we've had our fun, maybe you'd like to get on the radio with the description of my car and the man that took it.'

'What man are we talking about?' Trask said.

I told him, and added: 'If you don't mind my saying so, Sheriff, it might be a good idea for you to check with the Highway Patrol yourself. Our friend took off in the direction of San Francisco, but he may have circled back.'

'I'll put out the word.'

Trask started toward his radio car. I held him for a minute: 'One other thing. That Jaguar ought to be checked by an expert. It may be just another stolen car—'

'Yeah, let's hope it isn't.'

CHAPTER SIX

The dead man was lying where he had fallen, on a patch of blood-filmed grass, about ten feet from Sable's front door. The lower part of his white jacket was red-stained. His up-turned face was grey and impervious-looking, like the stone faces on tombs.

A Sheriff's identification man was taking pictures of him with a tripod camera. He was a white-haired officer with a long inquisitive nose. I waited until he moved his camera to get another angle:

'Mind if I have a look at him?'

'Long as you don't touch him. I'll be through here in a minute.'

When he had finished his work, I leaned over the body for a closer look. There was a single deep wound in the abdomen.

The right hand had cuts across the palm and inside the curled fingers. The knife that had done the damage, a bloody five-inch switch-blade, lay on the grass in the angle between the torso and the outstretched right arm.

I took hold of the hand: it was still warm and limp: and turned it over. The skin on the tattooed knuckles was torn, probably by teeth.

'He put up quite a struggle,' I said.

The identification officer hunkered down beside me. 'Yeah. Be careful with those fingernails. There's some kind of debris under 'em, might be human skin. You notice the tattoo marks?'

'I'd have to be blind to miss them.'

'I mean these.' He took the hand away from me, and pointed out four dots arranged in a tiny rectangle between the first and second fingers. 'Gang mark. He had it covered up later with a standard tattoo. A lot of old gang members do that. I see them on people we vag.'

'What kind of gang?'

'I don't know. This is a Sac or Frisco gang. I'm no expert on the northern California insignia. I wonder if Lawyer Sable knew he had an old gang member working for him.'

'We could ask him.'

The front door was standing open. I walked in and found Sable in the front sitting-room. He raised a limp arm, and waved me into a chair:

'Sit down, Archer. I'm sorry about what happened. I can't imagine what they thought they were pulling.'

'Eager-beavering. Forget it. We got off to a poor start, but the local boys seem to know what they're doing.'

'I hope so,' he said, not very hopefully.

'What do you know about your late houseman?'

'Not a great deal, I'm afraid. He only worked for me for a few months. I hired him originally to look after my yacht. He lived aboard the yacht until I sold it. Then he moved up here. He had no place to go, and he didn't ask for much. Peter wasn't very competent indoors, as you may have noticed. But it's hard for us to get help out in the country, and he was an obliging soul, so I let him stay on.'

'What sort of a background did he have?'

'I gathered he was pretty much of a floater. He mentioned various jobs he'd held: marine cook, longshoreman, house-painter.'

'How did you hire him? Through an employment agency?'

'No. I picked him up on the dock. I think he'd just come off a fishing-boat, a Monterey seiner. I was polishing brass, varnishing deck, and so on, and he offered to help me for a dollar an hour. He did a good day's work, so I took him on. He never failed to do a good day's work.'

A cleft of pain, like a knife-cut, had appeared between Sable's eyebrows. I guessed that he had been fond of the dead man. I hesitated to ask my next question:

'Would you know if Culligan had a criminal record?'

The cleft in his brow deepened. 'Good Lord, no. I trusted him with my boat and my house. What makes you ask such a question?'

'Two things mainly. He had a tattoo mark on his hand, four little black dots at the edge of the blue tattoo. Gangsters and drug addicts wear that kind of mark. Also, this has the look of a gang killing. The man who took my car is almost certainly the killer, and he has the earmarks of a pro.'

Sable looked down at the polished terrazzo as if at any moment it might break up under his feet. 'You think Peter Culligan was involved with criminals?'

'Involved is putting it mildly. He's dead.'

'I realize that,' he said rather shrilly.

'Did he seem nervous lately? Afraid of anything?'

'If he was, I never noticed. He didn't talk about himself.'

'Did he have any visitors, before this last one?'

'Never. At least, not to my knowledge. He was a solitary person.'

'Could he have been using your place and his job here as a sort of hide-out?'

'I don't know. It's hard to say.'

An engine started up in front of the house. Sable rose and moved to the glass wall, parting the drapes. I looked out over his shoulder. A black panel truck rolled away from the house and started down the hill.

'Come to think of it,' Sable said, 'he certainly kept out of sight. He wouldn't chauffeur for me, said he'd had bad luck with cars. But he may have wanted to avoid going to town. He never went to town.'

'He's on his way there now,' I said. 'How many people knew he was out here?'

'Just my wife and I. And you, of course. I can't think off-hand of anyone else.'

'Have you had visitors from out of town?'

'Not in the last few months. Alice has been having her ups and downs. It's one reason I took Peter on out here. We'd lost our housekeeper, and I didn't like to leave Alice by herself all day.'

'How is Mrs. Sable now?'

'Not so good, I'm afraid.'

'Did she see it happen?'

'I don't believe so. But she heard the sounds of the struggle, and saw the car drive away. That was when she phoned me. When I got here, she was sitting on the doorstep in a half daze. I don't know what it will do to her emotional state.'

'Any chance of my talking to her?'

'Not now, please. I've already spoken to Dr. Howell, and he told me to give her sedation. The Sheriff has agreed not to question her for the present. There's a limit to what the human mind can endure.'

Sable might have been talking about himself. His shoulders drooped as he turned from the window. In the harsh sunlight his face was a grainy white, and puffy like boiled rice. In murder cases, there are usually more victims than one.

Sable must have read the look on my face. 'This is an unsettling thing to me, too. It can't conceivably relate to Alice and me. And yet it does, very deeply. Peter was a member of the household. I believe he was quite devoted to us, and he died in our front yard. That really brings it home.'

'What?'

'*Timor mortis*,' he said. 'The fear of death.'

'You say Culligan was a member of your household. I take it he slept in.'

'Yes, of course.'

'I'd like to have a look at his room.'

He took me across the court and through a utility room to a back bedroom. The room was furnished with a single bed, a chest of drawers, a chair, and a reading-lamp.

'I'll just look in on Alice,' Sable said, and left me.

I went through Peter Culligan's meagre effects. The closet contained a pair of Levis, a couple of workshirts, boots, and a cheap blue suit which had been bought at a San Francisco department store. There was a Tanforan pari-mutuel stub in the outside breast pocket of the suit coat. A dirty comb and a safety razor lay on top of the chest of drawers. The drawers were practically empty: a couple of white shirts, a greasy blue tie, a T-shirt and a pair of floral shorts, socks and handkerchiefs, and a cardboard box containing a hundred shells for a .38-calibre automatic. Not quite a hundred: the box wasn't full. No gun.

Culligan's suitcase was under the bed. It was a limp old canvas affair, held together with straps, which looked as if it had been kicked around every bus station between Seattle and San Diego. I unstrapped it. The lock was broken, and it fell open. Its contents emitted a whiff of tobacco, sea water, sweat, and the subtler indescribable odour of masculine loneliness.

It contained a grey flannel shirt, a rough blue turtle-neck sweater, and other heavier work clothes. A broad-bladed fisherman's knife had fish scales still clinging like faded sequins to the cork handle. A crumpled greenish tuxedo jacket was preserved as a memento from some more sophisticated past.

A union card issued in San Francisco in 1941 indicated that Culligan had been a paid-up active member of the defunct Marine Cooks' Union. And there was a letter, addressed to Mr. Peter Culligan, General Delivery, Reno, Nevada. Culligan hadn't been a loner all his life. The letter was written on pink notepaper in an unformed hand. It said:

Dear Pete,

Dear is not the word after all I suffered from you, which is all over now and I'm going to keep it that way. I hope you realize. Just so you do I'll spell it out, you never realized a fact in your life until you got hit over the head with it. So here goes, no I don't love you anymore. Looking back now I don't see how I ever did love you, I was 'infatuated.' When I think of all you made me suffer, the jobs you lost and the fights and the drinking and all. You certainly didn't love me, so don't try to 'kid' me. No I'm not crying over 'spilt milk.' I had only myself to blame for staying with you. You gave me fair warning plenty of times. What kind of person you were. I must say you have your 'guts' writing to me. I don't know how you got hold of my address. Probably from one of your crooked cop friends, but they don't scare me.

I am happily married to a wonderful man. He knows that I was married before. But he does not know about 'us.' If you have any decency, stay away from me and don't write any more letters. I'm warning you, don't make trouble for me. I could make trouble for you, double trouble. Remember L. Bay.

Wishing you all success in your new life (I hope you're making as much money as you claim),

Marian
        Mrs. Ronald S. Matheson (and bear it in mind). Me come back to you? Don't ever give it another thought. Ronald is a very successful business exec! I wouldn't rub it in, only you really put me through the 'wringer' and you know it. No hard feelings on my part, just leave me alone, please.

The letter had no return address, but it was postmarked San Mateo, Calif. The date was indecipherable.

I put everything back and closed the suitcase and kicked it under the bed.

I went out into the court. In a room on the other side of it, a woman or an animal was moaning. Sable must have been watching for me. The sound became louder as he opened a sliding glass door, and was shut off as he closed it. He came toward me, his face tinged green by the reflected light from the foliage:

'Find anything significant?'

'He kept shells for an automatic in his drawer. I didn't come across the automatic.'

'I didn't know Peter had a gun.'

'Maybe he had, and sold it. Or it's possible the killer took it away from him.'

'Anything else?'

'I have a tentative lead to his ex-wife, if you want me to explore his background.'

'Why not leave it to the police? Trask is very competent, and an old friend of mine into the bargain. I wouldn't feel justified in taking you off the Galton case.'

'The Galton case doesn't seem so very urgent.'

'Possibly not. Still, I think you should stay with it for the present. Was Cassie Hildreth any help?'

'Some. I can't think of much more to be done around here. I was planning to drive to San Francisco.'

'You can take a plane. I wrote you a check for two hundred dollars, and I'll give you a hundred in cash.' He handed me the cheque and the money. 'If you need any more, don't hesitate to call on me.'

'I won't, but I'm afraid it's money down the drain.'

Sable shrugged. He had worse problems. The moaning behind the glass door was louder, rising in peaks of sound which pierced my eardrums.

CHAPTER SEVEN

I hate coincidences. Aboard the plane, I spent a fruitless hour trying to work out possible connections between Maria Galton's loss of her son and Peter Culligan's loss of life. I had a delayed gestalt after I'd given up on the subject.

I was flipping through the smudged pages of *Chisel*, the little magazine that Cassie Hildreth had given me. Somebody named Chad Bolling was listed on the masthead as editor and publisher. He also had a poem in the magazine, 'Elegy on the Death of Bix Beiderbecke.' It said that the inconsolable cornet would pipe Eurydice out of Boss Pluto's smoke-filled basement. I liked it better than the poem about Luna.

I reread Anthony Galton's poem, wondering if Luna was his wife. Then the gestalt clicked. There was a town named Luna Bay on the coast south of San Francisco. From where I sat, a few thousand feet above the Peninsula, I could practically spit on it. And Culligan's ex-wife had referred to an 'L. Bay' in her letter to him.

When the plane let down at International Airport, I headed for a telephone booth. The woman had signed herself Mrs. Ronald S. Matheson; the envelope had been postmarked in San Mateo.

I hardly expected a hit on such a random shot, after an indefinite lapse of time. But the name was in the directory: Ronald S. Matheson, 780 Sherwood Drive, Redwood City. I dialled the Emerson number.

I couldn't tell if it was a girl or a boy who answered. It was a child, pre-pubic: 'Hello?'

'Is Mrs. Matheson there?'

'Just a minute, please. Mummy, you're wanted on the phone.'

The child's voice trailed off, and a woman's took its place. It was cool and smooth and careful:

'Marian Matheson speaking. Who is calling, please?'

'My name is Archer. You've never heard of me.'

'That's right, I haven't.'

'Ever hear of a man named Culligan?'

There was a loud pause. 'Come again? I didn't catch the name.'

'Culligan,' I said. 'Peter Culligan.'

'What about him?'

'Did you ever know him?'

'Maybe I did, a long time ago. So what? Maybe I didn't.'

'Let's not play games, Mrs. Matheson. I have some information, if you're interested.'

'I'm not. Not if you're talking for Pete Culligan.' Her voice had become harsher and deeper. 'I don't care anything about him, as long as he leaves me alone. You can tell him for me.'

'I can't, though.'

'Why not?'

'Because he's dead.'

'Dead?' Her voice was a leaden echo.

'I'm investigating his murder.' I'd just decided I was. 'I'd like to talk to you about the circumstances.'

'I don't see why. I had nothing to do with it. I didn't even know it happened.'

'I'm aware of that. It's one reason I called.'

'Who killed him?'

'I'll tell you when I see you.'

'Who says you're seeing me?'

I waited.

'Where are you now?' she said.

'At the San Francisco Airport.'

'I guess I can come there, if it has to be. I don't want you coming to the house. My husband—'

'I understand that. It's good of you to come at all. I'll be in the coffee shop.'

'Are you in uniform?'

'Not at the moment.' Or for the last ten years, but let her go on thinking I was law. 'I'm wearing a grey suit. You won't miss me. I'll be sitting beside the windows close to the entrance.'

'I'll be there in fifteen minutes. Did you say Archer?'

'Yes. Archer.'

It took her twenty-five. I passed the time watching the big planes circling in, dragging their late-afternoon shadows along the runways.

A woman in a dark cloth coat came in, paused at the doorway, and looked around the huge room. Her eye lighted on me. She came toward the table, clutching her shiny leather purse as if it was a token of respectability. I got up to meet her:

'Mrs. Matheson?'

She nodded, and sat down hurriedly, as if she was afraid of being conspicuous. She was an ordinary-looking woman, decently dressed, who would never see forty again. There were flecks of grey in her carefully waved black hair, like little shards of iron.

She had once been handsome in a strong-boned way. Maybe she still was, under favourable lighting and circumstances. Her black eyes were her best feature, but they were hard with tension:

'I didn't want to come. But here I am.'

'Will you have some coffee?'

'No, thanks. Let's have the bad news. I'll take it straight.'

I gave it to her straight, leaving out nothing important. She began to twist the wedding ring on her finger, round and round.

'Poor guy,' she said when I finished. 'Why did they do it to him, do you know?'

'I was hoping you could help me answer that.'

'You say you're not a policeman?'

'No. I'm a private investigator.'

'I don't see why you come to me. We haven't been married for fifteen years. I haven't even seen him for ten. He wanted to come back to me, I guess he finally got tired of bucketing around. But I wasn't having any. I'm happily married to a good man—'

'When was the last time you heard from Culligan?'

'About a year ago. He wrote me a letter from Reno, claimed he'd struck it rich, that he could give me anything I wanted if I'd come back. Pete was always a dreamer. The first while after we were married, I used to believe in his dreams. But they all went blooey, one after another. I caught on to him so many years ago it isn't funny. I'm not laughing, notice.'

'What kind of dreams did he dream?'

'Great big ones, the kind that never come off. Like he was going to open a chain of restaurants where food of all nations would be served. He'd hire the best chefs in the country,

French, Chinese, Armenian, and so on. At which time he was a short-order cook on lower Market. Then there was the time he worked out a new system to beat the ponies. He took every cent we possessed to try it out. He even hocked my furniture. It took me all that winter to work it off.' Her voice had the driving energy of old anger that had found an outlet. 'That was Pete's idea of a honeymoon, me working and him playing the ponies.'

'How did you get hooked up with him?'

'I was a dreamer, too, I guess you'd say. I thought I could straighten him out, make a man of him. That all he needed was the love of a good woman. I wasn't a good woman, and I don't pretend to be. But I was better than he was.'

'Where did you meet?'

'In the San Francisco Hospital where I was working. I was a nurse's aide, and Pete was in the ward with a broken nose and a couple of broken ribs. He got beaten up in a gang fight.'

'A gang fight?'

'That's all I know. Pete just said it was some rumble on the docks. I should have taken warning, but after he got out of the hospital I went on seeing him. He was young and good-looking, and like I said I thought he had the makings of a man. So I married him—the big mistake of my life, and I've made some doozies.'

'How long ago was that?'

'Nineteen-thirty-six. That dates me, doesn't it? But I was only twenty-one at the time.' She paused, and raised her eyes to my face. 'I don't know why I'm telling you all this. I've never told a living soul in my life. Why don't you stop me?'

'I'm hoping you'll tell me something that will help. Did your husband go in for gambling?'

'Please don't call him that. I married Pete Culligan, but he was no husband to me.' She lifted her head. 'I have a real husband now. Incidentally, he'll be expecting me back to make his dinner.' She leaned forward in her chair and started to get up.

'Can't you give me a few minutes more, Mrs. Matheson? I've told you all I know about Peter—'

She laughed shortly. 'If I told you all *I* know, it would take all night. Okay, a few more minutes, if you promise me there won't be any publicity. My husband and me have a position to keep up. I'm a memer of the PTA, the League of Women Voters.'

'There won't be any publicity. Was he a gambler?'

'As much as he could afford to be. But he was always small-time.'

'This money he said he made in Reno—did he tell you how he made it?'

'Not a word. But I don't think it was gambling. He was never that lucky.'

'Do you still have his letter?'

'Certainly not. I burned it, the same day I got it.'

'Why?'

'Because I didn't want it around the house. I felt like it was dirt tracked into the house.'

'Was Culligan a crook, or a hustler?'

'Depends what you mean by that.' Her eyes were wary.

'Did he break the law?'

'I guess everybody does from time to time.'

'Was he ever arrested?'

'Yeah. Mostly for drunk and disorderly, nothing serious.'

'Did he carry a gun?'

'Not when I was with him. I wouldn't let him.'

'But the issue came up?'

'I didn't say that.' She was becoming evasive. 'I meant I wouldn't let him even if he wanted to.'

'Did he own a gun?'

'I wouldn't know,' she said.

I'd almost lost her. She wasn't talking frankly or willingly any more. So I threw her the question I didn't expect her to answer, hoping to gather something from her reaction to it:

'You mentioned an L. Bay in your letter to Culligan. What happened there?'

Her lips were pushed out stiff and pale, as if they were made of bone. The dark eyes seemed to shrink in her head:

'I don't know what makes you ask that.' The tip of her tongue moved along her upper lip, and she tried again: 'What was that about a bay in my letter? I don't remember any bay in my letter.'

'I do, Mrs. Matheson.' I quoted: ' "I could make trouble for you, double trouble. Remember L. Bay." '

'If I said that, I don't know what I meant.'

'There's a place called Luna Bay about twenty-five or thirty miles from here.'

'Is there?' she said stupidly.

'You know it. What did Pete Culligan do there?'

'I don't remember. It must have been some dirty trick he

played on me.' She was a poor liar, as most honest people are.
'Does it matter?'

'It seems to matter to you. Did you and Pete live in Luna Bay?'

'I guess you could call it living. I had a job there, doing practical nursing.'

'When?'

'Way back when. I don't remember what year.'

'Who were you working for?'

'Some people. I don't remember their name.' She leaned toward me urgently, her eyes pointed like flints. 'You have that letter with you?'

'I left it where I found it, in Culligan's suitcase in the house where he worked. Why?'

'I want it back. I wrote it, and it belongs to me.'

'You may have to take that up with the police. It's probably in their hands by now.'

'Will they be coming here?' She looked behind her, and all around the crowded restaurant, as if she expected to find a policeman bearing down on her.

'It depends on how soon they catch the killer. They may have him already, in which case they won't bother with secondary leads. Do you have any idea who it was, Mrs. Matheson?'

'How could I? I haven't seen Peter in ten years, I told you.'

'What happened in Luna Bay?'

'Change the record, can't you? If anything happened, which I can't remember, it was strictly between me and Pete. Nothing to do with anybody else, understand?'

Her voice and looks were altering under pressure. She seemed to have broken through into a lower stratum of experience and a coarser personality. And she knew it. She pulled her purse toward her and held on to it with both hands. It was a good purse, beautifully cut from genuine lizard. In contrast with it, her hands were rough, their knuckles swollen and cracked by years of work.

She raised her eyes to mine. I caught the red reflection of fear in their centres. She was afraid of me, and she was afraid to leave me.

'Mrs Matheson, Peter Culligan was murdered today—'

'You expect me to go into mourning?'

'I expect you to give me any information that might have a bearing on his death.'

'I already did. You can leave me alone, understand? You're not getting me mixed up in no murder. Any murder.'

'Did you ever hear of a man named Anthony Galton?'

'No.'

'John Brown?'

'No.'

I could see the bitter forces of her will gathering in her face. She exerted them, and got up, and walked away from me and her fear.

CHAPTER EIGHT

I went back to the telephone booths and looked up the name Chad Bolling in the Bay Area directories. I didn't expect to find it, after more than twenty years, but I was still running in luck. Bolling had a Telegraph Hill address. I immured myself in one of the booths and called him.

A woman's voice answered: 'This is the Bolling residence.'

'Is Mr. Bolling available?'

'Available for what?' she said abruptly.

'It has to do with magazine publication of a poem. The name is Archer,' I added, trying to sound like a wealthy editor.

'I see.' She softened her tone. 'I don't know where Chad is at the moment. And I'm afraid he won't be home for dinner. I do know he'll be at The Listening Ear later this evening.'

'The Listening Ear?'

'It's a new night club. Chad's giving a reading there to-night. If you're interested in poetry, you owe it to yourself to catch it.'

'What time does he go on?'

'I think ten.'

I rented a car and drove it up Bayshore to the city, where I parked it under Union Square. Above the lighted towers of the hotels, twilight had thickened into darkness. A damp chill had risen from the sea; I could feel it through my clothes. Even the coloured lights around the square had a chilly look.

I bought a pint of whisky to ward off the chill and checked in at the Salisbury, a small side-street hotel where I usually stayed in San Francisco. The desk clerk was new to me. Desk clerks are always moving up or down. This one was old and on his way down; his sallow face drooped in the pull of gravity. He handed me my key reluctantly:

'No luggage, sir?'

I showed him my bottle in its paper bag. He didn't smile.

'My car was stolen.'

'That's too bad.' His eyes were sharp and incredulous behind fussy little pince-nez. 'I'm afraid I'll have to ask you to pay in advance.'

'All right.' I gave him the five dollars and asked for a receipt.

The bellhop who took me up in the old open ironwork elevator had been taking me up in the same elevator for nearly twenty years. We shook hands. His was crumpled by arthritis.

'How are you, Coney?'

'Fine, Mr. Archer, fine. I'm taking a new pill, phenylbutasomething. It's doing wonders for me.'

He stepped out and did a little soft-shoe step to prove it. He'd once been half of a brother act that played the Orpheum circuit. He danced me down the corridor to the door of my room.

'What brings you up to the City?' he said when we were inside. To San Franciscans, there's only one city.

'I flew up for a little entertainment.'

'I thought Hollywood was the word's centre of entertainment.'

'I'm looking for something different,' I said. 'Have you heard of a new club called The Listening Ear?'

'Yeah, but you wouldn't like it.' He shook his white head. 'I hope you didn't come all the way up here for *that*.'

'What's the matter with it?'

'It's a culture cave. One of these bistros where guys read poems to music. It ain't your speed at all.'

'My taste is becoming more elevated.'

His grin showed all his remaining teeth. 'Don't kid an old man, eh?'

'Ever hear of Chad Bolling?'

'Sure. He promotes a lot of publicity for himself.' Coney looked at me anxiously. 'You really going in for the poetry kick, Mr. Archer? With music?'

'I have long yearned for the finer things.'

Such as a good French dinner at a price I could pay. I took a taxi to the Ritz Poodle Dog, and had a good French dinner. When I finished eating, it was nearly ten o'clock.

The Listening Ear was full of dark blue light and pale blue

music. A combo made up of piano, bass fiddle, trumpet, and drums was playing something advanced. I didn't have my slide rule with me, but the four musicians seemed to understand each other. From time to time they smiled and nodded like space jockeys passing in the night.

The man at the piano seemed to be the head technician. He smiled more distantly than the others, and when the melody had been done to death, he took the applause with more exquisite remoteness. Then he bent over his keyboard again like a mad scientist.

The tight-hipped waitress who brought my whisky-and-water was interchangeable with nightclub girls anywhere. Even her parts looked interchangeable. But the audience was different from other nightclub crowds. Most of them were young people with serious expressions on their faces. A high proportion of the girls had short straight hair through which they ran their fingers from time to time. Many of the boys had longer hair than the girls, but they didn't run their fingers through it so much. They stroked their beards instead.

Another tune failed to survive the operation, and then the lights went up. A frail-looking middle-aged man in a dark suit sidled through the blue curtains at the rear of the room. The pianist extended his hand and assisted him on to the bandstand. The audience applauded. The frail-looking man, by way of a bow, allowed his chin to subside on the big black bowtie which blossomed on his shirt front. The applause rose to a crescendo.

'I give you Mr. Chad Bolling,' the pianist said. 'Master of all the arts, singer of songs to be sung, painter of pictures, hepcat, man of letters. Mr. Chad Bolling.'

The clapping went on for a while. The poet lifted his hand as if in benediction, and there was silence.

'Thank you, friends,' he said. 'With the support of my brilliant young friend Fingers Donahue, I wish to bring to you tonight, if my larynx will permit, my latest poem.' His mouth twisted sideways as if in self-mockery. 'It ain't chopped liver.'

He paused. The instruments began to murmur behind him. Bolling took a roll of manuscript out of his inside breast pocket and unrolled it under the light.

' "Death Is Tabu," ' he said, and began to chant in a hoarse carrying voice that reminded me of a carnival spieler. He said that at the end of the night he sat in wino alley where the angels drink canned heat, and that he heard a beat. It seemed a girl came to the mouth of the alley and asked him what he was doing in death valley. "Death is the ultimate crutch," she said,' he said. She asked him to come home with her to bed.

He said that sex was the ultimate crutch, but he turned out to be wrong. It seemed he heard a gong. She fled like a ghost, and he was lost, at the end of the end of the night.

While the drummer and the bass fiddler made shock waves on the roof, Bolling raised his voice and began to belt it out. About how he followed her up and down and around and underground, up Russian Hill and Nob Hill and Telegraph Hill and across the Bay Bridge and back by way of the Oakland ferry. So he found the sphinx on Market Street cadging drinks and they got tight and danced on the golden asphalt of delight.

Eventually she fell upon her bed. 'I'm star-transfixed,' she said. He drank the canned hell of her lips, and it went on like that for quite a while, while the music tittered and moaned. She finally succeeded in convincing him that death was the ultimate crutch, whatever that meant. She knew, because it happened she was dead. 'Good night, mister,' she said, or he said she said. 'Good night, sister,' he said.

The audience waited to make sure that Bolling was finished, then burst into a surge of clapping, interspersed with *bravos* and *ole*'s. Bolling stood with pursed lips and absorbed it like a little boy sucking soda pop through a straw. While the lower part of his face seemed to be enjoying itself, his eyes were puzzled. His mouth stretched in a clownish grin:

'Thanks, cats. I'm glad you dig me. Now dig this.'

He read a poem about the seven blind staggers of the soul, and one about the beardless wonders on the psycho wards who were going to be the *gurus* of the new truth. At this point I switched off my hearing aid, and waited for it to be over. It took a long time. After the reading there were books to be autographed, questions to be answered, drinks to be drunk.

It was nearly midnight when Bolling left a tableful of admirers and made for the door. I got up to follow him. A large girl with a very hungry face cut in in front of me. She attached herself to Bolling's arm and began to talk into his ear, bending over because she was taller than he was.

He shook his head. 'Sorry, kiddie, I'm a married man. Also I'm old enough to be your father.'

'What are years?' she said. 'A woman's wisdom is ageless.'

'Let's see you prove it, honey.'

He shook her loose. Tragically clutching the front of her

baggy black sweater, she said: 'I'm not pretty, am I?'

'You're beautiful, honey. The Greek navy could use you for launching ships. Take it up with them, why don't you?'

He reached up and patted her on the head and went out. I caught up with him on the sidewalk as he was hailing a taxi.

'Mr. Bolling, do you have a minute?'

'It depends on what you want.'

'I want to buy you a drink, ask you a few questions.'

'I've had a drink. Several, in fact. It's late. I'm beat. Write me a letter, why don't you?'

'I can't write.'

He brightened a little. 'You mean to tell me you're not an unrecognized literary genius? I thought everybody was.'

'I'm a detective. I'm looking for a man. You may have known him at one time.'

His taxi had turned in the street and pulled into the kerb. He signalled the driver to wait:

'What's his name?'

'John Brown.'

'Oh sure, I knew him well at Harper's Ferry. I'm older than I look.' His empty clowning continued automatically while he sized me up.

'In 1936 you printed a poem of his in a magazine called *Chisel.*'

'I'm sorry you brought that up. What a lousy name for a magazine. No wonder it folded.'

'The name of the poem was "Luna." '

'I'm afraid I don't remember it. A lot of words have flowed under the bridge. I did know a John Brown back in the thirties. Whatever happened to John?'

'That's what I'm trying to find out.'

'Okay, buy me a drink. But not at the Ear, eh? I get tired of the shaves and the shave-nots.'

Bolling dismissed his taxi. We walked about sixty feet to the next bar. A pair of old girls on the two front stools flapped their eyelashes at us as we went in. There was nobody else in the place but a comatose bartender. He roused himself long enough to pour us a couple of drinks.

We sat down in one of the booths, and I showed Bolling my pictures of Tony Galton. 'Do you recognize him?'

'I think so. We corresponded for a while, but I only met him once or twice. Twice. He called on us when we were living in Sausalito. And then one Sunday when I was driving down the coast by Luna Bay, I returned the visit.'

'Were they living at Luna Bay?'

'A few miles this side of it, in an old place on the ocean. I had the very devil of a time finding it, in spite of the directions Brown had given me. I remember now, he asked me not to tell anyone else where he was living. I was the only one who knew. I don't know why he singled me out, except that he was keen to have me visit his home, and see his son. He may have had some sort of father feeling about me, though I wasn't much older than he was.'

He had a son?'

'Yes, they had a baby. He'd just been born, and he wasn't much bigger than my thumb. Little John was the apple of his father's eye. They were quite a touching little family.'

Bolling's voice was gentle. Away from the crowd and the music he showed a different personality. Like other performers, he had a public face and a private one. Each of them was slightly phony, but the private face suited him better.

'You met the wife, did you?'

'Certainly. She was sitting on the front porch when I got there, nursing the baby. She had lovely white breasts, and she didn't in the least mind exposing them. It made quite a picture, there on the bluff above the sea. I tried to get a poem out of her, but it didn't come off. I never really got to know her.'

'What sort of a girl was she?'

'Very attractive, I'd say, in the visual sense. She didn't have too much to say for herself. As a matter of fact, she massacred the English language. I suppose she had the fascination of ignorance for Brown. I've seen other young writers and artists fall for girls like that. I've been guilty of it myself, when I was in my pre-Freudian period.' He added wryly: 'That means before I got analyzed.'

'Do you remember her name?'

'Mrs Brown's name?' He shook his head. 'Sorry. In the poem I botched I called her Stella Maris, star of the sea. But that doesn't help you, does it?'

'Can you tell me when you were there? It must have been toward the end of the year 1936.'

'Yes. It was around Christmas, just before Christmas—I took along some bauble for the child. Young Brown was very pleased that I did.' Bolling pulled at his chin, lengthening his face. 'It's queer I never heard from him after that.'

'Did you ever try to get in touch with him?'

'No, I didn't. He may have felt I'd brushed him off. Perhaps I did, without intending to. The woods were full of young writers; it was hard to keep track of them all. I was doing valid work in those days, and a lot of them came to me. Frankly, I've hardly thought of Brown from that day to this. Is he still living on the coast?'

'I don't know. What was he doing in Luna Bay, did he tell you?'

'He was trying to write a novel. He didn't seem to have a job, and I can't imagine what they were living on. They couldn't have been completely destitute, either. They had a nurse to look after the mother and child.'

'A nurse?'

'I suppose she was what you'd call a practical nurse. One of those young women who take charge,' he added vaguely.

'Do you recall anything about her?'

'She had remarkable eyes, I remember. Sharp black eyes which kept watching me. I don't think she approved of the literary life.'

'Did you talk to her at all?'

'I may have. I have a distinct impression of her, that she was the only sensible person in the house. Brown and his wife seemed to be living in Cloud-Cuckoo-Land.'

'How do you mean?'

'They were out of touch with the ordinary run of life. I don't mean that as a criticism. I've been out of touch enough in my own life, God knows. I still am.' He gave me his clown grin. 'You can't make a Hamlet without breaking egos. But let's not talk about me.'

'Getting back to the nurse, do you think you can remember her name?'

'I know perfectly well I can't.'

'Would you recognize it if I said it?'

'That I doubt. But try me.'

'Marian Culligan,' I said. 'C-u-l-l-i-g-a-n.'

'It rings no bell with me. Sorry.'

Bolling finished his drink and looked around the bar as if he expected something to happen. I guessed that most of the things that can happen to a man had already happened to him. He changed expressions like rubber masks, but between the masks I could see dismay in his face.

'We might as well have another drink,' he said. 'This one will be on me. I'm loaded. I just made a hundred smackers at the Ear.' Even his commercialism sounded phony.

While I lit a fire under the bartender, Bolling studied the photographs I'd left on the table:

'That's John all right. A nice boy, and perhaps a talented one, but out of this world. All the way out of this world. Where did he get the money for horses and tennis?'

'From his family. They're heavily loaded.'

'Good Lord, don't tell me he's the missing heir. Is that why you're making a search for him?'

'That's why.'

'They waited long enough.'

'You can say that again. Can you tell me how to get to the house the Browns were living in when you visited them?'

'I'm afraid not. I might be able to *show* you, though.'

'When?'

'Tomorrow morning if you like.'

'That's good of you.'

'Not at all. I *liked* John Brown. Besides, I haven't been to Luna Bay for years. Eons. Maybe I'll rediscover my lost youth.'

'Maybe.' But I didn't think it likely.

Neither did he.

CHAPTER NINE

In the morning I picked up Bolling at his Telegraph Hill apartment. It was one of those sparkling days that make up for all the fog in San Francisco. An onshore wind had swept the air clear and tessellated the blue surface of the Bay. A white ship cutting a white furrow was headed out toward the Golden Gate. White gulls hung above her on the air.

Bolling looked at all this with a fishy eye. He was frowsy and grey and shivering with hangover. He crawled into the back seat and snored all the way to our destination. It was a dingy, formless town sprawling along the coast highway. Its low buildings were dwarfed by the hills rising behind it, the broad sea spreading out in front.

I stopped beside a filling-station where the inland road met Highway 1, and told Bolling to wake up.

'Wha' for?' he mumbled from the depths of sleep. 'Wha' happen?'

'Nothing yet. Where do we go from here?'

He groaned and sat up and looked around. The glare from the ocean made his eyes water. He shaded them with his hand. 'Where are we?'

'Luna Bay.'

'It doesn't look the same,' he complained. 'I'm not sure whether I can find the place or not. Anyway, we turn north here. Just drive along slowly, and I'll try to spot the road.'

Almost two miles north of Luna Bay, the highway cut inland across the base of a promontory. On the far side of the promontory, a new-looking asphalt road turned off toward the sea. A billboard stood at the intersection: 'Marvista Manor. Three bedrooms and rumpus room. Tile bathrooms. Built-in kitchens. All utilities in. See our model home.'

Bolling tapped my shoulder. 'This is the place, I think.'

I backed up and made a left turn. The road ran straight for several hundred yards up a gentle slope. We passed a rectangle of bare adobe as big as a football field, where earthmovers were working. A wooden sign at the roadside explained their activity: 'Site of the Marvista Shopping Centre.'

From the crest of the slope we looked down over the rooftops of a hundred or more houses. They stood along the hillside on raw earth terraces which were only just beginning to sprout grass. Driving along the winding street between them, I could see that most of the houses were occupied. There were curtains at the windows, children playing in the yards, clothes drying on the lines. The houses were painted different colours, which only seemed to emphasize their sameness.

The street unwound itself at the foot of the slope, paralleling the edge of the bluffs. I stopped the car and turned to look at Bolling.

'I'm sorry,' he said. 'It's changed so much, I can't be certain this is the place. There were some clapboard bungalows, five or six of them, scattered along the bluff. The Browns lived in one of them, if memory serves me.'

We got out and walked toward the edge of the bluff. A couple of hundred feet below, the sea wrinkled like blue metal against its base, and burst in periodic white explosions. A mile to the south, under the shelter of the promontory, a cove of quiet water lay in a brown rind of beach.

Bolling pointed toward the cove. 'This has to be the place. I remember Brown telling me that inlet was used as a harbour by rum-runners in the old Prohibition days. There used to be an old hotel on the bluff about it. You could see it from the Browns' front porch. Their bungalow must have stood quite near here.'

'They probably tore it down when they put in the road. It wouldn't have done me much good to see it, anyway. I was hoping I'd run across a neighbour who remembered the Browns.'

'I suppose you could canvass the tradesmen in Luna Bay.'

'I could.'

'Oh well, it's nice to get out in the country.'

Bolling wandered off along the edge of the bluff. Suddenly he said: 'Whee!' in a high voice like a gull's screak. He began to flap his arms.

I ran toward him. 'What's the matter?'

'Whee!' he said again, and let out a childish laugh. 'I was just imagining that I was a bird.'

'How did you like it?'

'Very much.' He flapped his arms some more. 'I can fly! I breast the windy currents of the sky. I soar like Icarus toward the sun. The wax melts. I fall from a great height into the sea. Mother Thalassa.'

'Mother who?'

'Thalassa, the sea, the Homeric sea. We could build another Athens. I used to think we could do it in San Francisco, build a new city of man on the great hills. A city measured with forgiveness. Oh, well.'

His mood sank again. I pulled him away from the edge. He was so unpredictable I thought he might take a flying leap into space, and I was beginning to like him.

'Speaking of mothers,' I said, 'if John Brown's wife had just had a baby, she must have been going to a doctor. Did they happen to mention where the baby was born?'

'Yes. Right in their house. The nearest hospital is in Redwood City, and Brown didn't want to take his wife there. The chances are she had a local doctor.'

'Let's hope he's still around.

I drove back through the housing-tract until I saw a young woman walking a pram. She shied like a filly when I pulled up beside her. In the daytime the tract was reserved for women and children; unknown men in cars were probably kidnappers.

I got out and approached her, smiling as innocuously as I could.

'I'm looking for a doctor.'

'Oh. Is somebody sick?'

'My friend's wife is going to have a baby. They're thinking of moving into Marvista Manor, and they thought they'd better check on the medical situation.'

'Dr. Meyers is very good,' she said. 'I go to him myself.'

'In Luna Bay?'

'That's right.'

'How long has he practised there?'

'I wouldn't know. We just moved out from Richmond month before last.'

'How old is Dr. Meyers?'

'Thirty, thirty-five, I dunno.'

'Too young,' I said.

'If your friend will feel safer with an older man, I think there is one in town. I don't remember his name, though. Personally I like a young doctor, they know all the latest wonder drugs and all.'

Wonder drugs. I thanked her, and drove back to Luna Bay in search of a drugstore. The proprietor gave me a run-down on the three local doctors. A Dr. George Dineen was the only one who had practised there in the thirties. He was an elderly man on the verge of retirement. I'd probably find him in his office if he wasn't out on a call. It was only a couple of blocks from the drugstore.

I left Bolling drinking coffee at the fountain, and walked to the doctor's office. It occupied the front rooms of a rambling house with green shingle walls which stood on a dusty side-street. A woman of about sixty answered the door. She had blue-white hair and a look on her face you don't see too often any more, the look of a woman who hasn't been disappointed:

'Yes, young man?'

'I'd like to see the doctor.'

'His office hours are in the afternoon. They don't start till one-thirty.'

'I don't want to see him as a patient.'

'If you're a pharmaceutical salesman, you'd better wait till after lunch. Dr. Dineen doesn't like his mornings to be disturbed.'

'I'm only in town for the morning. I'm investigating a disappearance. He may be able to help me to find a missing man.'

She had a very responsive face, in spite of its slack lines of age. Her eyes imagined what it would be like to lose a loved one. 'Well, that's different. Come in, Mr.—'

'Archer. I'm a private detective.'

'My husband is in the garden. I'll bring him in.'

She left me in the doctor's office. Several diplomas hung on the wall above the old oak desk. The earliest stated that Dr. Dineen had graduated from the University of Ohio Medical School in 1914. The room itself was like a preserve of prewar time. The cracked leather furniture had been moulded by use into comfortable human shapes. A set of old chessmen laid out on a board stood like miniature armies stalled in the sunlight that fell slanting from the window.

The doctor came in and shook hands with me. He was a tall high-shouldered old man. His eyes were noncommittal under shaggy grey brows which hung like bird's-nests on the cliff of his face. He lowered himself into the chair behind his desk. His head was partly bald; a few strands of hair lay lankly across the top of his scalp.

'You mentioned a missing person to my wife. One of my patients, perhaps?'

'Perhaps. His name was John Brown. In 1936 he and his wife lived a few miles up the coast where the Marvista tract is now.'

'I remember them very well,' the doctor said. 'Their son was in this office not so very long ago, sitting where you're sitting.'

'Their son?'

'John, Junior. You may know him. He's looking for his father, too.'

'No,' I said, 'I don't know him. But I'd certainly like to.'

'I daresay that could be arranged.' Dr. Dineen's deep voice rumbled to a stop. He looked at me intently, as if he was getting ready to make a diagnosis. 'First, I'd want to know the reasons for your interest in the family.'

'I was hired to make a search for the father, the senior John Brown.'

'Has your search had any results?'

'Not until now. You say this boy who came to see you is looking for his father?'

'That is correct.'

'What brought him to you?'

'He has the ordinary filial emotions. If his father is alive, he wants to be with him. If his father is dead, he wants to know.'

'I mean what brought him here to your office specifically? Had you known him before?'

'I brought him into the world. In my profession, that constitutes the best possible introduction.'

'Are you sure it's the same boy?'

'I have no reason to doubt it.' The doctor looked at me with some distaste, as if I'd criticized some work he'd done with his hands. 'Before we go any further, Mr Archer, you can oblige me with a fuller response to my question. You haven't told me who hired you.'

'Sorry, I can't do that. I've been asked to keep my client's identity confidential.'

'No doubt you have. I've been keeping such matters confidential for the past forty years.'

'And you won't talk unless I do, is that it?'

The doctor raised his hand and brushed the thought away from his face, like an annoying insect. 'I suggested no bargain. I simply want to know who I'm dealing with. There may be grave matters involved.'

'There are.'

'I think you ought to elucidate that remark.'

'I can't.'

We faced each other in a stretching silence. His eyes were steady, and bright with the hostility of a proud old man. I was afraid of losing him entirely, just as the case seemed to be breaking open. While I didn't doubt his integrity, I had my own integrity to think of, too. I'd promised Gordon Sable and Mrs. Galton to name no names.

Dr. Dineen produced a pipe, and began to pack its charred bowl with tobacco from an oilskin pouch. 'We seem to have reached a stalemate. Do you play chess, Mr. Archer?'

'Not as well as you do, probably. I've never studied the book.'

'I would have thought you had.' He finished packing his pipe, and lit it with a kitchen match. The blue smoke swirled in the hollow shafts of sunlight from the window. 'We're wasting both our times. I suggest you make a move.'

'I thought this was a stalemate.'

'New game.' A flicker of interest showed in his eyes for the first time. 'Tell me about yourself. Why would a man of your sort spend his life doing the kind of work you do? Do you make much money?'

'Enough to live on. I don't do it for the money, though. I

do it because I want to.'

'Isn't it dirty work, Mr. Archer?'

'It depends on who's doing it, like doctoring or anything else. I try to keep it clean.'

'Do you succeed?'

'Not entirely. I've made some bad mistakes about people. Some of them assume that a private detective is automatically crooked, and they act accordingly, as you're doing now.'

The old man emitted a grunt which sounded like a seal's bark. 'I can't act blindly in a matter of this importance.'

'Neither can I. I don't know what makes it important to you—'

'I'll tell you,' he said shortly. 'Human lives are involved. A boy's love for his parents is involved. I try to handle these things with the care they deserve.'

'I appreciate that. You seem to have a special interest in John Brown, Junior.'

'I do have. The young fellow's had a rough time of it. I don't want him hurt unnecessarily.'

'It's not my intention to hurt him. If the boy is actually John Brown's son, you'd be doing him a favour by leading me to him.'

'You're going to have to prove that to me. I'll be frank to say I've had one or two experiences with private detectives in my time. One of them had to do with the blackmailing of a patient of mine—a young girl who had a child out of wedlock. I don't mean that reflects on you, but it makes a man leery.'

'All right. I'll put my position hypothetically. Let's say I'd been hired to find the heir to several million dollars.'

'I've heard that one before. You'll have to invent a better gambit than that.'

'I didn't invent it. It happens to be the truth.'

'Prove it.'

'That will be easy to do when the time comes. Right now, I'd say the burden of proof is on this boy. Can he prove his identity?'

'The question never came up. As a matter of fact, the proof of his identity is on his face. I knew whose son he was as soon as he stepped in here. His resemblance to his father is striking.'

'How long ago did he turn up?'

'About a month. I've seen him since.'

'As a patient?'

'As a friend,' Dineen said.

'Why did he come to you in the first place?'

'My name is on his birth certificate. Now hold your horses, young man. Give me a chance to think.' The doctor smoked in silence for a while. 'Do you seriously tell me that this boy is heir to a fortune?'

'He will be, if his father is dead. His grandmother is still living. She has the money.'

'But you won't divulge her name.'

'Not without her permission. I suppose I could call her long distance. But I'd rather have a chance to talk to the boy first.'

The doctor hesitated. He held his right hand poised in the air, then struck the desk-top with the flat of it. 'I'll take a chance on you, though I may regret it later.'

'You won't if I can help it. Where can I find him?'

'We'll come to that.'

'What did he have to say about his origins?'

'It would be more appropriate if you got that from him. I'm willing to tell you what I know about his father and mother from my own direct observation. And this has more relevance than you may think.' He paused. 'What precisely did this anonymous client of yours hire you to do?'

'Find John Brown, Senior,' I said.

'I take it that isn't his real name.'

'That's right, it isn't.'

'I'm not surprised,' Dineen said. 'At the time I knew him, I did some speculating about him. It occurred to me he might be a remittance man—one of those ne'er-do-wells whose families paid them to stay away from home. I remember when his wife was delivered, Brown paid me with a hundred-dollar-bill. It didn't seem to suit with their scale of living. And there were other things, his wife's jewels, for example—diamonds and rubies in ornate gold settings. One day she came in here like a walking jewellery store.

'I warned her not to wear them. They were living out in the country, near the old Inn, and it was fairly raw territory in those days. Also, people were poor. A lot of them used to pay me for my services in fish. I had so much fish during the Depression I've never eaten it since. No matter. A public display of jewels was an incitement to robbery. I told the young lady so, and she left off wearing them, at least when I saw her.'

'Did you see her often?'

'Four or five times, I'd say. Once or twice before the boy

was born, and several times afterwards. She was a healthy enough wench, no complications. The main thing I did for her was to instruct her in the care of an infant. Nothing in her background had prepared her for motherhood.'

'Did she talk about her background?'

'She didn't have to. It had left marks on her body, for one thing. She'd been beaten half to death with a belt buckle.'

'Not by her husband?'

'Hardly. There had been other men in her life, as the phrase goes. I gathered that she'd been on her own from an early age. She was one of the wandering children of the thirties—quite a different sort from her husband.'

'How old was she?'

'I think nineteen or twenty, perhaps older. She looked older. Her experiences hadn't hardened her, but as I said they left her unprepared for motherhood. Even after she was back on her feet, she needed a nurse to help her care for the child. Actually, she was a child herself in emotional development.'

'Do you remember the nurse's name?'

'Let me see. I believe she was a Mrs. Kerrigan.'

'Or Culligan?'

'Culligan, that was it. She was a good young woman, fairly well trained. I believe she took off at the same time the Brown family did.'

'The Brown family took off?'

'They skipped, without a good-bye or a thank-you to anybody. Or so it appeared at the time.'

'When was this?'

'A very few weeks after the child was born. It was close to Christmas Day of 1936, I think a day or two after. I remember it so distinctly because I've gone into it since with the sheriff's men.'

'Recently?'

'Within the last five months. To make a long story short, when they were clearing the land for the Marvista tract, a set of bones were unearthed. The local deputy asked me to look them over to see what I could learn from them. I did so. They were human bones, which had probably belonged to a man of medium height, in his early twenties.

'It's not unlikely, in my opinion, that they are John Brown's bones. They were found buried under the house he lived in. The house was torn down to make way for the new road. Unfortunately, we had no means of making a positive identification. The skull was missing, which ruled out the possibility of dental evidence.'

'It rules in the possibility of murder.'

Dineen nodded gravely. 'There's rather more than a possibility of murder. One of the cervical vertebrae had been cut through by a heavy instrument. I'd say John Brown, if that is who he is, was decapitated with an axe.'

CHAPTER TEN

Before I left Dr. Dineen, he gave me a note of introduction to the deputy in charge of the local sheriff's office, written on a prescription blank; and the address of the gas station where John Brown, Jr., worked. I walked back to the drugstore in a hurry. Bolling was still at the fountain, with a grilled cheese sandwich in his left hand and a pencil in his right. He was simultaneously munching the sandwich and scribbling in a notebook.

'Sorry to keep you waiting—'

'Excuse me, I'm writing a poem.'

He went on scribbling. I ate an impatient sandwich while he finished, and dragged him out to the car:

'I want to show you somebody; I'll explain who he is later.' I started the car and turned south on the highway. 'What's your poem about?'

'The city of man. I'm making a break-through into the affirmative. It's going to be good—the first good poem I've written in years.'

He went on telling me about it, in language which I didn't understand. I found the place I was looking for on the southern outskirts of the town. It was a small independent station with three pumps, one attendant. The attendant was a young man in white drill coveralls. He was busy gassing a pickup truck whose bed was piled with brown fishermen's nets. I pulled in behind it and watched him.

There was no doubt that he looked like Anthony Galton. He had the same light eyes set wide apart, the same straight nose and full mouth. Only his hair was different; it was dark and straight.

Bolling was leaning forward in the seat. 'For Christ's sake!

Is it Brown? It can't be Brown. He's almost as old as I am.'

'He had a son, remember.'

'Is this the son?'

'I think so. Do you remember the colour of the baby's hair?'

'It was dark, what there was of it. Like his mother's.'

Bolling started to get out of the car.

'Wait a minute,' I said. 'Don't tell him who you are.'

'I want to ask him about his father.'

'He doesn't know where his father is. Besides, there's a question of identity. I want to see what he says without any prompting.'

Bolling gave me a frustrated look, but he stayed in the car. The driver of the pickup paid for his gas and rattled away. I pulled up even with the pumps, and got out for a better look at the boy.

He appeared to be about twenty-one or -two. He was very good-looking, as his putative father had been. His smile was engaging.

'What can I do for you, sir?'

'Fill her up. It'll only take a couple of gallons. I stopped because I want you to check the oil.'

'I'll be glad to, sir.'

He seemed like a willing boy. He filled the tank, and wiped the windshield spotless. But when he lifted the hood to check the oil, he couldn't find the dip-stick. I showed him where it was.

'Been working here long?'

He looked embarrassed. 'Two weeks. I haven't caught on to all the new cars yet.'

'Think nothing of it.' I looked across the highway at the windswept shore where the long combers were crashing. 'This is nice country. I wouldn't mind settling out here.'

'Are you from San Francisco?'

'My friend is.' I indicated Bolling, who was still in the car, sulking. 'I came up from Santa Teresa last night.'

He didn't react to the name.

'Who owns the beach property across the highway, do you know?'

'I'm sorry, I wouldn't know. My boss probably would, though.'

'Where is he?'

'Mr. Turnell has gone to lunch. He should be back pretty soon, if you want to talk to him.'

'How soon?'

He glanced at the cheap watch on his wrist. 'Fifteen or twenty minutes. His lunch-hour is from eleven to twelve. It's twenty to twelve now.'

'I might as well wait for him. I'm in no hurry.'

Bolling was in visible pain by this time. He made a con-spiratorial gesture, beckoning me to the car.

'Is it Brown's son?' he said in a stage whisper.

'Could be.'

'Why don't you ask him?'

'I'm waiting for him to tell me. Take it easy, Mr. Bolling.'

'May I talk to him?'

'I'd just as soon you didn't. This is a ticklish business.'

'I don't see why it should be. Either he is or he isn't.'

The boy came up behind me. 'Is something the matter, sir? Anything more I can do?'

'Nothing on both counts. The service was fine.'

'Thank you.'

His teeth showed bright in his tanned face. His smile was strained, though. He seemed to sense the tension in me and Bolling. I said as genially as I knew how:

'Are you from these parts?'

'I could say I was, I guess. I was born a few miles from here.'

'But you're not a local boy.'

'That's true. How can you tell?'

'Accent. I'd say you were raised in the middle west.'

'I was.' He seemed pleased by my interest. 'I just came out from Michigan this year.'

'Have you had any higher education?'

'College, you mean? As a matter of fact I have. Why do you ask?'

'I was thinking you could do better for yourself than jockey-ing a gas pump.'

'I hope to,' he said, with a look of aspiration. 'I regard this work as temporary.'

'What kind of work would you like to do?'

He hesitated, flushing under his tan. 'I'm interested in acting. I know that sounds ridiculous. Half the people who come to California probably want to be actors.'

'Is that why you came to California?'

'It was one of the reasons.'

'This is a way-stop to Hollywood for you, then?'

'I guess you could say that.' His face was closing up. Too many questions were making him suspicious.

'Ever been to Hollywood?'

'No. I haven't.'

'Had any acting experience?'

'I have as a student.'

'Where?'

'At the University of Michigan.'

I had what I wanted: a way to check on his background, if he was telling the truth; if he was lying, a way to prove that he was lying. Universities kept full dossiers on their students.

'The reason I'm asking you all these questions,' I said, 'is this. I have an office on Sunset Boulevard in Hollywood. I'm interested in talent, and I was struck by your appearance.'

He brightened up considerably. 'Are you an agent?'

'No, but I know a lot of agents.' I wanted to avoid the lie direct, on general principles, so I brought Bolling into the conversation: 'My friend here is a well-known writer. Mr. Chad Bolling. You may have heard of him.'

Bolling was confused. He was a sensitive man, and my underhand approach to the boy troubled him. He leaned out of the car to shake hands:

'Pleased to meet you.'

'I'm very glad to meet you, sir. My name is John Brown, by the way. Are you in the picture business?'

'No.'

Bolling was tongue-tied by the things he wanted to say and wasn't supposed to. The boy looked from Bolling to me, wondering what he had done to spoil the occasion. Bolling took pity on him. With a defiant look at me, he said:

'Did you say your name was John Brown? I knew a John Brown once, in Luna Bay.'

'That was my father's name. You must have known my father.'

'I believe I did.' Bolling climbed out of the car. 'I met you when you were a very small baby.'

I watched John Brown. He flushed up warmly. His grey eyes shone with pleasure, and then were moist with deeper feelings. I had to remind myself that he was a self-admitted actor.

He pumped Bolling's hand a second time. 'Imagine your knowing my father! How long is it since you've seen him?'

'Twenty-two years—a long time.'

'Then you don't know where he is now?'

'I'm afraid not, John. He dropped out of sight, you know, quite soon after you were born.'

The boy's face stiffened. 'And Mother?' His voice cracked on the word.

'Same story,' I said. 'Don't you remember either of your parents?'

He answered reluctantly: 'I remember my mother. She left me in an orphanage in Ohio when I was four. She promised to come back for me, but she never did come back. I spent nearly twelve years in that institution, waiting for her to come back.' His face was dark with emotion. 'Then I realized she must be dead. I ran away.'

'Where was it?' I said. 'What town?'

'Crystal Springs, a little place near Cleveland.'

'And you say you ran away from there?'

'Yes, when I was sixteen. I went to Ann Arbor, Michigan, to get an education. A man named Lindsay took me in. He didn't adopt me, but he let me use his name. I went to school under the name of John Lindsay.'

'Why the name change?'

'I didn't want to use my own name. I had good reason.'

'Are you sure it wasn't the other way around? Are you sure John Lindsay wasn't your real name, and you took the name of Brown later?'

'Why would I do that?'

'Somebody hired you, maybe.'

He flushed up darkly. 'Who are you?'

'A private detective.'

'If you're a detective, what was all that bushwa about Hollywood and Sunset Boulevard?'

'I have my office on Sunset Boulevard.'

'But what you said was deliberately misleading.'

'Don't worry about me so much. I needed some information, and I got it.'

'You could have asked me directly. I have nothing to hide.'

'That remains to be seen.'

Bolling stepped between us, sputtering at me in sudden anger: 'Leave the boy alone now. He's obviously genuine. He even has his father's voice. Your implications are an insult.'

I didn't argue with him. In fact, I was ready to believe he was right. The boy stepped back away from us as if we'd threatened his life. His eyes had turned the colour of slate, and there were white rims on his nostrils:

'What is this, anyway?'

'Don't get excited,' I said.

'I'm not excited.' He was trembling all over. 'You come here and ask me a bunch of questions and tell me you knew my father. Naturally I want to know what it means.'

Bolling moved toward him and laid an impulsive hand on his arm. 'It could mean a great deal to you, John. Your father belonged to a wealthy family.'

The boy brushed him off. He was young for his age in some ways. 'I don't care about that. I want to see my father.'

'Why is it so important?' Bolling said.

'I never had a father.' His working face was naked to the light. Tears ran down his cheeks. He shook them off angrily.

I bought him, and made a down payment: 'I've asked enough questions for now, John. Have you talked to the local police, by the way?'

'Yes, I have. And I know what you're getting at. They have a box of bones at the sheriff's station. Some of them claim that they're my father's bones, but I don't believe it. Neither does Deputy Mungan.'

'Do you want to come down there with me now?'

'I can't,' he said. 'I can't close up the station. Mr. Turnell expects me to stay on the job.'

'What time do you get off?'

'About seven-thirty, week nights.'

'Where can I get in touch with you tonight?'

'I live in a boardinghouse about a mile from here. Mrs. Gorgello's.' He gave me the address.

'Aren't you going to tell him who his father was?' Bolling said.

'I will when it's been proved. Let's go, Bolling.'

He climbed into the car reluctantly.

CHAPTER ELEVEN

The Sheriff's substation was a stucco shoebox of a building across the street from a sad-looking country hotel. Bolling said he would stay in the car, on the grounds that skeletons frightened him:

'It even horrifies me to think that I contain one. Unlike Webster in Mr. Eliot's poem, I like to remain oblivious to the skull beneath the skin.'

I never knew whether Bolling was kidding me.

Deputy Mungan was a very large man, half a head taller than I was, with a face like unfinished sculpture. I gave him my name and occupation, and Dineen's note of introduction. When he'd read it, he reached across the counter that divided his little office, and broke all the bones in my hand:

'Any friend of Doc Dineen's is a friend of mine. Come on in around behind and tell me your business.'

I went on in around behind and sat in the chair he placed for me at the end of his desk:

'It has to do with some bones that were found out in the Marvista tract. I understand you've made a tentative identification.'

'I wouldn't go so far as to say that. Doc Dineen thinks it was a man he knew—fellow by the name of John Brown. It fits in with the location of the body, all right. But we haven't been able to nail it down. The trouble is, no such man was ever reported missing in these parts. We haven't been able to turn up any local antecedents. Naturally we're still working on it.'

Mungan's broad face was serious. He talked like a trained cop, and his eyes were sharp as tacks. I said: 'We may be able to help each other to clarify the issue.'

'Any help you can give me will be welcome. This has been dragging on for five months now, more like six.' He threw out a quick hooked question: 'You represent his family, maybe?'

'I represent a family. They asked me not to use their name. And there's still a question whether they are the dead man's family. Was there any physical evidence found with the bones? A watch, or a ring? Shoes? Clothing?'

'Nothing. Not even a stitch of clothing.'

'I suppose it could rot away completely in twenty-two years. What about buttons?'

'No buttons. Our theory is he was buried the way he came into the world.'

'But without a head.'

Mungan nodded gravely. 'Doc Dineen filled you in, eh? I've been thinking about that head myself. A young fellow came in here a few weeks ago, claimed to be John Brown's son.'

'Don't you think he is?'

'He acted like it. He got pretty upset when I showed him the bones. Unfortunately, he didn't know any more about his father than I do. Which is nil, absolutely nil. We know this John Brown lived out on the old Bluff Road for a couple of months in 1936, and that's the sum-total of it. On top of that, the boy doesn't believe these are his father's bones. And he could just be right. I've been doing some thinking, as I said.

'This business about the head, now. We assumed when the body was first turned up, that he was killed by having his head cut off.' Mungan made a snicking sound between tongue and palate, and sheared the air with the edge of his huge hand. 'Maybe he was. Or maybe the head was chopped off after death to remove identification. You know how much we depend on teeth and fillings. Back in the thirties, before we developed our modern lab techniques, teeth and fillings were the main thing we had to go on.

'If my hypothesis is right, the killer was a pro. And that fits in with certain other facts. In the twenties and thirties, the Bluff Road area was a stamping ground for hoods. It was until quite recently, as a matter of fact. In those days it was a real hotbed. A lot of the liquor that kept San Francisco going during Prohibition came in by sea and was funnelled through Luna Bay. They brought in other things than liquor —drugs, for instance, and women from Mexico and Panama. You ever hear of the Red Horse Inn?'

'No.'

'It stood on the coast about a mile south of where we found the skeleton. They tore it down a couple of years ago, after we put the stopper on it. That was a place with a history. It used to be a resort hotel for well-heeled people from the City and the Peninsula. The rum-runners took it over in the twenties. They converted it into a three-way operation: liquor warehouse in the basement, bars and gaming on the first floor, women upstairs. The reason I know so much about it, I had my first drink there back about 1930. And my first woman.'

'You don't look that old.'

'I was sixteen at the time. I think that's one of the reasons I went into law enforcement. I wanted to put bastards like Lempi out of circulation. Lempi was the boss hood who ran the place in the twenties. I knew him personally, but the law got to him before I grew up to his size. They got him for income tax in 1932, he died on the Rock a few years later.

Some of his guns were sent up at the same time.

'I knew those boys, see, and this is the point I'm coming to. I knew what they were capable of doing. They killed for pay, and they killed because they enjoyed it. They bragged in public that nobody could touch them. It took a federal indictment to cool Lempi. Meantime a number of people lost their lives. Our Mr. Bones could be one of them.'

'But you say Lempi and his boys were cleaned out in '32. Our man was killed in '36.'

'We don't know that. We jumped to that conclusion on the basis of what Doc Dineen said, but we've got no concrete evidence to go on. The Doc himself admits that given the chemistry of that particular soil, he can't pinpoint time of burial closer than five years either way. Mr. Bones could have been knocked off as early as 1931. I say *could* have.'

'Or as late as 1941?' I said.

'That's right. You see how little we have to go on.'

'Do I get to take a look at what you have?'

'Why not?'

Mungan went into a back room and returned lugging a metal box about the size of a hope chest. He set it on top of his desk, unlocked it, lifted the lid. Its contents were jumbled like kindling. Only the vertebrae had been articulated with wire, and lay coiled on the heap like the skeleton of a snake. Mungan showed me where the neck bone had been severed by a cutting instrument.

The larger bones had been labelled: left femur, left fibula, and so on. Mungan picked out a heavy bone about a foot long; it was marked 'right humerus.'

'This is the bone of the upper arm,' he said in a lecturer's tone. 'Come along on over to the window here. I want to show you something.'

He held the bone to the light. Close to one knobbed end, I made out a thin line filled and surrounded by deposits of calcium.

'A break?' I said.

'I hope in more senses than one. It's a mended fracture, the only unusual thing in the entire skeleton. Dineen says it was probably set by a trained hand, a doctor. If we could find the doctor that set it, it would answer some of our questions. So if you've got any ideas . . .' Mungan let his voice trail off, but his eyes stayed hard on my face.

'I'll do some telephoning.'

'You can use my phone.'

'A pay phone would suit me better.'

'If you say so. There's one across the street, in the hotel.'

I found the telephone booth at the rear of the dingy hotel lobby, and placed a call to Santa Teresa. Sable's secretary put him on the line.

'Archer speaking, the one-man dragnet,' I said. 'I'm in Luna Bay.'

'You're where?'

'Luna Bay. It's a small town on the coast south of San Francisco. I have a couple of items for you: a dead man's bones, and a live boy. Let's start with the bones.'

'Bones?'

'Bones. They were dug up by accident about six months ago, and they're in the sheriff's substation here. They're unidentified, but the chances are better than even that they belong to the man I'm looking for. The chances are also better than even that he was murdered twenty-two years ago.'

The line was silent.

'Did you get that, Sable? He was probably murdered.'

'I heard you. But you say the remains haven't been identified.'

'That's where you can help me, if you will. You better write this down. There's a fracture in the right humerus, close to the elbow. It was evidently set by a doctor. I want you to check on whether Tony Galton ever had a broken right arm. If so, who was the doctor that looked after it? It may have been Howell, in which case there's no sweat. I'll call you back in fifteen minutes.'

'Wait. You mentioned a boy. What's he got to do with all this?'

'That remains to be seen. He thinks he's the dead man's son.'

'Tony's son?'

'Yes, but he isn't sure about it. He came here from Michigan in the hope of finding out who his father was.'

'Do you think he's Tony's son?'

'I wouldn't bet my life savings on it. I wouldn't bet against it, either. He bears a strong resemblance to Tony. On the other hand, his story is weak.'

'What story does he tell?'

'It's pretty long and complicated for the telephone. He was brought up in an orphanage, he says, went to college under an assumed name, came out here a month ago to find out who

72

he really is. I don't say it couldn't have happened the way he says, but it needs to be proved out.'

'What kind of a boy is he?'

'Intelligent, well spoken, fairly well mannered. If he's a con artist, he's smooth for his age.'

'How old is he?'

'Twenty-two.'

'You work very quickly,' he said.

'I was lucky. What about your end? Has Trask got anything on my car?'

'Yes. It was found abandoned in San Luis Obispo.'

'Wrecked?'

'Out of gas. It's in perfectly good shape, I saw it myself. Trask has it impounded in the county garage.'

'What about the man who stole it?'

'Nothing definite. He probably took another car in San Luis. One disappeared late yesterday afternoon. Incidentally, Trask tells me that the Jaguar, the murder car, as he calls it, was another stolen car.'

'Who was the owner?'

'I have no idea. The Sheriff is having the engine number traced.'

I hung up, and spent the better part of fifteen minutes thinking about Marian Culligan Matheson and her respectable life in Redwood City which I was going to have to invade again. Then I called Sable back. The line was busy. I tried again in ten minutes, and got him.

'I've been talking to Dr. Howell,' he said. 'Tony broke his right arm when he was in prep school. Howell didn't set the break himself, but he knows the doctor who did. In any case, it was a fractured humerus.'

'See if they can turn up the X-ray, will you? They don't usually keep X-ray pictures this long, but it's worth trying. It's the only means I can think of for making a positive identification.'

'What about teeth?'

'Everything above the neck is missing.'

It took Sable a moment to grasp this. Then he said: 'Good Lord!' After another pause: 'Perhaps I should drop everything and come up there. What do you think?'

'It might be a good idea. It would give you a chance to interview the boy.'

'I believe I'll do that. Where is he now?'

'Working. He works at a gas station in town. How long will it take you to get here?'

'I'll be there between eight and nine.'

'Meet me at the sheriff's substation at nine. In the meantime, is it all right if I take the local deputy into my confidence? He's a good man.'

'I'd just as soon you didn't.'

'You can't handle murder without publicity.'

'I'm aware of that,' Sable said acidly. 'But then we don't know for certain that the victim was Tony, do we?'

Before I could give him any further argument, Sable hung up.

CHAPTER TWELVE

I phoned the Santa Teresa courthouse. After some palaver, I got Sheriff Trask himself on the other end of the line. He sounded harried:

'What is it?'

'Gordon Sable just told me you traced the murder car in the Culligan case.'

'A fat lot of good it did us. It was stolen in San Francisco night before last. The thief changed the licence plates.'

'Who owns it?'

'San Francisco man. I'm thinking of sending somebody up to talk to him. Far as I can make out, he didn't report the theft.'

'That doesn't sound so good. I'm near San Francisco now, in Luna Bay. Do you want me to look him up?'

'I'd be obliged. I can't really spare anybody. His name is Roy Lemberg. He lives at a hotel called the Sussex Arms.'

An hour later, I drove into the garage under Union Square. Bolling said good-bye to me at the entrance:

'Good luck with your case.'

'Good luck with your poem. And thanks.'

The Sussex Arms was another side-street hotel like the one I had spent the night in. It was several blocks closer to Market Street, and several degrees more dilapidated. The desk clerk had large sorrowful eyes and a very flexible manner, as if he had been run through all the wringers of circumstance.

He said Mr. Lemberg was probably at work.

'Where does he work?'

'He's supposed to be a car salesman.'

'Supposed to be?'

'I don't think he's doing so good. He's just on commission with a secondhand dealer. The reason I know, he tried to sell *me* a car.' He snickered, as if he possessed the secret of a more advanced type of transportation.

'Has Lemberg lived here long?'

'A few weeks, more or less. This wouldn't happen to be a police matter?'

'I want to see him on personal business.'

'Maybe Mrs. Lemberg is up in the room. She usually is.'

'Try her, will you? My name is Archer. I'm interested in buying their car.'

He went to the switchboard and relayed the message. 'Mrs. Lemberg says come right on up. It's three-eleven. You can take the elevator.'

The elevator jerked me up to the third floor. At the end of the dust-coloured hallway, a blonde in a pink robe gleamed like a mirage. Closer up, her lustre was dimmer. She had darkness at the roots of her hair, and a slightly desperate smile.

She waited until I was practically standing on her feet; then she yawned and stretched elastically. She had wine and sleep on her breath. But her figure was very good, lush-breasted and narrow-waisted. I wondered if it was for sale or simply on exhibition by the owner.

'Mrs. Lemberg?'

'Yeah. What's all this about the Jag? Somebody phones this morning and he tells them it was stole. And now you want to buy it.'

'Was the car stolen?'

'That was just some of Roy's malarkey. He's full of it. You serious about buying?'

'Only if he has clear title,' I said fussily.

My show of reluctance made her eager, as it was intended to. 'Come in, we'll talk about it. The Jag is in his name, but I'm the one that makes the money decisions.'

I followed her into the little room. At the chinks in the drawn blinds, daylight peered like a spy. She turned on a lamp and waved her hand vaguely toward a chair. A man's shirt hung on the back of it. A half-empty half-gallon jug of muscatel stood on the floor beside it.

'Siddown, excuse the mess. With all the outside work I do, I don't get time to houseclean.'

'What do you do?'

'I model. Go ahead, siddown. That shirt is ready for the laundry, anyway.'

I sat down against the shirt. She flung herself on the bed, her body falling automatically into a cheesecake pose:

'Were you thinking of paying cash?'

'If I buy.'

'We sure could use a chunk of ready cash. What price did you have in mind? I'm warning you, I won't let it go too cheap. That's my chief recreation in life, driving out in the country. The trees and everything.' Her own words seemed to bewilder her. 'Not that he takes me out in it. I hardly ever see the car any more. That brother of his monopolizes it. Roy's so soft, he don't stick up for his rights the way he should. Like the other night.'

'What happened the other night?'

'Just more of the same. Tommy comes up full of the usual. He's got another one of these big job opportunities that never pan out. All he needs is a car, see, and he'll be making a fortune in no time. So Roy lends him the car, just like that. Tommy could talk the fillings right out of his teeth.'

'How long ago was this?'

'Night before last, I think. I lose count of the nights and days.'

'I didn't know Roy had a brother,' I prompted her.

'Yeah, he's got a brother.' Her voice was flat. 'Roy's all fixed up with a brother, till death doth us part. We'd still be in Nevada, living the life of O'Reilly, if it wasn't for that punk.'

'How so?'

'I'm talking too much.' But bad luck had dulled her brains, bad wine had loosened her tongue: 'The Adult Authority said they'd give him a parole if he had somebody willing to be responsible. So back we move to California, to make a home for Tommy.'

I thought: This is a home? She caught my look:

'We didn't always live here. We made a down payment on a real nice little place in Daly City. But Roy started drinking again, we couldn't hold on to it.' She turned over on to her stomach, supporting her chin on her hand. Her china-blue eyes looked fractured in the light. 'Not that I blame him,' she added more softly. 'That brother of his would drive a saint to drink. Roy never hurt nobody in his life. Except me, and you expect that from any man.'

I was touched by her asphalt innocence. The long curve of her hip and thigh, the rich flesh of her bosom, were like the disguise of a frightened adolescent.

'What was Tommy in for?'

'He beat up a guy and took his wallet. The wallet had three bucks in it, and Tommy was in for six months.'

'That works out to fifty cents a month. Tommy must be quite a mastermind.'

'Yeah, to hear him tell it. It was supposed to be longer, but I guess he's good when he's in, with somebody watching him. It's just when he gets out.' She cocked her head sideways, and her bright hair fell across her hand. 'I don't know why I'm telling you all this. In my experience, the guys do most of the talking. I guess you have a talkable-attable face.'

'You're welcome to the use of it.'

'Sanctuary mucho. But you came here to buy a car. I was almost forgetting. I worry so much, I forget things.' Her gaze slid down from my face to the muscatel jug. 'I had a few drinkies, too, if the truth be knownst.' She drew a lock of hair across her eyes and looked at me through it.

Her kittenish mood was depressing. I said: 'When can I have a look at the Jaguar?'

'Any time, I guess. Maybe you better talk to Roy.'

'Where can I find him?'

'Don't ask me. Tell you the truth, I don't even know if Tommy brought it back yet.'

'Why did Roy say the car was stolen?'

'I dunno. I was half asleep when he left. I didn't ask him.'

The thought of sleep made her yawn. She dropped her head and lay still. Traffic went by in the street like a hostile army. Then footsteps came down the corridor and paused outside the door. A man spoke softly through it:

'You busy, Fran?'

She raised herself on her arms like a fighter hearing a far-off count. 'Is that you, hon?'

'Yeah. You busy?'

'Not so's you'd notice. Come ahead in.'

He flung the door open, saw me, and hung back like an interloper. 'Excuse me.'

His dark eyes were quick and uncertain. He was still in his early thirties, but he had a look about him, intangible and definite as an odour. The look of a man who has lost his grip and is sliding. His suit was sharply pressed, but it hadn't been cleaned for too long. The very plumpness of his face gave it a lardlike inertness, as if it had stopped reacting to everything but crises.

His face interested me. Unless I was getting hipped on family resemblances, he was an older softer version of the boy who'd stolen my car. This one's dark curls were thinner and limper. And the violence of the younger man was petulance in him. He said to his wife:

'You told me you weren't busy.'

'I'm not. I'm only resting.' She rolled over and sat up. 'This gentleman wants to buy the Jaguar.'

'It's not for sale.' Lemberg closed the door behind him. 'Who told you it was?'

'Grapevine.'

'What else did you hear?'

He was quick on the uptake. I couldn't hope to con him for long, so I struck at his vulnerable spot:

'Your brother's in trouble.'

His gaze went to my shoulder, my hands, my mouth, and then my eyes. I think in his extremity he would have liked to hit me. But I could have broken him in half, and he must have known it. Still, anger or frustration made him foolish:

'Did Schwartz send you to tell me this?'

'Who?'

'You needn't play dumb. Otto Schwartz.' He gargled the words. 'If he sent you, you can take a message back for me. Tell him to take a running jump in the Truckee River and do us all a favour.'

I got up. Instinctively, one of Lemberg's arms rose to guard his face. The gesture told a lot about him and his background.

'Your brother's in very bad trouble. So are you. He drove down south to do a murder yesterday. You provided the car.'

'I didn't know whah—' His jaw hung open, and then clicked shut. 'Who are you?'

'A friend of the family. Show me where Tommy is.'

'But I don't know. He isn't in his room. He never came back.'

The woman said: 'Are you from the Adult Authority?'

'No.'

'Who are you?' Lemberg repeated. 'What do you want?'

'Your brother, Tommy.'

'I don't know where Tommy is. I swear.'

'What's Otto Schwartz got to do with you and Tommy?'

'I don't know.'

'You brought up his name. Did Schwartz give Tommy a contract to murder Culligan?'

'Who?' the woman said. 'Who did you say got murdered?'

'Peter Culligan. Know him?'

'No,' Lemberg answered for her. 'We don't know him.'

I advanced on him: 'You're lying, Lemberg. You better let down your back hair, tell me all about it. Tommy isn't the only one in trouble. You're accessory to any crime he did.'

He backed away until the backs of his legs were touching the bed. He looked down at his wife as if she was his only source of comfort. She was looking at me:

'What did you say Tommy did?'

'He committed a murder.'

'For gosh sake.' She swung her legs down and stood up facing her husband. 'And you lent him the car?'

'I had to. It was his car. It was only in my name.'

'Because he was on parole?' I said.

He didn't answer me.

The woman took hold of his arm and shook it. 'Tell the man where he is.'

'I don't know where he is.' Lemberg turned to me: 'And that's the honest truth.'

'What about Schwartz?'

'Tommy used to work for him, when we lived in Reno. They were always asking him to come back to work.'

'Doing what?'

'Any dirty thing they could dream up.'

'Including murder?'

'Tommy never did a murder.'

'Before this one, you mean.'

'I'll believe it when I hear it from him.'

The woman groaned. 'Don't be an idiot all your life. What did he ever do for you, Roy?'

'He's my brother.'

'Do you expect to hear from him?' I said.

'I hope so.'

'If you do, will you let me know?'

'Sure I will,' he lied.

I went down in the elevator and laid a ten-dollar bill on the counter in front of the room clerk. He raised a languid eyebrow:

'What's this for? You want to check in?'

'Not today, thanks. It's your certificate of membership in the junior G-men society. Tomorrow you get your intermediate certificate.'

'Another ten?'

'You catch on fast.'

'What do I have to do for it?'

'Keep track of Lemberg's visitors, if he has any. And any telephone calls, especially long-distance calls.'

'Can do.' His hand moved quickly, flicking the bill out of sight. 'What about *her* visitors?'

'Does she have many?'

'They come and go.'

'She pay you to let them come and go?'

'That's between me and her. Are you a cop?'

'Not me,' I said, as if his question was an insult. 'Just keep the best track you can. If it works out, I may give you a bonus.'

'If what works out?'

'Developments. Also I'll mention you in my memoirs.'

'That will be just ducky.'

'What's your name?'

'Jerry Farnsworth.'

'Will you be on duty in the morning?'

'What time in the morning?'

'Any time.'

'For a bonus I can be.'

'An extra five,' I said, and went outside.

There was a magazine shop on the opposite corner. I crossed to it, bought a *Saturday Review*, and punched a hole in the cover. For an hour or more, I watched the front of the Sussex Arms, trusting that Lemberg wouldn't penetrate my literate disguise.

But Lemberg didn't come out.

CHAPTER THIRTEEN

It was past five when I got to Redwood City. The commuting trains were running south every few minutes. The commuters in their uniforms, hat on head, brief-case in hand, newspaper under arm, marched wearily toward their waiting cars. The cop on traffic duty at the station corner told me how to get to Sherwood Drive.

It was in a junior-executive residential section, several cuts above the Marvista tract. The houses were set further apart, and differed from each other in architectural detail. Flowers bloomed competitively in the yards.

A bicycle lay on the grass in front of the Matheson house. A small boy answered my knock. He had black eyes like his mother's, and short brown hair which stuck up all over his head like visible excitement.

'I was doing pushups,' he said, breathing hard. 'You want my daddy? He ain't, I mean, he isn't home from the city yet.'

'Is your mother home?'

'She went to the station to get him. They ought to be back in about eleven minutes. That's how old I am.'

'Eleven minutes?'

'Eleven *years*. I had my birthday last week. You want to see me do some pushups?'

'All right.'

'Come in, I'll show you.'

I followed him into a living-room which was dominated by a large brick fireplace with a raised hearth. Everything in the room was so new and clean, the furniture so carefully placed around it, that it seemed forbidding. The boy flung himself down in the middle of the green broadloom carpet:

'Watch me.'

He did a series of pushups, until his arms collapsed under him. He got up panting like a dog on a hot day:

'Now that I got the knack, I can do pushups all night if I want to.'

'You wouldn't want to wear yourself out.'

'Shucks, I'm strong. Mr. Steele says I'm very strong for my age, it's just my co-ordination. Here, feel my muscle.'

He pulled up the sleeve of his jersey, flexed his biceps, and produced an egg-sized lump. I palpated this:

'It's hard.'

'That's from doing pushups. You think I'm big for my age, or just average?'

'A pretty fair size, I'd say.'

'As big as you when you were eleven?'

'Just about.'

'How big are you now?'

'Six feet or so.'

'How much do you weigh?'

'About one-ninety.'

'Did you ever play football?'

'Some, in high school.'

'Do you think, will I ever get to be a football player?' he said wistfully.

'I don't see why not.'

'That's my ambition, to be a football player.'

He darted out of the room and was back in no time with a football which he threw at me from the doorway.

'Y. A. Tittle,' he said.

I caught the ball and said: 'Hugh McElhenny.'

This struck him as very funny. He laughed until he fell down. Being in position, he did a few pushups.

'Stop it. You're making me tired.'

'I never get tired,' he bragged exhaustedly. 'When I get through doing pushups, I'm going to take a run around the block.'

'Don't tell me. It wears me out.'

A car turned into the driveway. The boy struggled to his feet:

'That's Mummy and Daddy now. I'll tell them you're here, Mr. Steele.'

'My name is Archer. Who's Mr. Steele?'

'My coach in the Little League. I got you mixed up with him, I guess.'

It didn't bother him, but it bothered me. It was a declaration of trust, and I didn't know what I was going to have to do to his mother.

She came in alone. Her face hardened and thinned when she saw me:

'What do you want? What are you doing with my son's football?'

'Holding it. He threw it to me. I'm holding it.'

'We were making like Forty-niners,' the boy said. But the laughter had gone out of him.

'Leave my son alone, you hear me?' She turned on the boy: 'James, your father is in the garage. You can help him bring in the groceries. And take that football with you.'

'Here.' I tossed him the ball. He carried it out as if it was made of iron. The door closed behind him. 'He's a likely boy.'

'A lot you care, coming here to badger me. I talked to the police this morning. I don't have to talk to you.'

'I think you want to, though.'

'I can't. My husband—he doesn't know.'

'What doesn't he know?'

'Please.' She moved toward me rapidly, heavily, almost as though she was falling, and grasping my arm. 'Ron will be coming in any minute. You won't force me to talk in front of him?'

'Send him away.'

'How can I? He wants his dinner.'

'You need something from the store.'

'But we just came from the store.'

'Think of something else.'

Her eyes narrowed to two black glittering slits. 'Damn you. You come in here disrupting my life. What did I do to bring this down on me?'

'That's the question that needs answering, Mrs. Matheson.'

'Won't you go away and come back later?'

'I have other things to do later. Let's get this over with.'

'I only wish I could.'

The back door opened. She pulled away from me. Her face smoothed out and became inert, like the face of someone dying.

'Sit down,' she said. 'You might as well sit down.'

I sat on the edge of an overstuffed chesterfield covered with hard shiny green brocade. Footsteps crossed the kitchen, and paper rustled. A man raised his voice:

'Marian, where are you?'

'I'm in here,' she said tightly.

Her husband appeared in the doorway. Matheson was a thin small man in a grey suit who looked about five years younger than his wife. He stared at me through his glasses with the belligerence of his size. It was his wife he spoke to:

'I didn't know you had a visitor.'

'Mr. Archer is Sally Archer's husband. You've heard me speak of Sally Archer, Ron.' In spite of his uncomprehending look, she rushed on: 'I promised to send her a cake for the church supper, and I forgot to bake it. What am I going to do?'

'You'll have to skip it.'

'I can't. She's depending on me. Ron, would you go downtown and bring me a cake for Mr. Archer to take to Sally? Please?'

'Now?' he said with disgust.

'It's for tonight. Sally's waiting for it.'

'Let her wait.'

'But I can't. You wouldn't want it to get around that I didn't do my share.'

He turned out his hands in resignation. 'How big a cake does it have to be?'

'The two-dollar size will do. Chocolate. You know the bakery at the shopping centre.'

'But that's way over on the other side of town.'

'It's got to be good, Ron. You don't want to shame me in front of my friends.'

Some of her real feeling was caught in the words. His eyes jabbed at me and returned to her face, searching it:

'Listen, Marian, what's the trouble? Are you okay?'

'Certainly I'm okay.' She produced a smile. 'Now run along like a good boy and bring me that cake. You can take Jimmy with you, and I'll have supper ready when you get back.'

Matheson went out, slamming the door behind him in protest. I heard his car engine start, and sat down again:

'You've got him well trained.'

'Please leave my husband out of this. He doesn't deserve trouble.'

'Does he know the police were here?'

'No, but the neighbours will tell him. And then I'll have to do some more lying. I hate this lying.'

'Stop lying.'

'And let him know I'm mixed up in a murder? That would be just great.'

'Which murder are you talking about?'

She opened her mouth. Her hand flew up to cover it. She forced her hand down to her side and stood very still, like a sentinel guarding her hearth.

'Culligan's?' I said. 'Or the murder of John Brown?'

The name struck her like a blow in the mouth. She was too shaken to speak for a minute. Then she gathered her forces and straightened up and said:

'I don't know any John Brown.'

'You said you hated lying, but you're doing it. You worked for him in the winter of 1936, looking after his wife and baby.'

She was silent. I brought out one of my pictures of Anthony Galton and thrust it up to her face:

'Don't you recognize him?'

She nodded resignedly. 'I recognize him. It's Mr. Brown.'

'And you worked for him, didn't you?'

'So what? Working for a person is no crime.'

'Murder is the crime we're talking about. Who killed him, Marian? Was it Culligan?'

'Who says anybody killed him? He pulled up stakes and went away. The whole family did.'

'Brown didn't go very far, just a foot or two underground. They dug him up last spring, all but his head. His head was missing. Who cut it off, Marian?'

The ugliness rose like smoke in the room, spreading to its far corners, fouling the light at the window. The ugliness entered the woman and stained her eyes. Her lips moved, trying to find the words that would exorcise it. I said:

'I'll make a bargain with you, and keep it if I can. I don't want to hurt your boy. I've got nothing against you or your husband. I suspect you're material witness to a murder. Maybe the law would call it accessory—'

'No.' She shook her head jerkily. 'I had nothing to do with it.'

'Maybe not. I'm not interested in pinning anything on you. If you'll tell me the whole truth as you know it. I'll do my best to keep you out of it. But it has to be the whole truth, and I have to have it now. A lot depends on it.'

'How could a lot depend, after all these years?'

'Why did Culligan die, after all these years? I think that the two deaths are connected. I also think that you can tell me how.'

Her deeper, cruder personality rose to the surface. 'What do you think I am, a crystal ball?'

'Stop fooling around,' I said sharply. 'We only have a few minutes. If you won't talk to me alone, you can talk in front of your husband.'

'What if I refuse to talk at all?'

'You'll be having another visit from the cops. It'll start here and end up at the courthouse. And everybody west of the Rockies will have a chance to read all about it in the papers. Now talk.'

'I need a minute to think.'

'You've had it. Who murdered Brown?'

'I didn't know he was murdered, not for sure. Culligan wouldn't let me go back to the house after that night. He said the Browns moved on, bag and baggage. He even tried to give me money he said they left for me.'

'Where did he get it?'

After a silence, she blurted: 'He stole it from them.'

'Did he murder Brown?'

'Not Culligan. He wouldn't have the nerve.'

'Who did?'

'There was another man. It must have been him.'

'What was his name?'

'I don't know.'

'What did he look like?'

'I hardly remember. I only saw him the once, and it was at night.'

Her story was turning vague, and it made me suspicious. 'Are you sure the other man existed?'

'Of course he did.'

'Prove it.'

'He was a jailbird,' she said. 'He escaped from San Quentin. He used to belong to the same gang Culligan did.'

'What gang is that?'

'I wouldn't know. It broke up long before I married Culligan. He never talked about his gang days. I wasn't interested.'

'Let's get back to this man who broke out of "Q." He must have had a name. Culligan must have called him something.'

'I don't remember what.'

'Try harder.'

She looked toward the window. Her face was drawn in the tarnished light.

'Shoulders. I think it was Shoulders.'

'No last name?'

'Not that I remember. I don't think Culligan ever told me his last name.'

'What did he look like?'

'He was a big man, dark-haired. I never really saw him, not in the light.'

'What makes you think he murdered Brown?'

She answered in a low voice, to keep her house from hearing: 'I heard them arguing that night, in the middle of the night. They were sitting out in my car arguing about money. The other man—Shoulders—said that he'd knock off Pete, too, if he didn't get his way. I heard him say it. The walls of the shack we lived in were paper thin. This Shoulders had a kind of shrill voice, and it cut through the walls like a knife. He wanted all the money for himself, and most of the jewels.

'Pete said it wasn't fair, that he was the finger man and should have an equal split. He needed money, too, and God knows that he did. He always needed money. He said that a couple of hot rubies were no good to him. That was how I guessed what happened. Little Mrs. Brown had these big red jewels, I always thought they were glass. But they were rubies.'

'What happened to the rubies?'

'The other man took them, he must of. Culligan settled for part of the money, I guess. At least he was flush for a while.'

'Did you ever ask him why?'

'No. I was afraid.'

'Afraid of Culligan?'

'Not him so much.' She tried to go on, but the words stuck in her throat. She plucked at the skin of her throat as if to dislodge them. 'I was afraid of the truth, afraid he'd tell me. I didn't want to believe what happened, I guess. That argument I heard outside our house—I tried to pretend to myself it was all a dream. I was in love with Culligan in those days. I couldn't face my own part in it.'

'You mean the fact that you didn't take your suspicions to the police?'

'That would have been bad enough, but I did worse. I was the one responsible for the whole thing. I've lived with it on my conscience for over twenty years. It was all my fault for not keeping my loud mouth shut.' She gave me an up-from-under look, her eyes burning with pain: 'Maybe I ought to be keeping it shut now.'

'How were you responsible?'

She hung her head still lower. Her eyes sank out of sight under her black brows. 'I told Culligan about the money,' she said. 'Mr. Brown kept it in a steel box in his room. I saw it when he paid me. There must have been thousands of dollars. And I had to go and mention it to my hus—to Culligan. I would have done better to go and cut my tongue out instead.' She raised her head, slowly, as if she was balancing a weight. 'So there you have it.'

'Did Brown ever tell you where *he* got the money?'

'Not really. He made a joke about it—said he stole it. But he wasn't the type.'

'What type was he?'

'Mr. Brown was a gentleman, at least he started out to be a gentleman. Until he married that wife of his. I don't know what he saw in her outside of a pretty face. She didn't know from nothing, if you ask me. But he knew plenty, he could talk your head off.'

She gasped. The enormity of the image struck her. 'God! They cut his head off?' She wasn't asking me. She was asking the dark memories flooding up from the basement of her life.

'Before death or after, we don't know which. You say you never went back to the house?'

'I never did. We went back to San Francisco.'

'Do you know what happened to the rest of the family, the wife and son?'

She shook her head. 'I tried not to think about them. What did happen to them?'

'I'm not sure, but I think they went east. The indications are they got away safe, at any rate.'

'Thank God for that.' She tried to smile, and failed. Her eyes were still intent on the guilty memory. She looked at the walls of her living-room as if they were transparent. 'I guess you wonder what kind of a woman I am, that I could run out on a patient like that. Don't think it didn't bother me. I almost went out of my mind for a while that winter. I used to wake up in the middle of the night and listen to Culligan's breathing and wish it would stop. But I stuck to him for five more years after that. Then I divorced him.'

'And now he's stopped breathing.'

'What do you mean by that?'

'You could have hired a gun to knock him off. He was threatening to make trouble for you. You have a lot to lose.' I didn't believe it, but I wanted to see what she would make of it.

Her two hands went to her breasts and grasped them cruelly. 'Me? You think I'd do that?'

'To keep your husband and son, you would. Did you?'

'No. For God's sake, no.'

'That's good.'

'Why do you say that?' Her eyes were dull with the sickness of the past.

'Because I want you to keep what you have.'

'Don't do me any favours.'

'I'm going to, though. I'm going to keep you out of the Culligan case. As for the information you've given me, I'm going to use it for private reference only. It would be easier for me if I didn't—'

'So you want to be paid for your trouble is that it?'

'Yes, but not in money. I want your confidence, and any other information you can give me.'

'But there isn't any more. That's all there is.'

'What happened to Shoulders?'

'I don't know. He must of got away. I never heard of him again.'

'Culligan never mentioned him?'

'No. Honest.'

'And you never brought the subject up?'

'No. I was too much of a coward.'

A car entered the driveway. She started, and went to the window. The light outside was turning dusky grey. In the yard across the street, red roses burned like coals. She rubbed her eyes with her knuckles, as if she wanted to wipe out all her past experiences, live innocent in an innocent world.

The little boy burst through the door. Matheson came at his heels, balancing a cake box in his hands.

'Well, I got the darn thing.' He thrust it into my hands. 'That takes care of the church supper.'

'Thanks.'

'Don't mention it,' he said brusquely, and turned to his wife: 'Is supper ready? I'm starved.'

She stood on the far side of the room, cut off from him by the ugliness. 'I didn't make supper.'

'You didn't make it? What is this? You said you'd have it ready when I got home.'

Hidden forces dragged at her face, widening her mouth, drawing deep lines between her eyes. Suddenly her eyes were blind with tears. The tears ran in the furrows of her face. Sobbing, she sat on the edge of the hearth like an urchin on a kerb.

'Marian? What's the matter? What's the trouble, kiddie?'

'I'm not a good wife to you.'

Matheson went across the room to her. He sat on the hearth beside her and took her in his arms. She buried her face in his neck.

The boy started toward them, and then turned back to me. 'Why is Mother crying?'

'People cry.'

'I don't cry,' he said.

CHAPTER FOURTEEN

I drove back across the ridge toward the last fading light in the sky. On the road that wound down to Luna Bay I passed an old man with a burlap bag on his back. He was one of the old-time hoboes who follow the sun like migratory birds. But the birds fly, and the men walk. The birds mate and nest; the old men have no nests. They pace out their lives along the road-sides.

I stopped and backed up and gave him the cake.

'Thank you very kindly.' His mouth was a rent in shaggy fur. He put the cake in his bag. It was a cheap gift, so I gave him a dollar to go with it. 'Do you want a ride into town?'

'No, thank you very kindly. I'd smell up your car.'

He walked away from me with a long, slow, swinging pur-poseless stride, lost in a dream of timeless space. When I passed him, he didn't raise his bearded head. He was like a moving piece of countryside on the edge of my headlight beam.

I had fish and chips at a greasy spoon and went to the sheriff's substation. It was eight by the clock on the wall above Mungan's desk. He looked up from his paperwork:

'Where you been? The Brown kid's been looking for you.'

'I want to see him. Do you know where he went?'

'Over to Doc Dineen's house. They're pretty good friends. He told me that the doc is teaching him how to play chess. That game was always a little over my head. Give me a hand of poker any time.'

I went around the end of the counter and complied with his request, in a way:

'I've been doing some asking around. A couple of things came up that ought to interest you. You say you knew some of the hoods in these parts, back in the early thirties. Does the name Culligan mean anything to you?'

'Yeah. Happy Culligan, they called him. He was in the Red Horse mob.'

'Who were his friends?'

'Let's see.' Mungan stroked his massive chin. 'There was Rossi, Shoulders Nelson, Lefty Dearborn—all of them Lempi's guns. Culligan was more the operator type, but he liked to hang around with the guns.'

'What about Shoulders Nelson?'

'He was about the hardest limb in the bunch. Even his buddies were afraid of him.' A trace of his boyhood admiration showed in Mungan's eyes. 'I saw him beat Culligan to a pulp one night. They both wanted the same girl.'

'What girl?'

'One of the girls upstairs at the Red Horse. I didn't know her name. Nelson shacked up with her for a while, I heard.'

'What did Nelson look like?'

'He was a big man, almost as big as me. The women went for him, he must have been good-looking to them. I never thought so, though. He was a mean-looking bastard, with a long sad face and mean eyes. Him and Rossi and Dearborn got sent up the same time as Lempi.'

'To Alcatraz?'

'Lempi went there, when the Government took it over. But the others took the fall on a larceny charge. Highjacking. The three of them went to San Quentin.'

'What happened to them after that?'

'I didn't keep any track of them. I wasn't in law enforcement at the time. Where is all this supposed to be leading?'

'Shoulders Nelson may be the killer you want,' I said. 'Would your Redwood City office have a dossier on him?'

'I doubt that. He hasn't been heard of around here in more than twenty-five years. It was a state case, anyway.'

'Then Sacramento should have it. You could have Redwood City teletype them.'

Mungan spread his hands on the desk-top and stood up, wagging his big head slowly from side to side. 'If all you got is a hunch, you can't use official channels to test it out for you.'

'I thought we were co-operating.'

'I am. You're not. I've been doing the talking, you've been doing the listening. And this has been going on for quite some time.'

'I told you Nelson's probably our killer. That's a fairly big mouthful.'

'By itself, it doesn't do anything for me.'

'It could if you let it. Try querying Sacramento.'

'What's your source of information?'

'I can't tell you.'

'Like that, eh?'

'I'm afraid so.'

Mungan looked down at me in a disappointed way. Not surprised, just disappointed. We had had the beginning of a beautiful friendship, but I had proved unworthy.

'I hope you know what you're doing.'

'I hope I do. You think about this Nelson angle. It's worth going into. You could earn yourself some very nice publicity.'

'I don't give a damn about publicity.'

'Good for you.'

'And you can go to hell.'

I didn't blame him for blowing off. It's tough to live with a case for half a year and then watch it elope with a casual pickup.

But I couldn't afford to leave him feeling sore. I didn't even want to. I went outside the counter and sat down on a wooden bench against the wall. Mungan resumed his place at his desk and avoided looking at me. I sat there like a penitent while the minute hand of the clock took little pouncing bites of eternity.

At eight-thirty-five Mungan got up and made an elaborate show of discovering me:

'You still here?'

'I'm waiting for a friend—a lawyer from down south. He said he'd be here by nine o'clock.'

'What for? To help you to pick my brains?'

'I don't know why you're browned off, Mungan. This is a big case, bigger than you realize. It's going to take more than one of us to handle it.'

'What makes it so big?'

'The people involved, the money, and the names. At this end we have the Red Horse gang, or what's left of it; at the other end, one of the richest and oldest families in California. It's their lawyer I'm expecting, a man named Sable.'

'So what? I get down on my knees? I give everybody an even shake, treat 'em all alike.'

'Mr. Sable may be able to identify those bones of yours.'

Mungan couldn't repress his interest. 'He the one you talked to on the phone?'

'He's the one.'

'You're working on this case for him?'

'He hired me. And he may be bringing some medical data that will help us identify the remains.'

Mungan went back to his paperwork. After a few minutes, he said casually:

'If you're working for a lawyer, it lets you off the hook. It gives you the same rights of privacy a lawyer has. You probably wouldn't know that, but I've made quite a study of the law.'

'It's news to me,' I lied.

He said magnanimously: 'People in general, even law officers, they don't know all the fine points of the law.'

His pride and his integrity were satisfied. He called the country courthouse and asked them to get a rundown on Nelson from Sacramento.

Gordon Sable walked in at five minutes to nine. He had on a brown topcoat and a brown Homburg, and a pair of yellow pigskin driving gloves. The lids of his grey eyes were slightly inflamed. His mouth was drawn down at the corners, and lines of weariness ran from them to the wings of his nose.

'You made a quick trip,' I said.

'Too quick to suit me. I didn't get away until nearly three o'clock.'

He looked around the small office as if he doubted that the trip had been worth making. Mungan rose expectantly.

'Mr. Sable, Deputy Mungan.'

The two men shook hands, each of them appraising the other.

'Glad to meet you,' Mungan said. 'Mr. Archer tells me you've got some medical information about this—these remains we turned up last spring.'

'That may be.' Sable glanced sideways at me. 'How much more detail did you go into?'

'Just that, and the fact that the family is important. We're not going to be able to keep them anonymous from here on in.'

'I realize that,' he snapped. 'But let's get the identification established first, if we can. Before I left, I talked to the doctor who set the broken arm. He did have X-ray pictures taken, but unfortunately they don't survive. He has his written record, however, and he gave me the—ah—specifications of the fracture.' Sable produced a folded piece of paper from an inner pocket. 'It was a clean break in the right humerus, two inches above the joint. The boy sustained it falling off a horse.'

Mungan said: 'It figures.'

Sable turned to him. 'May we see the exhibit in question?'

Mungan went into the back room.

'Where's the boy?' Sable said in an undertone.

'At a friend's house, playing chess. I'll take you to him when we finish here.'

'Tony was a chess-player. Do you really think he's Tony's son?'

'I don't know. I'm waiting to have my mind made up for me.'

'By the evidence of the bones?'

'Partly. I've got hold of another piece of evidence that fits in. Brown has been identified from one of Tony Galton's pictures.'

'You didn't tell me that before.'

'I didn't know it before.'

'Who's your witness?'

'A woman named Matheson in Redwood City. She's Culligan's ex-wife and Galton's ex-nurse. I've made a commitment to keep her name out of the police case.'

'Is that wise?' Sable's voice was sharp and unpleasant.

'Wise or not, it's the way it is.'

We were close to quarrelling. Mungan came back into the room and cut it short. The bones rattled in his evidence box. He hoisted it on to the counter and raised the lid. Sable looked down at John Brown's leavings. His face was grave.

Mungan picked out the arm bone and laid it on the counter. He went to his desk and came back with a steel foot-rule. The break was exactly two inches from the end.

Sable was breathing quickly. He spoke in repressed excitement: 'It looks very much as if we've found Tony Galton. Why is the skull missing? What was done to him?'

Mungan told him what he knew. On the way to the Dineen house I told Sable the rest of it.

'I have to congratulate you, Archer. You certainly get results.'

'They fell into my lap. It's one of the things that made me suspicious. Too many coincidences came together—the Culligan murder, the Brown-Galton murder, the Brown-Galton boy turning up, if that's who he is. I can't help feeling the whole business may have been planned to come out this way. There are mobsters involved, remember. Those boys look a long way ahead sometimes, and they're willing to wait for their payoff.'

'Payoff?'

'The Galton money. I think the Culligan killing was a gang killing. I think it was no accident that Culligan came to work for you three months ago. Your house was a perfect hide-out for him, and a place where he could watch developments in the Galton family.'

'For what possible purpose?'

'My thinking hasn't got that far,' I said. 'But I'm reasonably certain that Culligan didn't go there on his own.'

'Who sent him?'

'That's the question.' After a pause, I said: 'How is Mrs. Sable, by the way?'

'Not good. I had to put her in a nursing home. I couldn't leave her by herself at home.'

'I suppose it's the Culligan killing that got her down?'

'The doctors seem to think it's what triggered her breakdown. But she's had emotional trouble before.'

'What sort of emotional trouble?'

'I'd just as soon not go into it,' he said bleakly.

CHAPTER FIFTEEN

Dr. Dineen came to the door in an ancient smoking-jacket made of red velvet which reminded me of the plush in old railway coaches. His wrinkled face was set in a frown of concentration. He looked at me impatiently:

'What is it?'

'I think we've identified your skeleton.'

'Really? How?'

'Through the mended break in the arm bone. Dr. Dineen, this is Mr. Sable. Mr. Sable's an attorney representing the dead man's family.'

'Who were his family?'

Sable answered: 'His true name was Anthony Galton. His mother is Mrs. Henry Galton of Santa Teresa.'

'You don't say. I used to see her name on the society pages. She cut quite a swathe at one time.'

'I suppose she did,' Sable said. 'She's an old woman now.'

'We all grow older, don't we? But come in, gentlemen.'

He stood back to let us enter. I turned to him in the hall-way:

'Is John Brown with you?'

'He is, yes. I believe he was trying to locate you earlier in the evening. At the moment he's in my office studying the chessboard. Much good may it do him. I propose to beat him in six more moves.'

'Can you give us a minute, Doctor, by ourselves?'

'If it's important, and I gather it is.'

He steered us into a dining-room furnished in beautiful old mahogany. Light from a yellowing crystal chandelier fell on the dark wood and on the sterling tea set which stood in geometrical order on the tall buffet. The room recalled the feeling I'd had that morning, that the doctor's house was an enclave of the solid past.

He sat at the head of the table and placed us on either side of him. Sable leaned forward across the corner of the table. The events of the day and the one before it had honed his profile sharp:

'Will you give me your opinion of the young man's moral character?'

'I entertain him in my house. That ought to answer your question.'

'You consider him a friend?'

'I do, yes. I don't make a practice of entertaining casual strangers. At my age you can't afford to waste your time on second-rate people.'

'Does that imply that he's a first-rate person?'

'It would seem to.' The doctor's smile was slow, and almost indistinguishable from his frown. 'At least he has the makings. You don't ask much more from a boy of twenty-two.'

'How long have you known him?'

'All his life, if you count your initial introduction. Mr.

96

Archer may have told you that I brought him into the world.'

'Are you certain this is the same boy that you brought into the world?'

'I have no reason to doubt it.'

'Would you swear to it, Doctor?'

'If necessary.'

'It may be necessary. The question of his identity is a highly important one. A very great deal of money is involved.'

The old man smiled, or frowned. 'Forgive me if I'm not overly impressed. Money is only money, after all. I don't believe John is particularly hungry for money. As a matter of fact, this development will be quite a blow to him. He came here in the hope of finding his father, alive.'

'If he qualifies for a fortune,' Sable said, 'it ought to be some comfort to him. Were his parents legally married, do you know?'

'It happens that I can answer that question, in the affirmative. John has been making some inquiries. He discovered just last week that a John Brown and a Theodora Gavin were married in Benicia, by civil ceremony, in September 1936. That seems to make him legitimate, by a narrow margin.'

Sable sat in silence for a minute. He looked at Dineen like a prosecutor trying to weigh the credibility of a witness.

'Well,' the old man said. 'Are you satisfied? I don't wish to appear inhospitable, but I'm an early riser, and it happens to be my bedtime.'

'There are one or two other things, if you'll bear with me, Doctor. I'm wondering, for instance, just how you happen to be so close to the boy's affairs.'

'I choose to be,' Dineen said abruptly.

'Why?'

The doctor looked at Sable with faint dislike. 'My motives are no concern of yours, Counsellor. The young man knocked on my door a month ago, looking for some trace of his family. Naturally I did my best to help him. He has a moral right to the protection and support of his family.'

'If he can prove that he's a member of it.'

'There seems to be no question of that. I think you're being unnecessarily hard on him, and I see no reason why you should continue in that vein. Certainly there's no indication that he's an impostor. He has his birth certificate, which proves the facts of his birth. My name is on it as attending physician. It's why he came to me in the first place.'

'Birth certificates are easy to get,' I said. 'You can write in, pay your money, and take your choice.'

'I suppose you can, if you're a cheat and a scoundrel. I resent the implication that this boy is.'

'Please don't.' Sable moderated his tone. 'As Mrs. Galton's attorney, it's my duty to be sceptical of these claims.'

'John has been making no claims.'

'Perhaps not yet. He will. And very important interests are involved, human as well as financial. Mrs. Galton is in uncertain health. I don't intend to present her with a situation that's likely to blow up in her face.'

'I don't believe that's the case here. You asked me for my opinion, and now you have it. But no human situation is entirely predictable, is it?' The old man leaned forward to get up. His bald scalp gleamed like polished stone in the light from the chandelier. 'You'll be wanting to talk to John, I suppose. I'll tell him you're here.'

He left the room and came back with the boy. John was wearing flannel slacks and a grey sweater over an open-necked shirt. He looked like the recent college graduate that he was supposed to be, but he wasn't at ease in the situation. His eyes shifted from my face to Sable's. Dineen stood beside him in an almost protective posture.

'This is Mr. Sable,' he said in a neutral tone. 'Mr. Sable is an attorney from Santa Teresa, and he's very much interested in you.'

Sable stepped forward and gave him a brisk handshake. 'I'm glad to meet you.'

'Glad to meet you.' His grey eyes matched Sable's in watchfulness. 'I understand you know who my father is.'

'Was, John,' I said. 'We've identified those bones at the station, pretty definitely. They belonged to a man named Anthony Galton. The indications are that he was your father.'

'But my father's name was John Brown.'

'He used that name. It started out as a pen name, apparently.' I looked at the lawyer beside me. 'We can take it for granted, can't we, that Galton and Brown were the same man, and that he was murdered in 1936?'

'It appears so.' Sable laid a restraining hand on my arm. 'I wish you'd let me handle this. There are legal questions involved.'

He turned to the boy, who looked as if he hadn't absorbed

the fact of his father's death. The doctor laid an arm across his shoulders:

'I'm sorry about this, John. I know how much it means to you.'

'It's funny, it doesn't seem to mean a thing. I never knew my father. It's simply words, about a stranger.'

'I'd like to talk to you in private.' Sable said. 'Where can we do that?'

'In my room, I suppose. What are we going to talk about?'

'You.'

He lived in a workingmen's boardinghouse on the other side of town. It was a ramshackle frame house standing among others which had known better days. The landlady intercepted us at the front door. She was a large-breasted Portuguese woman with rings in her ears and spice on her breath. Something in the boy's face made her say:

'Whatsamatter, Johnny? You in trouble?'

'Nothing like that, Mrs. Gorgello,' he said with forced lightness. 'These men are friends of mine. Is it all right if I take them up to my room?'

'It's your room, you pay rent. I cleaned it up today for you, real nice. Come right in, gentlemen,' she said royally.

Not so royally, she jostled the boy as he passed her in the doorway. 'Lift up the long face, Johnny. You look like judgment day.'

His room was a small bare cubicle on the second floor at the rear. I guessed that it had been a servant's room in the days when the house was a private residence. Torn places and stains among the faded roses of the wallpaper hinted at a long history of decline.

The room was furnished with an iron cot covered by an army blanket, a stained pine chest of drawers topped by a clouded mirror, a teetery wardrobe, a kitchen chair standing beside a table. In spite of the books on the table, something about the room reminded me of the dead man Culligan. Perhaps it was the smell, compound of hidden dirt and damp and old grim masculine odours.

My mind skipped to Mrs. Galton's grandiose estate. It would be quite a leap from this place to that. I wondered if the boy was going to make it.

He was standing by the single window, looking at us with a sort of defiance. This was his room, his bearing seemed to say, and we could take it or leave it. He lifted the kitchen chair and turned it away from the table:

'Sit down if you like. One of you can sit on the bed.'

'I'd just as soon stand, thanks,' Sable said. 'I had a long drive up here, and I'm going to have to drive back tonight.'

The boy said stiffly: 'I'm sorry to put you to all this trouble.'

'Nonsense. This is my job, and there's nothing personal about it. Now I understand you have your birth certificate with you. May I have a look at it?'

'Certainly.'

He pulled out the top drawer of the chest of drawers and produced a folded document. Sable put on horn-rimmed spectacles to read it. I read it over his shoulder. It stated that John Brown, Jr., had been born on Bluff Road in San Mateo County on December 2, 1936; father, John Brown; mother, Theodora Gavin Brown; attending physician, Dr. George T. Dineen.

Sable glanced up, snatched off his glasses like a politician:

'You realize this document means nothing in itself? Anyone can apply for a birth certificate, any birth certificate.'

'This one happens to be mine, sir.'

'I notice it was issued only last March. Where were you in March?'

'I was still in Ann Arbor. I lived there for over five years.'

'Going to the University all that time?' I asked.

'Most of it. I attended high school for a year and a half, then I shifted over to the University. I graduated this spring.' He paused, and caught with his teeth at his full lower lip. 'I suppose you'll be checking all this, so I might as well explain that I didn't go to school under my own name.'

'Why? Didn't you know your own name?'

'Of course I did. I always have. If you want me to go into the circumstances, I will.'

'I think that's very much to be desiderated,' Sable said.

The boy picked up one of the books from the table. Its title was *Dramas of Modernism*. He opened it to the flyleaf and showed us the name 'John Lindsay' written in ink there.

'That was the name I used, John Lindsay. The Christian name was my own, of course. The surname belonged to Mr. Lindsay, the man who took me into his home.'

'He lived in Ann Arbor?' Sable said.

'Yes, at 1028 Hill Street.' The boy's tone was faintly sardonic. 'I lived there with him for several years. His full name was Mr. Gabriel R. Lindsay. He was a teacher and counsellor at the high school.'

'Isn't it rather odd that you used his name?'

'I didn't think so, under the circumstances. The circumstances were odd—that's putting it mildly—and Mr. Lindsay was the one who took a real interest in my case.'

'Your case?'

The boy smiled wryly. 'I was a case, all right. I've come a long way in five years, thanks to Mr. Lindsay. I was a mess when I showed up at that high school—a mess in more ways than one. I'd been two days on the road, and I didn't have decent clothes, or anything. Naturally they wouldn't let me in. I didn't have a school record, and I wouldn't tell them my name.'

'Why not?'

'I was mortally scared that they'd drag me back to Ohio and put me in training-school. They did that to some of the boys who ran away from the orphanage. Besides, the superintendent didn't like me.'

'The superintendent of the orphanage?'

'Yes. His name was Mr. Merriweather.'

'What was the name of the orphanage?'

'Crystal Springs. It's near Cleveland. They didn't call it an orphanage. They called it a Home. Which didn't make it any more homelike.'

'You say your mother put you there?' I said.

'When I was four.'

'Do you remember your mother?'

'Of course. I remember her face, especially. She was very pale and thin, with blue eyes. I think she must have been sick. She had a bad cough. Her voice was husky, very low and soft. I remember the last thing she ever said to me: 'Your daddy's name was John Brown, too, and you were born in California.' I didn't know what or where California was, but I held on to the word. You can see why I had to come here, finally.' His voice seemed to have the resonance of his life behind it.

Sable was unimpressed by his emotion. 'Where did she say that to you?'

'In the Superintendent's office, when she left me there. She promised to come back for me, but she never did. I don't know what happened to her.'

'But you remember her words from the age of four?'

'I was bright for my age,' he answered matter-of-factly. 'I'm bright, and I'm not ashamed of it. It stood me in good stead when I was trying to get into the high school in Ann Arbor.'

'Why did you pick Ann Arbor?'

'I heard it was a good place to get an education. The teachers in the Home were a couple of ignorant bullies. I wanted an education more than anything. Mr. Lindsay gave me an aptitude test, and he decided that I deserved an education, even if I didn't have any transcript. He put up quite a battle for me, getting me into the high school. And then he had to fight the welfare people. They wanted to put me in Juvenile, or find a foster-home for me. Mr. Lindsay convinced them that his home would do, even if he didn't have a wife. He was a widower.'

'He sounds like a good man,' I said.

'He was the best, and I ought to know. I lived with him for nearly four years. I looked after the furnace, mowed the lawn in the summer, worked around the house to pay for my board and room. But board and room was the least of what he gave me. I was a little bum when he took me in. He made a decent person out of me.'

He paused, and his eyes looked past us, thousands of miles. Then they focused on me:

'I had no right today, to tell you that I never had a father. Gabe Lindsay was a father to me.'

'I'd like to meet him,' I said.

'So that you can check up on me?'

'Not necessarily. Don't take all this so hard, John. As Mr. Sable said, there's nothing personal about it. It's our business to get the facts.'

'It's too late to get them from Mr. Lindsay. Mr. Lindsay died the winter before last. He was good to me right up to the end, and past it. He left me enough money to finish my studies.'

'How much did he leave you?' Sable said.

'Two thousand dollars. I still have a little of it left.'

'What did he die of?'

'Pneumonia. He died in the University Hospital in Ann Arbor. I was with him when he died. You can check that. Next question.'

His irony was young and vulnerable. It failed to mask his feeling. I thought if his feeling was artificial, he didn't need the Galton money: he could make his fortune as an actor.

'What motivated you to come here to Luna Bay?' Sable said. 'It couldn't have been pure coincidence.'

'Who said it was?' Under the pressure of cross-questioning, the boy's poise was breaking down. 'I had a right to come here. I was born here, wasn't I?'

'Were you?'

'You just saw my birth certificate.'

'How did you get hold of it?'

'I wrote to Sacramento. Is there anything wrong with that? I gave them my birthdate, and they were able to tell me where I was born.'

'Why the sudden interest in where you were born?'

'It wasn't a sudden interest. Ask any orphan how important it is to him. The only sudden part of it was my bright idea of writing to Sacramento. It hadn't occurred to me before.'

'How did you know your birthdate?'

'My mother must have told the orphanage people. They always gave me a birthday present on December second.' He grinned wryly. 'Winter underwear.'

Sable smiled, too, in spite of himself. He waved his hand in front of his face, as if to dissipate the tension in the room: 'Are you satisfied, Archer?'

'I am for now. We've all had a long day. Why don't you lay over for the night?'

'I can't. I have an important probate coming up at ten tomorrow morning. Before that, I have to talk to the Judge in his chambers.' He turned suddenly to the boy: 'Do you drive a car?'

'I don't have one of my own, but I can drive.'

'How would you like to drive me to Santa Teressa? Now.'

'To stay?'

'If it works out. I think it will. Your grandmother will be eager to see you.'

'But Mr. Turnell's counting on me at the station.'

'He can get himself another boy,' I said. 'You better go, John. You're due for a big change, and this is the beginning of it.'

'I'll give you ten minutes to pack,' Sable said.

The boy seemed dazed for a minute. He looked around the walls of the mean little room as if he hated to leave it. Perhaps he was afraid to make the big leap.

'Come on,' Sable said. 'Snap into it.'

John shook himself out of his apathy, and dragged an old leather suitcase from the wardrobe. We stood and watched him pack his meagre belongings: a suit, a few shirts and socks, shaving gear, a dozen books, his precious birth certificate.

I wondered if we were doing him a favour. The Galton household had hot and cold running money piped in from an inexhaustible reservoir. But money was never free. Like any other commodity, it had to be paid for.

CHAPTER SIXTEEN

I sat up late in my motel room, making notes on John Brown's story. It wasn't a likely story, on the face of it. His apparent sincerity made it plausible; that, and the fact that it could easily be checked. Some time in the course of the interview I'd made a moral bet with myself that John Brown was telling the truth. John Galton, that is.

In the morning I mailed my notes to my office in Hollywood. Then I paid a visit to the sheriff's substation. A young deputy with a crewcut was sitting at Mungan's desk.

'Yessir?'

'Is Deputy Mungan anywhere around?'

'Sorry, he's off duty. If you're Mr. Archer, he left a message for you.'

He took a long envelope out of a drawer and handed it across the counter. It contained a hurried note written on yellow scratch-pad paper:

R.C. phoned me some dope on Fred Nelson. Record goes back to S.F. docks in twenties. Assault with intent, nolle-prossed. Lempi gang enforcer 1928 - on. Arrested suspicion murder 1930, habeas-corpused. Convicted grand theft 1932 sentenced 'Q.' Attempted escape 1933, extended sentence. Escaped December 1936, never apprehended.

Mungan.

I walked across the street to the hotel and phoned Roy Lemberg's hotel, the Sussex Arms. The desk clerk answered:

'Sussex Arms. Mr Farnsworth speaking.'

'This is Archer. Is Lemberg there?'

'Who did you say it was?'

'Archer. I gave you ten dollars yesterday. Is Lemberg there?'

'Mr. and Mrs. Lemberg both checked out.'

'When?'

'Yesterday aft, right after you left.'

'Why didn't I see them go?'

'Maybe because they went out the back way. They didn't even leave a forwarding address. But Lemberg made a long-distance call before they took off. A call to Reno.'

'Who did he call in Reno?'

'Car-dealer name of Generous Joe. Lemberg used to work for him, I think.'

'And that's all there is?'

'That's all,' Farnsworth said. 'I hope it's what you want.'

I drove across country to International Airport, turned in my rented car, and caught a plane to Reno. By noon I was parking another rented car in front of Generous Joe's lot.

A huge billboard depicted a smiling Santa Claus type scattering silver dollars. The lot had a kiosk on one corner, and a row of late-model cars fronting for half an acre of clunks. A big corrugated metal shed with a Cars Painted sign on the wall stood at the rear of the lot.

An eager young man with a rawhide tie cantered out of the kiosk almost before I'd brought my car to a halt. He patted and stroked the fender:

'Nice. Very nice. Beautiful condition, clean inside and out. Depending on your equity, you can trade up and still carry cash away.'

'They'd put me in jail. I just rented this crate.'

He gulped, performed a mental back somersault, and landed on his feet: 'So why pay rent? On our terms, you can *own* a car for less money.'

'You wouldn't be Generous Joe?'

'Mr. Culotti's in the back. You want to talk to him?'

I said I did. He waved me toward the shed, and yelled: 'Hey. Mr. Culotti, customer!'

A grey-haired man came out, looking cheaply gala in an ice-cream suit. His face was swarthy and pitted like an Epstein bronze, and its two halves didn't quite match. When I got closer to him, I saw that one of his brown eyes was made of glass. He looked permanently startled.

'Mr. Culotti?'

'That's me.' He smiled a money smile. 'What can I do for you?' A trace of Mediterranean accent added feminine endings to some of his words.

'A man named Lemberg called you yesterday.'

'That's right, he used to work for me, wanted his old job back. Nix.' A gesture of his spread hand swept Lemberg into the dust-bin.

'Is he back in Reno? I'm trying to locate him.'

Culotti picked at his nose and looked wise, in a startled way. He smiled expansively, and put a fatherly arm around my back. 'Come in, we'll talk.'

He propelled me toward the door. Hissing sounds came from the shed, and the sweet anaesthetic odour of sprayed paint. Culotti opened the door and stepped back. A goggled man with a paint-gun turned from his work on a blue car.

I was trying to recognize him, when Culotti's shoulder caught me like a trunk-bumper in the small of the back. I staggered toward the goggled man. The paint-gun hissed in his hands.

A blue cloud stung my eyes. In the burning blue darkness, I recalled that the room clerk Farnsworth hadn't asked me for more money. Then I felt the sap's soft explosion against the back of my head. I glissaded down blue slopes of pain to a hole which opened for me.

Later there was talking.

'Better wash out his eyes,' the first gravedigger said. 'We don't want to blind him.'

'Let him go blind,' the second gravedigger said. 'Teach him a lesson. I got a hook in the eye.'

'Did it teach you a lesson, Blind-eye? Do what I tell you.'

I heard Culotti breathe like a bull. He spat, but made no answer. My hands were tied behind me. My face was on cement. I tried to blink. My eyelids were stuck tight.

The fear of blindness is the worst fear there is. It crawled on my face and entered my mouth. I wanted to beg them to save my eyes. A persistent bright speck behind my eyes stared me down and shamed me into continued silence.

Liquid gurgled in a can.

'Not with gasoline, greaseball.'

'Don't call me that.'

'Why not? You're a blind-eye greaseball, hamburger that used to be muscle.' This voice was light and featureless, without feeling, almost without meaning. 'You got any olive oil?'

'At home, plenty.'

'Go and get it. I'll keep store.'

My consciousness must have lapsed. Oil ran on my face like

tears. I thought of a friend named Angelo who made his own oil from olives he grew on his hillside in the Valley. The Mafia had killed his father.

A face came into blurred focus, Culotti's face, hanging slack-mouthed over me. I twisted from my side on to my back, and lashed at him with both feet. One heel caught him under the chin, and he went down. Something bounced and rolled on the floor. Then he stood one-eyed over me, bleeding at the mouth. He stamped my head back down into earthy darkness.

It was a bad afternoon. Quite suddenly it was a bad evening. Somebody had awakened me with his snoring. I listened to the snoring for a while. It stopped when I held my breath and started again when I let my breath out. For a long time I missed the significance of this.

There were too many other interesting things to do and think about. The staring speck was back again in the centre of my mind. It moved, and my hands moved with it. They felt my face. It bored me. Ruins always bored me.

I was lying in a room. The room had walls. There was a window in one of the walls. Snow-capped mountains rose against a yellow sky, which darkened to green, then blue. Twilight hung like blue smoke in the room.

I sat up; springs creaked under me. A man I hadn't noticed moved away from the wall he'd been leaning on. I dropped my feet to the floor and turned to face him, slowly and carefully, so as not to lose my balance.

He was a thick young man with shiny black curls tumbling over his forehead. One of his arms was in a sling. The other arm had a gun at the end of it. His hot eyes and the cold eye of the gun triangulated my breastbone.

'Hello, Tommy,' I tried to say. It came out: 'Huddo, Tawy.'

My mouth contained ropes of blood. I tried to spit them out. That started a chain-reaction which flung me back on the bed retching and cawing. Tommy Lemberg stood and watched me.

He said when I was still: 'Mr. Schwartz is waiting to talk to you. You want to clean up a little?'

'When do I do dat?' I said in my inimitable patois.

'There's a bathroom down the hall. Think you can walk?'

'I can walk.'

But I had to lean on the wall to reach the bathroom. Tommy Lemberg stood and watched me wash my face and gargle. I tried to avoid looking into the mirror over the sink. I looked, though, finally, when I was drying my nose. One of my front teeth was broken off short. My nose resembled a boiled potato.

All of this made me angry. I moved on Tommy. He stepped back into the doorway. I lost my footing and fell to my knees, took the barrel of his gun in the nape of my neck. Pain went through me so large and dull it scared me. I got up, supporting myself on the sink.

Tommy was grinning in an excited way. 'Don't *do* things like that. I don't want to hurt you.'

'Or Culligan, either, I bet.' I was talking better now, but my eyes weren't focusing properly.

'Culligan? Who he? I never heard of any Culligan.'

'And you've never been in Santa Teresa?'

'Where's that?'

He ushered me to the end of the corridor and down a flight of steps into a big dim room. In its picture windows, the mountains now stood black against the darkening sky. I recognized the mountains west of Reno. Tommy turned on lights which blotted them out. He moved around the room as if he was at home there.

I suppose it was the living-room of Otto Schwartz's house, but it was more like the lobby of a hotel or the recreation room of an institution. The furniture stood around in impersonal groupings, covered with plastic so that nothing could harm it. An antique bar and a wall of bottles took up one whole end. A jukebox, an electric player piano, a roulette layout, and several slot machines stood against the rear wall.

'You might as well sit down.' Tommy waved his gun at a chair.

I sat down and closed my eyes, which still weren't focusing. Everything I looked at had a double outline. I was afraid of concussion. I was having a lot of fears.

Tommy turned on the player piano. It started to tinkle out a tune about a little Spanish town. Tommy did a few dance steps to it, facing me and holding the gun in his hand. He didn't seem to know what to do with himself.

I concentrated on wishing that he would put his gun away and give me some kind of chance at him. He never would, though. He loved holding the gun. He held it different ways, posturing in front of his reflection in the window. I began to draft a mental letter to my congressman advocating legislation prohibiting the manufacture of guns except for millitary purposes.

Mr. J. Edgar Hoover entered the room at this point. He must have been able to read minds, because he said that he approved of my plan and intended to present it to the President. I felt my forehead. It was hot and dry, like a heating-pad. Mr. Hoover faded away. The player piano went on hammering out the same tune: music to be delirious by.

The man who came in next radiated chill from green glacial eyes. He had a cruel nose and under it the kind of mouth that smiles by stretching horizontally. He must have been nearly sixty but he had a well-sustained tan and a lean quick body. He wore a light fedora and a topcoat.

So did the man who moved a step behind him and towered half a foot over him. This one had the flat impervious eyes, the battered face and pathological nervelessness of an old-fashioned western torpedo. When his boss paused in front of me, he stood to one side in canine watchfulness. Tommy moved up beside him, like an apprentice.

'You're quite a mess.' Schwartz's voice was chilly, too, and very soft, expecting to be listened to. 'I'm Otto Schwartz, in case you don't know. I got no time to waste on two-bit private eyes. I got other things on my mind.'

'What kind of things have you got on it? Murder?'

He tightened up. Instead of hitting me, he took off his hat and threw it to Tommy. His head was completely bald. He put his hands in his coat pockets and leaned back on his heels and looked down the curve of his nose at me:

'I was giving you the benefit, that you got in over your head without knowing. What's going to happen, you go on like this, talk about murder, crazy stuff like that?' He wagged his head solemnly from side to side. 'Lake Tahoe is very deep. You could take a long dive, no Aqualung, concrete on the legs.'

'You could sit in a hot seat, no cushion, electrodes on the bald head.'

The big man took a step toward me, watching Schwartz with a doggy eye, and lunged around with his big shoulders. Schwartz surprised me by laughing, rather tinnily:

'You are a brave young man. I like you. I wish you no harm. What do you suggest? A little money, and that's that?'

'A little murder. Murder everybody. Then you can be the bigshot of the world.'

'I am a bigshot, don't ever doubt it.' His mouth pursed suddenly and curiously, like a wrinkled old wound: 'I take in-

109

sults from nobody! And nobody steals from me.'

'Did Culligan steal from you? Is that why you ordered him killed?'

Schwartz looked down at me some more. His eyes had dark centres. I thought of the depths of Tahoe, and poor drowned Archer with concrete on his legs. I was in a susceptible mood, and fighting it. Tommy Lemberg spoke up:

'Can I say something, Mr. Schwartz? I didn't knock the guy off. The cops got it wrong. He must of fell down on the knife and stabbed himself.'

'Yah! Moron!' Schwartz turned his contained fury on Tommy: 'Go tell that to the cops. Just leave me out of it, please.'

'They wouldn't believe me,' he said in a misunderstood whine. 'They'd pin it on me, just because I tried to defend myself. I was the one got shot. He pulled a gun on me.'

'Shut up! Shut up!' Schwartz spread one hand on top of his head and pulled at imaginary hair. 'Why is there no intelligence left in the world? All morons!'

'The intelligent ones wouldn't touch your rackets with a ten-foot pole.'

'I heard enough out of you.'

He jerked his head at the big man, who started to take off his coat:

'Want me to work him over, Mr. Schwartz?'

It was the light and meaningless voice that had argued with Culotti. It lifted me out of my chair. Because Schwartz was handy, I hit him in the stomach. He jack-knifed, and went down gasping. It doesn't take much to make me happy, and that gave me a happy feeling which lasted through the first three or four minutes of the beating.

Then the big man's face began to appear in red snatches. When the light in the room failed entirely, the bright staring speck in my mind took over for a while. Schwartz's voice kept making tinny little jokes:

'Just promise to forget it, that will be that.'

'All you gotta do, give me your word. I'm a man of my word, you're another.'

'Back to L.A., that's all you gotta do. No questions asked, no harm done.'

The bright speck stood like a nail in my brain. It wouldn't let me let go of the room. I cursed it, but it wouldn't go away.

It wrote little luminous remarks on the red pounding darkness: This is it. You take a stand.

Then it was a light surging away from me like the light of a ship. I swam for it, but it rose away, hung in the dark heaven still as a star. I let go of the pounding room, and swung from it up and over the black mountains.

CHAPTER SEVENTEEN

I came to early next morning in the accident ward of the Reno hospital. When I had learned to talk with a packed nose and a wired jaw, a couple of detectives asked me who took my wallet. I didn't bother disturbing their assumption that I was a mugging victim.

Anything I told them about Schwartz would be wasted words. Besides, I needed Schwartz. The thought of him got me through the first bad days, when I doubted from time to time that I would be very active in the future. Everything was still fuzzy at the edges. I got very tired of fuzzy nurses and earnest young fuzzy doctors asking me how my head felt.

By the fourth day, though, my vision was clear enough to read some of yesterday's newspapers which the voluntary aides brought around for the ward patients. There was hardware in the sky, and dissension on earth. A special dispatch in the back pages told how a real-life fairy-tale had reached its happy ending when the long-lost John Galton was restored to the bosom of his grandmother, the railroad and oil widow. In the accompanying photograph, John himself was wearing a new-looking sports jacket and a world-is-my-oyster grin.

This spurred me on. By the end of the first week, I was starting to get around. One morning after my Cream of Wheat I sneaked out to the nurses' station and put in a collect call to Santa Teresa. I had time to tell Gordon Sable where I was, before the head nurse caught me and marched me back to the ward.

Sable arrived while I was eating my Gerber's-baby-food dinner. He waved a chequebook. Before I knew it I was in a private room with a bottle of Old Forester which Sable had brought me. I sat up late with him, drinking highballs through a glass tube and talking through my remaining teeth like a gangster in very early sound.

'You're going to need a crown on that tooth,' Sable said comfortingly. 'Also, plastic surgery on the nose. Do you have any hospital insurance?'

'No.'

'I'm afraid I can't commit Mrs. Galton.' Then he took another look at me, and his manner softened: 'Well, yes, I think I can. I think I can persuade her to underwrite the expense, even though you did exceed your instructions.'

'That's mighty white of you and her.' But the words didn't come out ironic. It had been a bad eight days. 'Doesn't she give a good goddam about who murdered her son? And what about Culligan?'

'The police are working on both cases, don't worry.'

'They're the same case. The cops are sitting on their tails. Schwartz put the fix in.'

Sable shook his head. 'You're way off in left field, Lew.'

'The hell I am. Tommy Lemberg's his boy. Have they arrested Tommy?'

'He dropped out of sight. Don't let it ride you. You're a willing man, but you can't take on responsibility for all the trouble in the world. Not in your present condition, anyway.'

'I'll be on my feet in another week. Sooner.' The whisky in the bottle was falling like a barometer. I was full of stormy optimism. Give me another week after that and I'll break the case wide open for you.'

'I hope so, Lew. But don't take too much on yourself. You've been hurt, and naturally your feelings are a bit exaggerated.'

He was sitting directly under the light, but his face was getting fuzzy. I leaned out of bed and grabbed his shoulder. 'Listen, Sable, I can't prove it, but I can feel it. That Galton boy is a phony, part of a big conspiracy, with the Organization behind it.'

'I think you're wrong. I've spent hours on his story. It checks out. And Mrs. Galton is quite happy, for the first time in many years.'

'I'm not.'

He rose, and pushed me gently back against the pillows. I was still as weak as a cat. 'You've talked enough for one night. Let it rest, and don't worry, eh? Mrs. Galton will take care of everything, and if she doesn't want to, I'll make her. You've earned her gratitude. We're all sorry this had to happen.'

He shook my hand and started for the door.

'Flying back tonight?' I asked him.

'I have to. My wife's in bad shape. Take it easy, now, you'll hear from me. And I'll leave some money for you at the desk.'

CHAPTER EIGHTEEN

I sprung myself out of the hospital three days later, and assembled myself aboard a plane for San Francisco. From International Airport I took a cab to the Sussex Arms Hotel.

The room clerk, Farnsworth, was sitting behind the counter at the rear of the dim little lobby, looking as if he hadn't moved in two weeks. He was reading a muscle magazine, and he didn't look up until I was close enough to see the yellow of his eyes. Even then he didn't recognize me right away: the bandages on my face made an effective mask.

'You wish a room, sir?'

'No. I came to see you.'

'Me?' His eyebrows jumped, and then came down in a frown of concentration.

'I owe you something.'

The colour left his face. 'No. No, you don't. That's all right.'

'The other ten and the bonus. That makes fifteen I owe you. Excuse the delay. I got held up.'

'That's too bad.' He craned his neck around and looked behind him. There was nothing there but the switchboard, staring like a wall of empty eyes.

'Don't let it bother you, Farnsworth. It wasn't your fault. Was it?'

'No.' He swallowed several times. 'It wasn't my fault.'

I stood and smiled at him with the visible parts of my face.

'What happened?' he said after a while.

'It's a long sad story. You wouldn't be interested.'

I took the creaking new wallet out of my hip pocket and laid a five and a ten on the counter between us. He sat and looked at the money.

'Take it,' I said.

He didn't move.

'Go ahead, don't be bashful. The money belongs to you.'

'Well. Thanks.'

Slowly and reluctantly, he reached out for the bills. I caught his wrist in my left hand, and held it. He jerked convulsively, reached under the counter and came up with a gun in his left hand:

'Turn me loose.'

'Not a chance.'

'I'll shoot!' But the gun was wavering.

I reached for his gun wrist, and twisted it until the gun dropped on the counter between us. It was a .32 revolver, a little nickel-plated suicide gun. I let go of Farnsworth and picked it up and pointed it at the knot of his tie. Without moving, he seemed to draw away from it. His eyes got closer together.

'Please. I couldn't help it.'

'What couldn't you help?'

'I had orders to give you that contact in Reno.'

'Who gave you the orders?'

'Roy Lemberg. It wasn't my fault.'

'Lemberg doesn't give orders to anybody. He's the kind that takes them.'

'Sure, he passed the word, that's what I meant.'

'Who gave him the word?'

'Some gambler in Nevada, name of Schwartz.' Farnsworth wet his mauve lips with his tongue. 'Listen, you don't want to ruin me. I make a little book, lay off the heavy bets. If I don't do like the money boys say, I'm out of business. So have a heart, mister.'

'If you level with me. Does Lemberg work for Schwartz?'

'His brother does. Not him.'

'Where are the Lembergs now?'

'I wouldn't know about the brother. Roy took off like I said, him and his wife both. Put the gun down, mister. Jeez. I got a nervous stomach.'

'You'll have a perforated ulcer if you don't talk. Where did the Lembergs go?'

'Los Angeles, I think.'

'Where in Los Angeles?'

'I dunno.' He spread his hands. They had a tremor running through them, like dry twigs in a wind. 'Honest.'

'You know, Farnsworth,' I said in my menacing new lockjaw voice, 'I'll give you five seconds to tell me.'

He looked around at the switchboard again, as if it was an

instrument of execution, and swallowed audibly. 'All right, I'll tell you. They're at a motor court on Bayshore, down by Moffett Field. The Triton Motor Court. At least, that's where they said they were going. Now will you put down the gun, mister?'

Before the rhythm of his fear ran down, I said: 'Do you know a man named Peter Culligan?'

'Yeah. He roomed here for a while, over a year ago.'

'What did he do for a living?'

'He was a horseplayer.'

'That's a living?'

'I guess he hacked a little, too. Put the gun down, eh? I told you what you wanted to know.'

'Where did Culligan go from here?'

'I heard he got a job in Reno.'

'Working for Schwartz?'

'Could be. He told me once he used to be a stickman.'

I dropped the gun in my jacket pocket.

'Hey,' he said. 'That's my gun. I bought it myself.'

'You're better off without it.'

Looking back from the door, I saw that Farnsworth was halfway between the counter and the switchboard. He stopped in mid-motion. I went back across the lobby:

'If it turns out you're lying, or if you tip off the Lembergs, I'll come back for you. Is that clear?'

A kind of moral wriggle moved up his body from his waist to his fish-belly face. 'Yeah. Sure. Okay.'

This time I didn't look back. I walked up to Union Square, where I made a reservation on an afternoon flight to L.A. Then I rented a car and drove down Bayshore past the airport.

The hangars of Moffett Field loomed up through the smog like grey leviathans. The Triton Motor Court stood in a wasteland of shacks on the edge of the flight pattern. Its buildings were a fading salmon pink. Its only visible attraction was the $3.00 Double sign. Jets snored like flies in the sky.

I parked on the cinder driveway beside the chicken-coop office. The woman who ran it wore a string of fake pearls dirtied by her neck. She said that Mr. and Mrs. Lemberg weren't registered there.

'They may be going under their maiden name.' I described them.

'Sounds like the girl in seven, maybe. She don't want to be disturbed, not in the daytime.'

'She won't mind. I have no designs on her.'

She bridled. 'Who said you had? What kind of a place do you think this is, anyway?'

It was a tough question to answer. I said: 'What name is she going under?'

'You from the cops? I don't want trouble with the cops.'

'I was in an accident. She may be able to help me find the driver.'

'That's different.' The woman probably didn't believe me, but she chose to act as if she did. 'They registered under the name Hamburg. Mr. and Mrs. Rex Hamburg.'

'Is her husband with her?'

'Not for the last week. Maybe it's just as well,' she added cryptically.

I knocked on the weathered door under the rusted iron seven. Footsteps dragged across the floor behind it. Fran Lemberg blinked in the light. Her eyes were puffed. The roots of her hair were darker. Her robe was taking on a grimy patina.

She stopped blinking when she recognized me.

'Go away.'

'I'm coming in for a minute. You don't want trouble.'

She looked past me, and I followed her look. The woman with the dirty pearls was watching us from the window of the office.

'All right, come in.'

She let me come in past her, and slammed the door on daylight. The room smelled of wine and smoke, stale orange-peel and a woman's sleep, and a perfume I didn't recognize, Original Sin perhaps. When my eyes became night-adapted, I saw the confusion on the floor and the furniture: clothes and looped stockings and shoes and empty bottles, ashes and papers, the congealed remains of hamburgers and french fries.

She sat in a defensive posture on the edge of the unmade bed. I cleared a space for myself on the chair.

'What happened to you?' she said.

'I had a run-in with some of Tommy's playmates. Your husband set me up for the fall.'

'Roy did?'

'Don't kid me, you were with him at the time. I thought he was a straight joe trying to help his brother, but he's just another errandboy for mobsters.'

'No. He isn't.'

'Is that what he told you?'

'I lived with him nearly ten years, I ought to know. He worked one time for a crooked car-dealer in Nevada. When Roy found out about the crookedness, he quit. That's the kind of guy he is.'

'If you mean Generous Joe, that hardly qualifies Roy as a boy scout.'

'I didn't say he was. He's just a guy trying to get through life.'

'Some of us make it harder for the others.'

'You can't blame Roy for trying to protect himself. He's wanted for accessory in a murder. But it isn't fair. You can't blame him for what Tommy did.'

'You're a loyal wife,' I said. 'But where is it getting you?'

'Who says I want to get any place?'

'There are better places than this.'

'You're telling me. I've lived in some of them.'

'How long has Roy been gone?'

'Nearly two weeks, I guess. I don't keep track of the time. It goes faster that way.'

'How old are you, Fran?'

'None of your business.' After a pause she added: 'A hundred and twenty-eight.'

'Is Roy coming back?'

'He says he is. But he always sides with his brother when the chips are down.' Emotion flooded up in her eyes, but drained away again. 'I guess I can't blame him. This time the chips are really down.'

'Tommy's staying in Nevada,' I said, trying to find the wedge that would open her up.

'Tommy's in Nevada?'

'I saw him there. Schwartz is looking after him. And Roy, too, probably.'

'I don't believe you. Roy said they were leaving the country.'

'The state, maybe. Isn't that what he said, that they were leaving the state?'

'The country,' she repeated stubbornly. 'That's why they couldn't take me along.'

'They were stringing you. They just don't want a woman in the way. So here you sit in a rundown crib on Bayshore. Hustling for hamburgers, while the boys are living high on the hog in Nevada.'

'You're a liar!' she cried. 'They're in Canada!'

'Don't let them kid you.'

'Roy is going to send for me as soon as he can swing it.'

'You've heard from him, then.'

'Yeah, I've heard from him.' Her loose mouth tightened, too late to hold back the words. 'Okay, so you got it out of me. That's all you're going to get out of me.' She folded her arms across her half-naked breasts, and looked at me grimly: 'Why don't you beat it? You got nothing on me, you never will have.'

'As soon as you show me Roy's letter.'

'There was no letter. I got the message by word of mouth.'

'Who brought it?'

'A guy.'

'What guy?'

'Just a guy. Roy told him to look me up.'

'He sent him from Nevada, probably.'

'He did not. The guy drove a haulaway out from Detroit. He talked to Roy in Detroit.'

'Is that where Roy and Tommy crossed the border?'

'I guess so.'

'Where were they headed?'

'I don't know, and I wouldn't tell you if I did know.'

I sat on the bed beside her. 'Listen to me, Fran. You want your husband back, don't you?'

'Not in a convict suit, or on a slab.'

'It doesn't have to be that way. Tommy's the one we're after. If Roy will turn him over to us, he'll be taking a long step out of trouble. Can you get that message to Roy from me?'

'Maybe if he phones me or something. All I can do is wait.'

'You must have some idea where they went.'

'Yeah, they said something about this town in Ontario near Windsor. Tommy was the one that knew about it.'

'What's the name of the place?'

'They didn't say.'

'Was Tommy ever in Canada before?'

'No, but Pete Culligan—'

She covered the lower part of her face with her hand and looked at me over it. Fear and distress hardened her eyes, but not for long. Her feelings were too diffuse to sustain themselves.

I said: 'Tommy did know Culligan, then?'

She nodded.

'Did he have a personal reason for killing Culligan?'

'Not that I know of. Him and Pete were palsy-walsy.'

'When did you see them together?'

'Last winter in Frisco. Tommy was gonna jump parole until Roy talked him out of it, and Pete told him about this place in Canada. It's sort of an irony of fate like, now Tommy's hiding out there for knocking Pete off.'

'Did Tommy admit to you that he killed Culligan?'

'No, to hear him tell it he's innocent as an unborn babe. Roy even believes him.'

'But you don't?'

'I swore off believing Tommy the day after I met him. But we won't go into that.'

'Where is this hide-out in Canada?'

'I don't know.' Her voice was taking on an edge of hysteria. 'Why don't you go away and leave me alone?'

'Will you contact me if you hear from them?'

'Maybe I will, maybe I won't.'

'How are you fixed for money?'

'I'm loaded,' she said. 'What do you think? I park in this crib because I like the homey atmosphere.'

I dropped a ten in her lap as I went out. Before my plane took off for Los Angeles, I had time to phone Sheriff Trask. I filled him in, with emphasis on Culligan's probable connection with Schwartz. In the rational light of day, I didn't want Schwartz all to myself.

CHAPTER NINETEEN

In the morning, after a session with my dentist, I opened up my office on Sunset Boulevard. The mailbox was stuffed with envelopes, mostly bills and circulars. There were two envelopes mailed from Santa Teresa in the past few days.

The first one I opened contained a cheque for a thousand dollars and a short letter from Gordon Sable typed on the letterhead of his firm. Sad as was the fact of Anthony Galton's death, his client and he both felt that the over-all outcome was better than could have been hoped for. He hoped and trusted that I was back in harness, and none the worse for wear, and would I forward my medical bills as I received them.

The other letter was a carefully hand-written note from John Galton:

Dear Mr. Archer—

Just a brief note to thank you for your labours on my behalf. My father's death is a painful blow to all of us here. There is tragedy in the situation, which I have to learn to face up to. But there is also opportunity, for me. I hope to prove myself worthy of my patrimony.

Mr. Sable told me how you 'fell among thieves.' I hope that you are well again, and Grandmother joins me in this wish. For what it's worth, I did persuade Grandmother to send you an additional cheque in token of appreciation. She joins me in inviting you to visit us when you can make the trip up this way.

I myself would like very much to talk to you.

Respectfully yours,
John Galton.

It seemed to be pure gratitude undiluted by commercialism, until I reflected that he was taking credit for the cheque Sable had sent me. His letter stirred up the suspicions that had been latent in my mind since I'd talked to Sable in the hospital. Whatever John was, he was a bright boy and a fast worker. I wondered what he wanted from me.

After going through the rest of my mail, I called my answering-service. The girl at the switchboard expressed surprise that I was still in the land of the living, and told me that a Dr. Howell had been trying to reach me. I called the Santa Teresa number he'd left.

A girl's voice answered: 'Dr. Howell's residence.'

'This is Lew Archer. Miss Howell?' The temporary crown I'd just acquired that morning pushed out against my upper lip, and made me lisp.

'Yes, Mr. Archer.'

'Your father has been trying to get in touch with me.'

'Oh. He's just leaving for the hospital. I'll see if I can catch him.'

After a pause, Howell's precise voice came over the line: 'I'm glad to hear from you, Archer. You may recall that we met briefly at Mrs. Galton's house. I'd like to buy you a lunch.'

'Lunch will be fine. What time and place do you have in mind?'

'The time is up to you—the sooner the better. The Santa Teresa Country Club would be the most convenient place for me.'

120

'It's a long way for me to come for lunch.'

'I had a little more than lunch in mind.' He lowered his voice as though he suspected eavesdroppers. 'I'd like to engage your services, if you're free.'

'To do what?'

'I'd much prefer to discuss that in person. Would today be possible for you?'

'Yes. I'll be at the Country Club at one.'

'You can't drive it in three hours, man.'

'I'll take the noon plane.'

'Oh, fine.'

I heard the click as he hung up, and then a second click. Someone had been listening on an extension. I found out who it was when I got off the plane at Santa Teresa. A young girl with doe eyes and honey-coloured hair was waiting for me at the barrier.

'Remember me? I'm Sheila Howell. I thought I'd pick you up.'

'That was a nice thought.'

'Not really. I have an ulterior motive.'

She smiled charmingly. I followed her through the sunlit terminal to her car. It was a convertible with the top down.

Sheila turned to me as she slid behind the wheel: 'I might as well be frank about it. I overheard what was said, and I wanted to talk to you about John before Dad does. Dad is a well-meaning person, but he's been a widower for ten years, and he has certain blind spots. He doesn't understand the modern world.'

'But you do?'

She coloured slightly, like a peach in the sun. 'I understand it better than Dad does. I've studied social science at college, and people just don't go around any more telling other people who to be interested in. That sort of thing is as dead as the proverbial dodo. Deader.' She nodded her small head, once, with emphasis.

'First-year social science?'

The colour in her cheeks deepened. Her eyes were candid, the colour of the sky. 'How did you know? Anyway, I'm a sophomore now.' As if this made all the difference between adolescence and maturity.

'I'm a mind reader. You're interested in John Galton.'

Her pure gaze didn't waver. 'I love John. I think he loves me.'

'Is that what you wanted to say to me?'

'No.' She was suddenly flustered. 'I didn't mean to say it. But it's true.' Her eyes darkened. 'The things that Dad believes aren't true, though. He's just a typical patriarch type, full of prejudices against the boy I happen to like. He believes the most awful things against John, or pretends to.'

'What things, Sheila?'

'I wouldn't even repeat them, so there. Anyway, you'll be hearing them from him. I know what Dad wants you to do, you see. He let the cat out of the bag last night.'

'What does he want me to do?'

'Please,' she said, 'don't talk to me as if I were a child. I know that tone so well, and I'm so tired of it. Dad uses it on me all the time. He doesn't realize I'm practically grown up. I'm going to be nineteen on my next birthday.'

'Wow,' I said softly.

'All right, go ahead and patronize me. Maybe I'm not mature. I'm mature enough to know good people from bad people.'

'We all make mistakes about people, no matter how ancient we are.'

'But I couldn't be mistaken about John. He's the nicest boy I ever met in my life.'

I said: 'I like him, too.'

'I'm so glad.' Her hand touched my arm, like a bird alighting and then taking off again: 'John likes you, or I wouldn't be taking you into our confidence.'

'You wouldn't be planning on getting married?'

'Not just yet,' she said, as if this was a very conservative approach. 'John has a lot of things he wants to do first, and of course I couldn't go against Father's wishes.'

'What things does John want to do?'

She answered vaguely: 'He wants to make something of himself. He's very ambitious. And of course the one big thing in his life is finding out who killed his father. It's all he thinks about.'

'Has he done anything about it?'

'Not yet, but I know he has plans. He doesn't tell me all he has on his mind. I probably wouldn't understand, anyway. He's much more intelligent than I am.'

'I'm glad you realize that. It's a good thing to bear in mind.'

'What do you mean?' she said in a small voice. But she knew what I meant: 'It isn't true, what Father says, that John is an impostor. It can't be true!'

'What makes you so sure?'

'I know it here.' Her hand touched her breast, ever so lightly. 'He couldn't be lying to me. And Cassie says he's the image of his dad. So does Aunt Maria.'

'Does John ever talk about his past to you?'

She regarded me with deepening distrust. 'Now you sound just like Father again. You mustn't ask me questions about John. It wouldn't be fair to John.'

'Give yourself some thought, too,' I said. 'I know it doesn't seem likely, but if he is an impostor, you could be letting yourself in for a lot of pain and trouble.'

'I don't even care if he is!' she cried, and burst into tears.

A young man in airline coveralls came out of the terminal and glared at me. I was making a pretty girl cry, and there ought to be a law. I assumed a very legal expression. He went back inside again.

My plane took off with a roar. The roar diminished to a cicada humming in the northern sky. Sheila's tears passed like a summer shower. She started the engine and drove me into town, very efficiently, like a chauffeur who happened to be a deaf-mute.

John was a very fast worker.

CHAPTER TWENTY

Before she deposited me in the main lounge of the clubhouse, Sheila apologized for her emotional outburst, as she called it, and said something inarticulate about not telling Daddy. I said that no apology was necessary, and that I wouldn't.

The windows of the lounge overlooked the golf course. The players were a shifting confetti of colour on the greens and fairways. I watched them until Howell came in at five minutes after one.

He shook my hand vigorously. 'Good to see you, Archer. I hope you don't mind eating right away. I have to meet a committee shortly after two.'

He led me into a huge dining-room. Most of the tables were roped off and empty. We took one by a window which looked out across a walled swimming-pool enclosure where young people were romping and splashing. The waiter deferred to Howell as if he was a member of the stewardship committee.

Since I knew nothing about the man, I asked him the first question that occurred to me: 'What kind of a committee are you meeting?'

'Aren't all committees alike? They spend hours making up their collective mind to do something which any one of their members could accomplish in half the time. I'm thinking of setting up a committee to work for the abolition of committees.' His smile was a rapid flash. 'As a matter of fact, it's a Heart Association committee. We're laying plans for a fund campaign, and I happen to be chairman. Will you have something to drink? I'm going to have a Gibson.'

'That will do for me.'

He ordered two Gibsons from the hovering waiter. 'As a medical man, I feel it's my duty to perpetuate the little saving vices. It's probably safer to overdrink than it is to overeat. What will you have to eat?'

I consulted the menu.

'If you like sea food,' he said executively, 'the lobster Newberg is easy to chew. Gordon Sable told me about your little accident. How's the jaw?'

'Mending, thanks.'

'What precisely was the trouble about, if you don't object to the question?'

'It's a long story, which boils down to something like this: Anthony Galton was killed for his money by a criminal named Nelson who had just escaped from prison. Your original guess was very close to the truth. But there's more to the case. I believe Tony Galton's murder and Pete Culligan's murder are related.'

Howell leaned forward across the table, his short grey hair bristling. 'How related?'

'That's the problem I was trying to solve when I got my jaw broken. Let me ask you a question, Doctor. What's your impression of John Galton?'

'I was going to ask you the same question. Since you got to it first, I'll take first turn in answering. The boy *seems* open and aboveboard. He's certainly intelligent, and I suppose prepossessing if you like obvious charm. His grand—Mrs. Galton seems to be charmed with him.'

'She doesn't question his identity?'

'Not in the slightest, she hasn't from the beginning. For

Maria, the boy is practically the reincarnation of her son Tony. Her companion, Miss Hildreth, feels very much the same way. I have to admit myself that the resemblance is striking. But such things can be arranged, when a great deal of money is involved. I suppose there's no man alive who doesn't have a double somewhere in the world.'

'You're suggesting that he was searched out and hired?'

'Hasn't the possibility occurred to you?'

'Yes, it has. I think it should be explored.'

'I'm glad to hear you say that. I'll be frank with you. It occurred to me when the boy turned up here, that you might be a part of the conspiracy. But Gordon Sable vouches for you absolutely, and I've had other inquiries made.' His grey eyes probed mine. 'In addition to which, you have the marks of honesty on your face.'

'It's the hard way to prove you're honest.'

Howell smiled slightly, looking out over the pool. His daughter, Sheila, had appeared at the poolside in a bathing-suit. She was beautifully made, but the fact seemed to give her no pleasure. She sat by herself, with a pale closed look, undergoing the growing pains of womanhood. Howell's glance rested on her briefly, and a curious woodenness possessed his face.

The waiter brought our drinks, and we ordered lunch. When the waiter was out of hearing, Howell said:

'It's the boy's story that bothers me. I understand you were the first to hear it. What do you think about it?'

'Sable and I gave him quite a going-over. He took it well, and his story stood up. I made notes on it the same night. I've gone over the notes since I talked to you this morning, and couldn't find any self-contradictions.'

'The story may have been carefully prepared. Remember that the stakes are very high. You may be interested to know that Maria is planning to change her will in his favour.'

'Already?'

'Already. She may already have done. Gordon wouldn't agree to it, so she called in another attorney to draw up a will. Maria's half out of her mind—she's pent up her generous feelings for so long, that she's intoxicated with them.'

'Is she incompetent?'

'By no means,' he said hastily. 'I don't mean to overstate the case. And I concede her perfect right to do what she wants to do with her own money. On the other hand, we can't let her be defrauded by a—confidence man.'

'How much money is involved?'

He raised his eyes over my head as if he could see a mountain of gold in the distance. 'I couldn't estimate. Something like the national debt of a medium-sized European country. I know Henry left her oil property that brings in a weekly income in the thousands. And she has hundreds of thousands in securities.'

'Where does it all go if it doesn't go to the boy?'

Howell smiled mirthlessly. 'I'm not supposed to know that. It happens that I do, but I'm certainly not supposed to tell.'

'You've been frank with me,' I said. 'I'll be frank with you. I'm wondering if you have an interest in the estate.'

He scratched at his jaw, violently, but gave no other sign of discomposure. 'I have, yes, in several senses. Mrs. Galton named me executor in her original will. I assure you personal considerations are not influencing my judgment. I think I know my own motives well enough to say that.'

It's a lucky man who does, I thought. I said: 'Apart from the amount of money involved, what exactly is bothering you?'

'The young man's story. As he tells it, it doesn't really start till age sixteen. There's no way to go beyond that to his origins, whatever they may be. I tried, and came up against a stone wall.'

'I'm afraid I don't follow you. The way John tells it, he was in an orphanage until he ran away at the age of sixteen. The Crystal Springs Home, in Ohio.'

'I've been in touch with a man I know in Cleveland—chap I went to medical school with. The Crystal Springs Home burned to the ground three years ago.'

'That doesn't make John a liar. He says he left there five and a half years ago.'

'That doesn't make John a liar, no. But if he is, it leaves us with no way to prove that he is. The records of the Home were completely destroyed in the fire. The staff was scattered.'

'The Superintendent should be traceable. What was his name —Merriweather?'

'Merriweather died in the fire of a heart attack. All of this suggests the possibility—I'd say probability—that John provided himself with a story *ex post facto*. Or was provided with one. He or his backers looked around for a foolproof background to equip him with—one that was uncheckable. Crystal Springs was it—a large institution which no longer existed, which had no surviving records. Who knows if John Brown ever spent a day there?'

'You've been doing a lot of thinking about this.'

'I have, and I haven't told you all of it. There's the question of his speech, for instance. He represents himself as an American, born and raised in the United States.'

'You're not suggesting he's a foreigner?'

'I am, though. National differences in speech have always interested me, and it happens I've spent some time in central Canada. Have you ever listened to a Canadian pronounce the word "about"?'

'If I did, I never noticed. "About"?'

'You say aba-oot, more or less. A Canadian pronounces the word more like "aboat." And that's the way John Brown pronounces it.'

'Are you certain?'

'Of course I'm certain.'

'About the theory, I mean?'

'It isn't a theory. It's a fact. I've taken it up with specialists in the subject.'

'In the last two weeks?'

'In the last two days,' he said. 'I hadn't meant to bring this up, but my daughter, Sheila is—ah—interested in the boy. If he's a criminal, as I suspect—' Howell broke off, almost choking on the words.

Both our glances wandered to the poolside. Sheila was still alone, sitting on the edge and paddling her feet in the water. She turned to look toward the entrance twice while I watched her. Her neck and body were stiff with expectancy.

The waiter brought our food, and we ate in silence for a few minutes. Our end of the dining-room was slowly filling up with people in sports clothes. Slice and sand-trap seemed to be the passwords. Dr. Howell glanced around independently from time to time, as if to let the golfers know that he resented their intrusion on his privacy.

'What do you intend to do, Doctor?'

'I propose to employ you myself. I understand that Gordon has terminated your services.'

'So far as I know. Have you taken it up with him?'

'Naturally I have. He's just as keen as I am that there

should be further investigation. Unfortunately Maria won't hear of it, and as her attorney he can't very well proceed on his own. I can.'

'Have you discussed it with Mrs. Galton?'

'I've tried to.' Howell grimaced. 'She won't listen to a word against the blessed youth. It's frustrating, to say the least, but I can understand why she has to believe in him. The fact of her son Anthony's death came as a great shock to her. She had to hold on to something, and there was Anthony's putative son, ready and willing. Perhaps it was planned that way. At any rate, she's clinging to the boy as if her life depended on it.'

'What will the consequences be if we prove he's crooked?'

'Naturally we'll put him in prison where he belongs.'

'I mean the consequences to Mrs. Galton's health. You told me yourself that any great shock might kill her.'

'That's true, I did.'

'Aren't you concerned about that?'

His face slowly reddened, in blotches. 'Of course I'm concerned. But there are ethical priorities in life. We can't sit still for a criminal conspiracy, merely because the victim has diseases. The longer we permit it to go on, the worse it will be in the long run for Maria.'

'You're probably right. Anyway, her health is your responsibility. I'm willing to undertake the investigation. When do I begin?'

'Now.'

'I'll probably have to go to Michigan, for a start. That will cost money.'

'I understand that. How much?'

'Five hundred.'

Howell didn't blink. He produced a chequebook and a fountain pen. While he was making out the cheque, he said:

'It might be a good idea if you talked to the boy first. That is, if you can do it without arousing suspicion.'

'I think I can do that. I got an invitation from him this morning.'

'An invitation?'

'A written invitation to visit the Galton house.'

'He's making very free with Mrs. Galton's property. Do you happen to have the document with you?'

I handed him the letter. He studied it with growing signs of excitement. 'I was right, by God!'

'What do you mean?'

'The dirty little hypocrite is a Canadian. Look here.' He put the letter on the table between us, and speared at it with his forefinger. 'He spells the word "labor" l, a, b, o, u, r. It's the British spelling, still current in Canada. He isn't even American. He's an impostor.'

'It's going to take more than this to prove it.'

'I realize that. Get busy, man.'

'If you don't mind, I'll finish my lunch first.'

Howell didn't hear me. He was looking out of the window again, half out of his seat.

A dark-headed youth in a tan sport shirt was talking to Sheila Howell at the poolside. He turned his head slightly. I recognized John Galton. He patted the shoulder of her terrycloth robe familiarly. Sheila smiled up full into his face.

Howell's light chair fell over backwards. He was out of the room before I could stop him. From the front door of the clubhouse, I saw him striding across the lawn toward the entrance of the swimming-pool enclosure.

John and Sheila came out hand-in-hand. They were so intent on each other that they didn't see Howell until he was on top of them. He thrust himself between them, shaking the boy by the arm. His voice was an ugly tearing rent in the quietness:

'Get out of here, do you hear me? You're not a member of this club.'

John pulled away and faced him, white and rigid. 'Sheila invited me.'

'I dis-invite you.' The back of Howell's neck was carbuncle red.

Sheila touched his arm. 'Please, Daddy, don't make a scene. There's nothing to be gained.'

John was encouraged to say: 'My grandmother won't like this, Doctor.'

'She will when she knows the facts.' But the threat had taken the wind out of Howell's sails. He wasn't as loud as he had been.

'Please,' Sheila repeated. 'John's done no harm to anyone.'

'Don't you understand, Sheila, I'm trying to protect you?'

'From what?'

'From corruption.'

'That's silly, Dad. To hear you talk, you'd think John was a criminal.'

The boy's head tilted suddenly, as if the word had struck a

nerve in his neck. 'Don't argue with him, Sheila. I oughtn't to've come here.'

He turned on his heel and walked head down toward the parking-lot. Sheila went in the other direction. Moulded in terry-cloth, her body had a massiveness and mystery that hadn't struck me before. Her father stood and watched her until she entered the enclosure. She seemed to be moving heavily and fatally out of his control.

I went back to the dining-room and let Howell find me there. He came in pale and slack-faced, as if he'd had a serious loss of blood. His daughter was in the pool now, swimming its length back and forth with slow and powerful strokes. Her feet churned a steady white wake behind her.

She was still swimming when we left. Howell drove me to the courthouse. He scowled up at the barred windows of the county jail:

'Put him behind bars, that's all I ask.'

CHAPTER TWENTY-ONE

Sheriff Trask was in his office. Its walls were hung with testimonials from civic organizations and service clubs; recruiting certificates from Army, Navy, and Air Force; and a number of pictures of the Sheriff himself taken with the Governor and other notables. Trask's actual face was less genial than the face in the photographs.

'Trouble?' I said.

'Sit down. You're the trouble. You stir up a storm, and then you drop out of the picture. The trouble with you private investigators is irresponsibility.'

'That's a rough word, Sheriff.' I fingered the broken bones in my face, thoughtfully and tenderly.

'Yeah, I know you got yourself hurt, and I'm sorry. But what can I do about it? Otto Schwartz is outside my jurisdiction.'

'Murder raps cross state lines, or haven't you heard.'

'Yeah, and I also heard at the same time that you can't extradite without a case. Without some kind of evidence, I can't even get to Schwartz to question him. And you want to know why I have no evidence?'

'Let me guess. Me again.'

'It isn't funny, Archer. I was depending on you for some discretion. Why did you have to go and spill your guts to Roy Lemberg? Scare my witnesses clear out of the damn country?'

'I got overeager, and made a mistake. I wasn't the only one.'

'What is that supposed to mean?'

'You told me Lemberg's car had been stolen.'

'That's what switched licence plates usually mean.' Trask sat and thought about this for a minute, pushing out his lower lip. 'Okay. We made mistakes. I made a medium-sized dilly and you made a peacheroo. So you took a beating for it. We don't sit around and cry. Where do we go from here?'

'It's your case, Sheriff. I'm just your patient helper.'

He leaned toward me, heavy-shouldered and earnest. 'You really mean to help? Or have you got an angle?'

'I mean to help, that's my angle.'

'We'll see. Are you still working for Sable—for Mrs. Galton, that is?'

'Not at the moment.'

'Who's bankrolling you, Dr. Howell?'

'News travels fast.'

'Heck, I knew it before you did. Howell came around asking me to check your record with L.A. You seem to have some good friends down south. If you ever conned any old ladies, you never got caught.'

'Young ones are more my meat.'

Trask brushed aside the badinage with an impatient gesture. 'I assume you're being hired to go into the boy's background. Howell wanted me to. Naturally I told him I couldn't move without some indication that law's been broken. You got any such indication?'

'Not yet.'

'Neither have I. I talked to the boy, and he's as smooth as silk. He doesn't even make any definite claims. He merely says that people tell him he's his father's son, so it's probably so.'

'Do you think he's been coached, Sheriff?'

'I don't know. He may be quarterbacking his own plays. When he came in to see me, it had nothing to do on the face of it with establishing his identity. He wanted information about his father's murder, if this John Brown was his father.'

'Hasn't that been proved?'

'As close as it ever will be. There's still room for doubt, in my opinion. But what I started to say, he came in here to tell *me* what to do. He wanted more action on that old killing. I told him it was up to the San Mateo people, so what did he do? He made a trip up there to build a fire under the San Mateo sheriff.'

'It's barely possible he's serious.'

'Either that, or he's a psychologist. That kind of behaviour doesn't go with consciousness of guilt.'

'The Syndicate hires good lawyers.'

Trask pondered this, his eyes withdrawing under the ledges of his brows. 'You think it's a Syndicate job, eh? A big conspiracy?'

'With a big payoff, in the millions. Howell tells me Mrs. Galton's rewriting her will, leaving everything to the boy. I think her house should be watched.'

'You honestly believe they'd try to knock her off?'

'They kill people for peanuts. What wouldn't they do to get hold of the Galton property?'

'Don't let your imagination run away. It won't happen, not in Santa Teresa County.'

'It started to happen two weeks ago, when Culligan got it. That has all the marks of a gang killing, and in your territory.'

'Don't rub it in. That case isn't finished yet.'

'It's the same case,' I said. 'The Brown killing and the Culligan killing and the Galton impersonation, if it is one, all hang together.'

'That's easy to say. How do we prove it?'

'Through the boy. I'm taking off for Michigan tonight. Howell thinks his accent originated in central Canada. That ties in with the Lembergs. Apparently they crossed the border into Canada from Detroit, and were headed for an address Culligan gave them. If you could trace Culligan that far back—'

'We're working on it.' Trask smiled, rather forbiddingly. 'Your Reno lead was a good one, Archer. I talked long distance last night to a friend in Reno, captain of detectives. He called me back just before lunch. Culligan was working for Schwartz about a year ago.'

'Doing what?'

'Steerer for his casino. Another interesting thing: Culligan was arrested in Detroit five-six years ago. The FBI has a rap sheet on him.'

'What was this particular rap?'

'An old larceny charge. It seems he left the country to evade it, got nabbed as soon as he showed his face on American soil, spent the next couple of years in Southern Michigan pen.'

'What was the date of his arrest in Detroit?'

'I don't remember exactly. It was about five-and-a-half years ago. I could look it up, if it matters.'

'It matters.'

'What's on your mind?'

'John Galton turned up in Ann Arbor five-and-a-half years ago. Ann Arbor is practically a suburb of Detroit. I'm asking myself if he crossed the Canadian border with Culligan.'

Trask whistled softly, and flicked on the switch of his squawk-box:

'Conger, bring me the Culligan records. Yeah, I'm in my office.'

I remembered Conger's hard brown face. He didn't remember me at first, then did a double take:

'Long time no see.'

I quipped lamely: 'How's the handcuff business?'

'Clicking.'

Trask rustled the papers Conger had brought, and frowned impatiently. When he looked up his eyes were crackling bright:

'A little over five-and-a-half years. Culligan got picked up in Detroit January 7. Does that fit with your date?'

'I haven't pinned it down yet, but I will.'

I rose to go. Trask's parting handshake was warm. 'If you run into anything, call me collect, anytime day or night. And keep the hard nose out of the chopper.'

'That's my aspiration.'

'By the way, your car's in the county garage. I can release it to you if you want.'

'Save it for me. And take care of the old lady, eh?'

The Sheriff was giving Conger orders to that effect before I reached the door.

CHAPTER TWENTY-TWO

I cashed Howell's cheque at his bank just before it closed for business at three. The teller directed me to a travel agency where I made a plane reservation from Los Angeles to Detroit. The connecting plane didn't leave Santa Teresa for nearly three hours.

I walked the few blocks to Sable's office. The private elevator let me out into the oak-panelled anteroom.

Mrs. Haines looked up from her work, and raised her hand to smooth her dyed red hair. She said in maternal dismay:

'Why, Mr. Archer, you were *badly* injured. Mr. Sable *told* me you'd been hurt, but I had no idea——'

'Stop it. You're making me feel sorry for myself.'

'What's the matter with feeling sorry for yourself? I do it all the time. It bucks me up no end.'

'You're a woman.'

She dipped her bright head as if I'd paid her a compliment. 'What's the difference?'

'You don't want me to spell it out.'

She tittered, not unpleasantly, and tried to blush, but her experienced face resisted the attempt. 'Some other time, perhaps. What can I do for you now?'

'Is Mr. Sable in?'

'I'm sorry, he isn't back from lunch.'

'It's three-thirty.'

'I know. I don't expect he'll be in again today. He'll be sorry he missed you. The poor man's schedule has been all broken up, ever since that trouble at his house.'

'The murder, you mean?'

'That, and other things. His wife isn't well.'

'So I understand. Gordon told me she had a breakdown.'

'Oh, did he tell you that? He doesn't do much talking about it to anyone. He's awfully sensitive on the subject.' She made a confidential gesture, raising her red-tipped hand vertically beside her mouth. 'Just between you and me, this isn't the first time he's had trouble with her.'

'When was the other time?'

'Times, in the plural. She came here one night in March

when we were doing income tax, and accused me of trying to steal her husband. I could have told her a thing or two, but of course I couldn't say a word in front of Mr. Sable. I tell you, he's a living saint, what he's taken from that woman, and he goes right on looking after her.'

'What did she do to him?'

Colour dabbed her cheekbones. She was slightly drunk with malice. 'Plenty. Last summer she took off and went rampaging around the country spending his good money like water. Spending it on other men, too, can you imagine? He finally tracked her down in Reno, where she was *living* with another man.'

'Reno?'

'Reno,' she repeated flatly. 'She probably intended to divorce him or something, but she gave up on the idea. She'd have been doing him a favour, if you ask me. But the poor man talked her into coming back with him. He seems to be infatuated with her.' Her voice was disconsolate. After a moment's thought, she said: 'I oughtn't to be telling you all this. Ought I?'

'I knew she had a history of trouble. Gordon told me himself that he had to put her in a nursing home.'

'That's right, he's probably there with her now. He generally goes over to eat lunch with her, and most of the time he stays the rest of the day. Wasted devotion, I call it. If you ask me, that's one marriage doomed to failure. I did a horoscope on it, and you never saw such antagonism in the stars.'

Not only in the stars.

'Where is the nursing home she's in, Mrs. Haines?'

'It's Dr. Trenchard's, on Light Street. But I wouldn't go there, if that's what you're thinking of. Mr. Sable doesn't like to be disturbed when he's visiting Mrs. Sable.'

'I'll take my chances. And I won't mention that I've been here. Okay?'

'I guess so,' she said dubiously. 'It's over on the west side, 235 Light Street.'

I took a cab across town. The driver looked me over curiously as I got out. Perhaps he was trying to figure out if I was a patient or just a visitor.

'You want me to wait?'

'I think so. If I don't come out, you know what that will mean.'

I left him having a delayed reaction. The 'home' was a long stucco building set far back from the street on its own acre.

Nothing indicated its specialness, except for the high wire fence which surrounded the patio at the side.

A man and a woman were sitting in a blue canvas swing behind the fence. Their backs were to me, but I recognized Sable's white head. The woman's blonde head rested on his shoulder.

I resisted the impulse to call out to them. I climbed the long veranda, which was out of sight of the patio, and pressed the bellpush beside the front door. The door was unlocked and opened by a nurse in white, without a cap. She was unexpectedly young and pretty.

'Yes, sir?'

'I'd like to speak to Mr. Sable.'

'And who shall I say is calling?'

'Lew Archer.'

She left me in a living-room or lounge whose furniture was covered with bright chintz. Two old ladies in shawls were watching a baseball game on television. A young man with a beard squatted on his heels in a corner, watching the opposite corner of the ceiling. His lips were moving.

One of the half-curtained windows looked out across the sun-filled patio. I saw the young nurse cross to the blue swing, and Sable's face come up as if from sleep. He disengaged himself from his wife. Her body relaxed into an awkward position. Blue-shadowed by the canvas shade of the swing, her face had the open-eyed blankness of a doll's.

Sable dragged his shadow across the imitation flagstone. He looked small, oddly diminished, under the sky's blue height. The impression persisted when he entered the lounge. Age had fallen on him. He needed a haircut, and his tie was pulled to one side. The look he gave me was red-eyed; his voice was cranky.

'What brings you here, anyway?'

'I wanted to see you. I don't have much time in town.'

'Well. You see me.' He lifted his arms from his sides, and dropped them.

The old ladies, who had greeted him with smiles and nods, reacted like frightened children to his bitterness. One of them hitched her shawl high around her neck and slunk out of the room. The other stretched her hand out toward Sable as if she wanted to comfort him. She remained frozen in that position while she went on watching the ball game. The bearded man watched the corner of the ceiling.

'How is Mrs. Sable?'

'Not well.' He frowned, and drew me out into the corridor. 'As a matter of fact, she's threatened with melancholia. Dr. Trenchard tells me she's had a similar illness before—before I married her. The shock she suffered two weeks ago stirred up the old trouble. Good Lord, was that only two weeks ago?'

I risked asking: 'What sort of background does she have?'

'Alice was a model in Chicago, and she's been married before. She lost a child, and her first husband treated her badly. I've tried to make it up to her. With damn poor success.'

His voice sank toward despair.

'I take it she's having therapy.'

'Of course. Dr. Trenchard is one of the best psychiatrists on the coast. If she gets any worse, he's going to try shock treatment.' He leaned on the wall, looking down at nothing in particular. His red eyes seemed to be burning.

'You should go home and get some sleep.'

'I haven't been sleeping much lately. It's easy to say, sleep. But you can't will yourself to sleep. Besides, Alice needs me with her. She's much calmer when I'm around.' He shook himself and straightened. 'But you didn't come here to discuss my woes with me.'

'That's true, I didn't. I came to thank you for the cheque, and to ask you a couple of questions.'

'You earned the money. I'll answer the questions if I can.'

'Dr. Howell has hired me to investigate John Galton's background. Since you brought me into the case, I'd like to have your go-ahead.'

'Of course. You have it, as far as I'm concerned. I can't speak for Mrs. Galton.'

'I understand that. Howell tells me she's sold on the boy. Howell himself is convinced that he's a phony.'

'We've discussed it. There seems to be some sort of romance between John and Howell's daughter.'

'Does Howell have any other special motive?'

'For doing what?'

'Investigating John, trying to prevent Mrs. Galton from changing her will.'

Sable looked at me with some of his old sharpness. 'That's a good question. Under the present will, Howell stands to benefit in several ways. He himself is executor, and due to inherit a substantial sum, I really mustn't say how much. His daughter, Sheila, is in for another substantial sum, very substantial. And after various other bequests have been met, the bulk of the estate goes to various charities, one of which is the Heart Association. Henry Galton died of cardiovascular trouble. Howell is an officer of the Heart Association. All of which makes him a highly interested party.'

'And highly interesting. Has the will been changed yet?'

'I can't say. I told Mrs. Galton I couldn't conscientiously draw up a new will for her under the circumstances. She said she'd get someone else. Whether she has or not, I can't say.'

'Then you're not sold on the boy, either.'

'I was. I no longer know what to think. Frankly, I haven't been giving the matter much thought.' He moved impatiently, and made a misstep to one side, his shoulder thudding against the wall. 'If you don't mind, I think I'll get back to my wife.'

The young nurse let me out.

I looked back through the wire fence. Mrs. Sable remained in the same position on the swing. Her husband joined her in the blue shadow. He raised her inert head and insinuated his shoulder behind it. They sat like a very old couple waiting for the afternoon shadows to lengthen and merge into night.

CHAPTER TWENTY-THREE

The cab-driver stopped at the kerb opposite the gates of the Galton estate. He hung one arm over the back of the seat and gave me a quizzical look:

'No offence, Mister, but you want the front entrance or the service entrance?'

'The front entrance.'

'Okay. I just didn't want to make a mistake.'

He let me off under the port-cochère. I paid him, and told him not to wait. The Negro maid let me into the reception hall, and left me to cool my heels among the ancestors.

I moved over to one of the tall, narrow windows. It looked out across the front lawn, where the late afternoon sunlight lay serenely. I got some sense of the guarded peace that walled estates like this had once provided. In the modern world the walls were more like prison walls, or the wire fence around a nursing-home garden. When it came right down to it, I preferred the service entrance. The people in the kitchen usually had more fun.

Quick footsteps descended the stairs, and Cassie Hildreth came into the room. She had on a skirt and a sweater which emphasized her figure. She looked more feminine in other, subtler ways. Something had happened to change her style.

She gave me her hand. 'It's good to see you, Mr. Archer. Sit down. Mrs. Galton will be down in a minute.'

'Under her own power?'

'Yes, isn't it remarkable? She's becoming much more active than she was. John takes her out for a drive nearly every day.'

'That's nice of him.'

'He actually seems to enjoy it. They hit it off from the start.'

'He's the one I really came to see. Is he around?'

'I haven't seen him since lunch. Probably he's out in his car somewhere.'

'His car?'

'Aunt Maria bought him a cute little Thunderbird. John's crazy about it. He's like a child with a new toy. He told me he's never had a car of his own before.'

'I guess he has a lot of things he never had before.'

'Yes. I'm so happy for him.'

'You're a generous woman.'

'Not really. I've a lot to be thankful for. Now that John's come home, I wouldn't trade my life for any other. It may sound like a strange thing to say, but life is suddenly just as it was in the old days—before the war, before Tony died. Everything seems to have fallen into harmony.'

She sounded as if she had transferred her lifelong crush from Tony to John Galton. A dream possessed her face. I wanted to warn her not to bank too heavily on it. Everything could fall into chaos again.

Mrs. Galton was fussing on the stairs. Cassie went to the door to meet her. The old lady had on a black tailored suit with something white at her throat. Her hair was marcelled in hard grey corrugations which resembled galvanized iron. She extended her bony hand:

'I'm most pleased to see you. I've been wanting to express my personal appreciation to you. You've made my house a happier one.'

'Your cheque was a very nice expression,' I said.

'The labourer is worthy of his hire.' Perhaps she sensed that

that wasn't the most tactful way to put it, because she added: 'Won't you stay for tea? My grandson will want to see you. I expect him back for tea. He should be here now.'

The querulous note was still in her voice. I wondered how much of her happiness was real, how much sheer will to believe that something good could happen to a poor old rich lady. She lowered herself into a chair, exaggerating the difficulty of her movements. Cassie began to look anxious.

'I think he's at the country club, Aunt Maria.'

'With Sheila?'

'I think so,' Cassie said.

'Is he still seeing a lot of her?'

'Just about every day.'

'We'll have to put a stop to that. He's much too young to think of taking an interest in any one girl. Sheila is a dear sweet child, of course, but we can't have her monopolizing John. I have other plans for him.'

'What plans,' I said, 'if you don't mind my asking?'

'I'm thinking of sending John to Europe in the fall. He needs broadening, and he's very much interested in the modern drama. If the interest persists, and deepens, I'll build him a repertory theatre here in Santa Teresa. John has great talent, you know. The Galton distinction comes out in a different form in each generation.'

As if to demonstrate this proposition, a red Thunderbird convertible careened up the long driveway. A door slammed. John came in. His face was flushed and sullen. He stood inside the doorway and pushed his fists deep in his jacket pockets, his head thrust forward in a peering attitude.

'Well!' he said. 'Here we all are. The three fates, Clotho, Lachesis, and Mr. Archer.'

'That isn't funny, John,' Cassie said in a voice of warning.

'I think it's funny. Very, very funny.'

He came toward us, weaving slightly, exaggerating the movement of his shoulders. I went to meet him:

'Hello, John.'

'Get away from me. I know why you're here.'

'Tell me.'

'I'll tell you all right.'

He threw a wild fist in my direction, staggering off balance. I moved in close, turned him with his back to me, took hold of his jacket collar with both hands and pulled it halfway down his arms. He sputtered words at me which smelled like

140

the exhalations from a still. But I could feel the lethal force vibrating through him.

'Straighten up and quiet down,' I said.

'I'll knock your block off.'

'First you'll have to load yourself up with something solider than whisky.'

Mrs. Galton breathed at my shoulder. 'Has he been drinking?'

John answered her himself, in a kind of small-boy defiance: 'Yes I have been drinking. And I've been thinking. Thinking and drinking. I say it's a lousy setup.'

'What?' she said. 'What's happened?'

'A lot of things have happened. Tell this man to turn me loose.'

'Let him go,' Mrs. Galton said commandingly.

'Do you think he's ready?'

'Damn you, let me go.'

He made a violent lunge, and tore loose from the arms of his jacket. He whirled and faced me with his fists up:

'Come on and fight. I'm not afraid of you.'

'This is hardly the time and place.'

I tossed his jacket to him. He caught and held it, looking down at it stupidly. Cassie stepped between us. She took the jacket and helped him on with it. He submitted almost meekly to her hands.

'You need some black coffee, John. Let me get you some black coffee.'

'I don't want coffee, I'm not drunk.'

'But you've been drinking.' Mrs. Galton's voice rose almost an octave and stayed there on a querulous monotone: 'Your *father* started drinking young, you mustn't let it happen all over again. Please, you must promise me.'

The old lady hung on John's arm, making anxious noises, while Cassie tried to soothe her. John's head swung around, his eyes on me:

'Get that man out of here! He's spying for Dr. Howell.'

Mrs. Galton turned on me, the bony structure of her face pushing out through the seamed flesh:

'I trust my grandson is mistaken about you. I know Dr. Howell is incapable of committing disloyal acts behind my back.'

'Don't be too sure of that,' John said. 'He doesn't want me seeing Sheila. There's nothing he wouldn't do to break it up.'

'I'm asking you, Mr. Archer. Did Dr. Howell hire you?'

'I'll have to ask you to take it up with Howell.'

'It is true, then?'

'I can't answer that, Mrs. Galton.'

'In that case please leave my house. You entered it under false pretences. If you trespass again, I'll have you prosecuted. I've a good mind to go to the authorities as it is.'

'No, don't do that,' John said. 'We can handle it, Grandma.' He seemed to be sobering rapidly. Cassie chimed in:

'You mustn't get so excited about nothing. You know what Dr. Howell—'

'Don't mention his name in my presence. To be betrayed by an old and trusted friend—well, that's what it is to have money. They think they have a right to it simply because it's there. I see now what August Howell has been up to, insinuating himself and his chit of a daughter into my life. Well, he's not getting a cent of my money. I've seen to that.'

'Please calm down, Aunt Maria.'

Cassie tried to lead her back to her chair. Mrs. Galton wouldn't budge. She called hoarsely in my direction:

'You can go and tell August Howell he's overreached himself. He won't get a cent of my money, not a cent. It's going to my own kith and kin. And tell him to keep that daughter of his from flinging herself at my grandson. I have other plans for him.'

The breath rustled and moaned in her head. She closed her eyes; her face was like a death mask. She tottered and almost fell. John held her around the shoulders.

'Get out,' he said to me. 'My grandmother is a sick woman. Can't you see what you're doing to her?'

'Somebody's doing it to her.'

'Are you going to get out, or do I call the police?'

'You'd better go,' Cassie said. 'Mrs. Galton has a heart condition.'

Mrs. Galton's hand went to her heart automatically. Her head fell loosely on to John's shoulder. He stroked her grey hair. It was a very touching scene.

I wondered as I went out how many more scenes like that the old lady's heart would stand. The question kept me awake on the night plane to Chicago.

CHAPTER TWENTY-FOUR

I put in two days of legwork in Ann Arbor, where I represented myself as a personnel investigator for a firm with overseas contracts. John's account of his high school and college life checked out in detail. I established one interesting additional detail: He had enrolled in the high school under the name of John Lindsay five-and-a-half years before, on January 9. Peter Culligan had been arrested in Detroit, forty miles away on January 7 of the same year. Apparently it had taken the boy just two days to find a new protector in Gabriel Lindsay.

I talked to friends of Lindsay's, mostly high school teachers. They remembered John as a likely boy, though he had been, as one of them said: 'A tough little egg to start with.' They understood that Lindsay had taken him off the streets.

Gabriel Lindsay had gone in for helping young people in trouble. He was an older man who had lost a son in the war, and his wife soon after the war. He died himself in the University Hospital in February of the previous year, of pneumonia.

His doctor remembered John's constant attendance at his bedside. The copy of his will on file in the Washtenaw County courthouse left two thousand dollars to 'my quasi-foster-son, known as John Lindsay, for the furtherance of his education.' There were no other specific bequests in Lindsay's will; which probably meant it was all the money he had.

John had graduated from the University in June, as a Speech major, with honours. His counsellor in the Dean's office said that he had been a student without any overt problems; not exactly popular perhaps: he seemed to have no close friends. On the other hand, he had been active in campus theatrical productions, and moderately successful as an actor in his senior year.

His address at the time of his graduation had been a rooming-house on Catherine Street, over behind the Graduate School. The landlady's name was Mrs. Haskell. Maybe she could help me.

Mrs. Haskell lived on the first floor of an old three-story gingerbread mansion. I guessed from the bundles of mail on the table inside the door that the rest of her house was given over to roomers. She led me along the polished parquetry hallway into a half-blinded parlour. It was a cool oasis in the heat of the Michigan July.

Somewhere over our heads, a typewriter pecked at the silence. The echo of a southern drawl twanged like a mandolin in Mrs. Haskell's voice:

'Do sit down and tell me how John is. And how is he doing in his position?' Mrs. Haskell clapsed her hands enthusiastically on her flowered print bosom. The curled bangs on her forehead shook like silent bells.

'He hasn't started with us yet, Mrs. Haskell. The purpose of my investigation is to clear him for a confidential assignment.'

'Does that mean the other thing has fallen through?'

'What other thing is that?'

'The acting thing. You may not know it, but John Lindsay's a very fine actor. One of the most talented boys I've ever had in my house. I never missed an appearance of his at the Lydia Mendelssohn. In *Hobson's Choice* last winter, he was rich.'

'I bet he was. And you say he had acting offers?'

'I don't know about offers in the plural, but he had one very good one. Some big producer wanted to give him a personal contract and train him professionally. The last I heard, John had accepted it. But I guess he changed his mind, if he's going with your firm. Security.'

'It's interesting about his acting.' I said. 'We like our employees to be well-rounded people. Do you remember the producer's name?'

'I'm afraid I never knew it.'

'Where did he come from?'

'I don't know. John was very secretive about his private affairs. He didn't even leave a forwarding address when he left in June. All I really know about this is what Miss Reichler told me after he left.'

'Miss Reichler?'

'His friend. I don't mean she was his girlfriend exactly. Maybe she thought so, but he didn't. I warned him not to get mixed up with a rich young lady like her, riding around in her Cadillacs and her convertibles. My boys come and go, but I try to keep them from overstepping themselves. Miss Reichler is several years older than John.' Her lips moved over his name with a kind of maternal greed. The mandolin twang was becoming more pronounced.

'He sounds like the kind of young man we need. Socially mobile, attractive to the ladies.'

'Oh, he was always that. I don't mean he's girl-crazy. He paid the girls no mind, unless they forced themselves on his attention. Ada Reichler practically beat a path to his door. She used to drive up in her Cadillac every second or third day. Her father's a big man in Detroit. Auto parts.'

'Good,' I said. 'A high-level business connection.'

Mrs. Haskell sniffed. 'Don't count too much on that one. Miss Reichler was sore as a boil when John left without even saying good-bye. She was really let down. I tried to explain to her that a young man just starting out in the world couldn't carry any excess baggage. Then she got mad at me, for some god-forsaken reason. She slam-banged into her car and ground those old Cadillac gears to a pulp.'

'How long did they know each other?'

'As long as he was with me, at least a year. I guess she had her nice qualities, or he wouldn't have stuck with her so long. She's pretty enough, if you like the slinky type.'

'Do you have her address? I'd like to talk to her.'

'She might tell you a lot of lies. You know: "Hell hath no fury like a woman scorned." '

'I can discount anything like that.'

'See that you do. John's a fine young man, and your people will be lucky if he decides to go with them. Her father's name is Ben, I think, Ben Reichler. They live over in the section by the river.'

I drove on winding roads through a semi-wooded area. Eventually I found the Reichlers' mailbox. Their driveway ran between rows of maples to a low brick house with a sweeping roof. It looked small from a distance, and massive when I got up close to it. I began to understand how John could have made the leap from Mrs. Gorgello's boarding-house to the Galton house. He'd been training for it.

A man in overalls with a spraygun in his hands climbed up the granite steps of a sunken garden.

'The folks aren't home,' he said. 'They're never home in July.'

'Where can I find them?'

'If it's business, Mr. Reichler's in his office in the Reichler Building three-four days a week.'

'Miss Ada Reichler's the one I want.'

'Far as I know, she's in Kingsville with her mother. Kingsville, Canada. They have a place up there. You a friend of Miss Ada's?'

'Friend of a friend,' I said.

It was early evening when I drove into Kingsville. The heat hadn't let up, and my shirt was sticking to my back. The lake lay below the town like a blue haze in which white sails hung upright by their tips.

The Reichlers' summer place was on the lakeshore. Green terraces descended from the house to a private dock and boathouse. The house itself was a big old lodge whose brown shingled sides were shaggy with ivy. The Reichlers weren't camping out, though. The maid who answered the door wore a fresh starched uniform, complete with cap. She told me that Mrs. Reichler was resting and Miss Ada was out in one of the boats. She was expected back at any time, if I cared to wait.

I waited on the dock, which was plastered with No Trespassing signs. A faint breeze had begun to stir, and the sailboats were leaning shoreward. Mild little land-locked waves lapped at the pilings. A motorboat went by like a bird shaking out wings of white water. Its wash rocked the dock. The boat turned and came in, slowing down. A girl with dark hair and dark glasses was at the wheel. She pointed a finger at her brown chest, and cocked her head questioningly.

'You want me?'

I nodded, and she brought the boat in, I caught the line she threw and helped her on to the dock. Her body was lean and supple in black Capris and a halter. Her face, when she took off her glasses, was lean and intense.

'Who are you?'

I had already decided to discard my role. 'My name is Archer. I'm a private detective from California.'

'You came all this way to see me?'

'Yes.'

'Why on earth?'

'Because you knew John Lindsay.'

Her face opened up, ready for anything, wonderful or otherwise.

'John sent you here?'

'Not exactly.'

'Is he in some kind of trouble?'

I didn't answer her. She jerked at my arm like a child wanting attention.

'Tell me, is John in trouble? Don't be afraid, I can take it.'

'I don't know whether he is or not, Miss Reichler. What makes you jump to the conclusion that he is?'

'Nothing, I don't mean that.' Her speech was staccato. 'You said that you're a detective. Doesn't that indicate trouble?'

'Say he is in trouble. What then?'

'I'd want to help him, naturally. Why are we talking in riddles?'

I liked her rapid, definite personality, and guessed that honesty went along with it:

'I don't like riddles any more than you do. I'll make a bargain with you, Miss Reichler. I'll tell you my end of the story it you'll tell me yours.'

'What is this, true confession hour?'

'I'm serious, and I'm willing to do my talking first. If you're interested in John's situation—'

'Situation is a nice neutral word.'

'That's why I used it. Is it a bargain?'

'All right.' She gave me her hand on it, as a man would have. 'I warn you in advance, though, I won't tell you anything against him. I don't *know* anything against him, except that he treated me—well, I was asking for it.' She lifted her high thin shoulders, shrugging off the past. 'We can talk in the garden, if you like.'

We climbed the terraces to a walled garden in the shadow of the house. It was crowded with the colours and odours of flowers. She placed me in a canvas chair facing hers. I told her where John was and what he was doing.

Her eyes were soft and black, lit tremulously from within. Their expression followed all the movements of my story. She said when I'd finished:

'It sounds like one of Grimm's fairy tales. The goatherd turns out to be the prince in disguise. Or like Œdipus. John had an Œdipus theory of his own, that Œdipus killed his father because he banished him from the kingdom. I thought it was very clever.' Her voice was brittle. She was marking time.

'John's a clever boy,' I said. 'And you're a clever girl, and you knew him well. Do you believe he's who he claims to be?'

'Do you?' When I failed to answer, she said: 'So he has a girl in California, already.' Her hands lay open on her slender thighs. She hugged them between her thighs.

'The girl's father hired me. He thinks John is a fraud.'

'And you do, too?'

'I don't like to think it, but I'm afraid I do. There are some indications that his whole story was invented to fit the occasion.'

'To inherit money?'

'That's the general idea. I've been talking to his landlady in Ann Arbor, Mrs. Haskell.'

'I know her,' the girl said shortly.

'Do you know anything about this offer John had from a producer?'

'Yes, he mentioned it to me. It was one of these personal contacts that the movie producers give to promising young actors. This man saw him in *Hobson's Choice*.'

'When?'

'Last February.'

'Did you meet the man?'

'I never did. John said he flew back to the coast. He didn't want to discuss it after that.'

'Did he mention any names before he dried up?'

'Not that I recall. Do you think John was lying about him, that it wasn't an acting job he was offered?'

'That could be. Or it could be John was sucked in. The conspirators made their approach as movie producers or agents, and later told him what was required of him.'

'Why would John fall in with their plans? He's not a criminal.'

'The Galton estate is worth millions. He stands to inherit all of it, any day. Even a small percentage of it would make him a rich man.'

'But he never cared about money, at least not the kind you inherit. He could have married me: Barkis was willing. My father's money was one of the reasons he didn't. At least that's what he said. The real reason, I guess, was that he didn't love me. Does he love her?'

'My client's daughter? I couldn't say for sure. Maybe he doesn't love anybody.'

'You're very honest, Mr. Archer. I gave you an opening, but you didn't try to use her on me as a wedge. You could have said that he was crazy about her, thus fanning the fires of jealousy.' She winced at her own self-mockery.

'I try to be honest with honest people.'

She gave me a flashing look. 'That's intended to put me on the spot.'

'Yes.'

She turned her head and looked out over the lake as if she could see all the way to California. The last sails were converging toward shore, away from the darkness falling like soot along the horizon. As light drained from the sky, it seemed to gather more intensely on the water.

'What will they do to him if they find out he's an impostor?'

'Put him in jail.'

'For how long?'

'It's hard to say. It'll be easier on him if we get it over with soon. He hasn't made any big claims yet, or taken any big money.'

'You really mean, really and truly, that I'd be doing him a favour by puncturing his story?'

'That's my honest opinion. If it's all a pack of lies, we'll find out sooner or later. The sooner the better.'

She hesitated. Her profile was stark. One cord in her neck stood out under the skin. 'You say that he claims that he was brought up in an orphanage in Ohio.'

'Crystal Springs, Ohio. Did he ever mention the place to you?'

She shook her head in a quick short arc. I said:

'There are some indications that he was raised here in Canada.'

'What indications?'

'Speech. Spelling.'

She rose suddenly, walked to the end of the garden, stooped to pick a snapdragon, threw it away with a spurning gesture. She came back toward me and stood with her face half-averted. She said in a rough dry voice:

'Just don't tell him I was the one that told you. I couldn't bear to have him hate me, even if I never see him again. The poor damn silly fool was born and raised right here in Ontario. His real name is Theodore Fredericks, and his mother runs a boardinghouse in Pitt, not more than sixty miles from here.'

I stood up, forcing her to look at me. 'How do you know, Miss Reichler?'

'I talked to Mrs. Fredericks. It wasn't a very fortunate meeting. It didn't do anything for either of us. I should never have gone there.'

'Did he take you to meet his mother?'

'Hardly. I went to see her myself a couple of weeks ago, after John left Ann Arbor. When I didn't hear from him I got it into my head that perhaps he'd gone home to Pitt.'

'How did you learn about his home in Pitt? Did he tell you?'

'Yes, but I don't believe he intended to. It happened on the spur of the moment, when he was spending a week-end here with us. It was the only time he ever came to visit us here in Kingsville, and it was a bad time for me—the worst. I hate to think of it.'

'Why?'

'If you have to know, he turned me down. We went for a drive on Sunday morning. I did the driving, of course. He'd never touch the wheel of my car. That's the way he was with me, so proud, and I had no pride at all with him. I got carried away by the flowers and the bees, or something, and I asked him to marry me. He gave me a flat refusal.

'He must have seen how hurt I was, because he asked me to drive him to Pitt. We weren't too far from there, and he wanted to show me something. When we got there he made me drive down a street that runs along by the river on the edge of the Negro section. It was a dreadful neighbourhood, filthy children of all colours playing in the mud, and slatternly women screaming at them. We stopped across from an old red brick house where some men in their undershirts were sitting on the front steps passing around a wine jug.

'John asked me to take a good look, because he said he belonged there. He said he'd grown up in that neighbourhood, in that red house. A woman came out on the porch to call the men in for dinner. She had a voice like a kazoo, and she was a hideous fat pig of a woman. John said that she was his mother.

'I didn't believe him. I thought he was hoaxing me, putting me to some kind of silly test. It was a test, in a way, but not in the way I imagined. He wanted to be *known*, I think. He wanted me to accept him as he actually was. But by the time I understood that, it was too late. He'd gone into one of his deep freezes.' She touched her mournful mouth with the tips of her long fingers.

'When did this happen?'

'Last spring. It must have been early in March, there was still some snow on the ground.'

'Did you see John after that?'

'A few times, but it wasn't any good. I think he regretted telling me about himself. In fact I know he did. That Sunday in Pitt was the end of any real communication between us. There were so many things we couldn't talk about, finally we couldn't talk at all. The last time I saw him was humiliating, for him, and for me, too. He asked me not to mention what he'd said about his origins, if anyone ever brought it up.'

'Who did he expect to bring it up? The police?'

'The immigration authorities. Apparently there was something irregular about his entry into the United States. That fitted in with what his mother told me afterwards. He'd run away with one of her boarders when he was sixteen, and apparently crossed over into the States.'

'Did she give you the boarder's name?'

'No. I'm surprised Mrs. Fredericks told me as much as she did. You know how the lower classes are, suspicious, but I gave her a little money, and that loosened her up.' Her tone was contemptuous, and she must have overheard herself: 'I know, I'm just what John said I was, a dollar snob. Well, I had my comeuppance. There I was prowling around the Pitt slums on a hot summer day like a lady dog in season. And I might as well have stayed at home. His mother hadn't laid eyes on him for over five years, and she never expected to see him again, she said. I realized that I'd lost him for good.'

'He was easy to lose,' I said, 'and no great loss.'

She looked at me like an enemy. 'You don't know him. John's a fine person at heart, fine and deep. I was the one who failed in our relationship. If I'd been able to understand him that Sunday, say the right thing and hold him, he mightn't have gone into this fraudulent life. I'm the one who wasn't good for anything.'

She screwed up her face like a monkey and tugged at her hair, making herself look ugly.

'I'm just a hag.'

'Be quiet.'

She looked at me incredulously, one hand flat against her temple. 'Who do you think you're talking to?'

'Ada Reichler. You're worth five of him.'

'I'm not. I'm no good. I betrayed him. Nobody could love me. *No*body could.'

'I told you to be quiet.' I'd never been angrier in my life.

'Don't you dare speak to me like that. Don't you dare!'

Her eyes were as bright and heavy as mercury. She ran blind to the end of the garden, knelt at the edge of the grass, and buried her face in flowers.

Her back was long and beautiful. I waited until she was still, and lifted her to her feet. She turned toward me.

The last light faded from the flowers and from the lake. Night came on warm and moist. The grass was wet.

CHAPTER TWENTY-FIVE

The town of Pitt was dark except for occasional street lights and the fainter lights that fell from the heavily starred sky. Driving along the street Ada Reichler had named, I could see the moving river down between the houses. When I got out of the car, I could smell the river. A chanting chorus of frogs made the summer night pulsate at its edges.

On the second floor of the old red house, a bleary light outlined a window. The boards of the veranda groaned under my weight. I knocked on the alligatored door. A card offering 'Rooms for Rent' was stuck inside the window beside the door.

A light went on over my head. Moths swirled up around it like unseasonable snow. An old man peered out, cocking his narrow grey head at me out of a permanent stoop.

'Something you want?' His voice was a husky whisper.

'I'd like to speak to Mrs. Fredericks, the landlady.'

'I'm Mr. Fredericks. If it's a room you want, I can rent you a room just as good as she can.'

'Do you rent by the night?'

'Sure, I got a nice front room you can have. It'll cost you—let's see.' He stroked the bristles along the edge of his jaw, making a rasping noise. His dull eyes looked me over with stupid cunning. 'Two dollars?'

'I'd like to see the room first.'

'If you say so. Try not to make too much noise, eh? The old woman—Mrs. Fredericks is in bed.'

He must have been just about to go himself. His shirt was open so that I could have counted his ribs, and his broad striped suspenders were hanging down. I followed him up the stairs. He moved with elaborate secrecy, and turned at the top to set a hushing finger to his lips. The light from the hall below cast his hunched condor shadow on the wall.

A woman's voice rose from the back of the house: 'What are you creeping around for?'

'Didn't want to disturb the boarders,' he said in his carrying whisper.

'The boarders aren't in yet, and you know it. Is somebody with you?'

'Nope. Just me and my shadow.'

He smiled a yellow-toothed smile at me, as if he expected me to share the joke.

'Come to bed then,' she called.

'In a minute.'

He tiptoed to the front of the hallway, beckoned me through an open door, and closed the door quietly behind me. For a moment we were alone in the dark, like conspirators. I could hear his emotional breathing.

Then he reached up to pull on a light. It swung on its cord, throwing lariats of shadow up to the high ceiling, and shifting gleam and gloom on the room's contents. These included a bureau, a washstand with pitcher and bowl, and a bed which had taken the impress of many bodies. The furnishings reminded me of the room John Brown had had in Luna Bay.

John Brown? John Nobody.

I looked at the old man's face. It was hard to imagine what quirk of his genes had produced the boy. If Fredericks had ever possessed good looks, time had washed them out. His face was patchily furred leather, stretched on gaunt bones, held in place by black nailhead eyes.

'The room all right?' he said uneasily.

I glanced at the flowered paper on the walls. Faded morning-glories climbed brown lattices to the watermarked ceiling. I didn't think I could sleep in a room with morning-glories crawling up the walls all night.

'If it's bugs you're worried about,' he said, 'we had the place fumigated last spring.'

'Oh. Good.'

'I'll let in some fresh air.' He opened the window and sidled back to me. 'Pay me cash in advance, and I can let you have it for a dollar and a half.'

I had no intention of staying the night, but I decided to let him have the money. I took out my wallet and gave him two ones. His hand trembled as he took them:

'I got no change.'

'Keep it. Mr. Fredericks, you have a son.'

He gave me a long slow cautious look. 'What if I have?'

'A boy named Theodore.'

'He's no boy. He'll be grown up now.'

'How long is it since you've seen him?'

'I dunno. Four-five years, maybe longer. He ran away when he was sixteen. It's a tough thing to have to say about your own boy, but it was good riddance of bad rubbish.'

'Why do you say that?'

'Because it's the truth. You acquainted with Theo?'

'Slightly.'

'Is he in trouble again? Is that why you're here?'

Before I could answer, the door of the room flew open. A short stout woman in a flannelette nightgown brushed past me and advanced on Fredericks: 'What you think you're doing, renting a room behind my back?'

'I didn't.'

But the money was still in his hand. He tried to crumple it in his fist and hide it. She grabbed for it:

'Give me my money.'

He hugged his valuable fist against his washboard chest. 'It's just as much my money as it is yours.'

'Aw no it isn't. I work myself to the bone keeping our heads above water. And what do you do? Drink it up as fast as I can make it.'

'I ain't had a drink for a week.'

'You're a liar.' She stamped her bare foot. Her body shook under the nightgown, and her grey braids swung like cables down her back. 'You were drinking wine last night with the boys in the downstairs bedroom.'

'That was free,' he said virtuously. 'And you got no call to talk to me like this in front of a stranger.'

She turned to me for the first time. 'Excuse us, mister. It's no fault of yours, but he can't handle money.' She added unnecessarily: 'He drinks.'

While her eyes were off him, Fredericks made for the door. She intercepted him. He struggled feebly in her embrace. Her upper arms were as thick as hams. She pried open his bony fist and pushed the crumpled bills down between her breasts. He watched the money go as though it represented his hope of heaven:

'Just give me fifty cents. Fifty cents won't break you.'

'Not one red cent,' she said. 'If you think I'm going to help you get the d.t.'s again, you got another think coming.'

'All I want is one drink.'

'Sure, and then another and another. Until you feel the

154

rats crawling up under your clothes, and I got to nurse you out of it again.'

'There's all different kinds of rats. A woman that won't give her lawful husband four bits to settle his stomach is the worst kind of rat there is.'

'Take that back.'

She moved on him, arms akimbo. He backed into the hall-way:

'All right, I take it back. But I'll get a drink, don't worry. I got good friends in this town, they know my worth.'

'Sure they do. They feed you stinking rotgut across the river, and then they come to me asking for money. Don't you set foot outside this house tonight.'

'You're not going to order me around, treat me like a has-been. It ain't my fault I can't work, with a hole in my belly. It ain't my fault I can't sleep without a drink to ease the pain.'

'Scat,' she said. 'Go to bed, old man.'

He shambled away, trailing his slack suspenders. The fat woman turned to me.

'I apologize for my husband. He's never been the same since his accident.'

'What happened to him?'

'He got hurt bad.' Her answer seemed deliberately vague. Under folds of fat, her face showed traces of her son's stub-born intelligence. She changed the subject: 'I notice you paid with American money. You from the States?'

'I just drove over from Detroit.'

'You live in Detroit? I never been over there, but I hear it's an interesting place.'

'It probably is. I was just passing through on my way from California.'

'What brings you all the way from California?'

'A man named Peter Culligan was murdered there several weeks ago. Culligan was stabbed to death.'

'Stabbed to death?'

I nodded. Her head moved slightly in unison with mine. Without shifting her eyes from my face, she moved around me and sat on the edge of the bed.

'You know him, don't you, Mrs. Fredericks?'

'He boarded with me for a while, years ago. He had this very room.'

'What was he doing in Canada?'

'Don't ask me. I don't ask my boarders where their money

comes from. Mostly he sat in this room and studied his racing sheets.' She looked up shrewdly from under frowning brows. 'Would you be a policeman?'

'I'm working with the police. Are you sure you don't know why Culligan came here?'

'I guess it was just a place like any other. He was a loner and a drifter—I get quite a few of them. He probably covered a lot of territory in his time.' She looked up at the shadows on the ceiling. The light was still now, and the shadows were concentric, spreading out like ripples on a pool. 'Listen, mister, who stabbed him?'

'A young hoodlum.'

'My boy? Was it my boy that done it? Is that why you come to me?'

'I think your son is involved.'

'I knew it.' Her cheeks shuddered. 'He took a knife to his father before he was out of high school. He would of killed him, too. Now he really is a murderer.' She pressed her clenched hands deep into her bosom; it swelled around her fists like rising dough. 'I didn't have enough trouble in my life. I had to give birth to a murderer.'

'I don't know about that, Mrs. Fredericks. He committed fraud. I doubt that he committed murder.' Even as I said it, I was wondering if he had been within striking distance of Culligan, and if he had an alibi for that day. 'Do you have a picture of your son?'

'I have when he was in high school. He ran away before he graduated.'

'May I have a look at the picture, Mrs. Fredericks? It's barely possible we're talking about two different people.'

But any hope of this died a quick death. The boy in the snapshot she brought was the same one, six years younger. He stood on the riverbank, his back to the water, smiling with conscious charm into the camera.

I gave the picture back to Mrs. Fredericks. She held it up to the light and studied it as if she could re-create the past from its single image.

'Theo was a good-looking boy,' she said wistfully. 'He was doing so good in school and all, until he started getting those ideas of his.'

'What kind of ideas did he have?'

'Crazy ideas, like he was the son of an English lord, and the gypsies stole him away when he was a baby. When he was just a little tyke, he used to call himself Percival Fitzroy, like in a book. That was always his way—he thought he was too good for his own people. I worried about where all that day-dreaming was going to land him.'

'He's still dreaming,' I said. 'Right now he's representing himself as the grandson of a wealthy woman in Southern California. Do you know anything about that?'

'I never hear from him. How would I know about it?'

'Apparently Culligan put him up to it. I understand he ran away from here with Culligan.'

'Yeah. The dirty scamp talked him into it, turned him against his own father.'

'And you say he knifed his father?'

'That very same day.' Her eyes widened and glazed. 'He stabbed him with a butcher knife, game him an awful wound. Fredericks was on his back for weeks. He's never got back on his feet entirely. Neither have I, to think my own boy would do a thing like that.'

'What was the trouble about, Mrs. Fredericks?'

'Wildness and wilfulness,' she said. 'He wanted to leave home and make his own way in the world. That Culligan en-couraged him. He pretended to have Theo's welfare at heart and I know what you're thinking, that Theo did right to run away from home with his old man a bum and the kind of boarders I get. But the proof of the pudding is in the eating. Look at how Theo turned out.'

'I have been, Mrs. Fredericks.'

'I knew he was headed for a bad end,' she said. 'He didn't show natural feelings. He never wrote home once since he left. Where has he been all these years?'

'Going to college.'

'To college? He went to college?'

'Your son's an ambitious boy.'

'Oh, he always had an ambition, if that's what you want to call it. Is that what he learned in college, how to cheat people?'

'He learned that someplace else.'

Perhaps in this room, I thought, where Culligan spun his fantasies and laid a long-shot bet on an accidental resemblance to a dead man. The room had Culligan's taint on it.

The woman stirred uncomfortably, as if I'd made a subtle accusation:

'I don't claim we were good parents to him. He wanted more than we could give him. He always had a dream of himself, like.'

Her face moved sluggishly, trying to find the shape of truth and feeling. She leaned back on her arms and let her gaze rest on the swollen slopes of her body, great sagging breasts, distended belly from which a son had struggled headfirst into the light. Over her bowed head, insects swung in eccentric orbits around the hanging bulb, tempting hot death.

She managed to find some hope in the situation: 'At least he didn't murder anybody, eh?'

'No.'

'Who was it that knifed Culligan? You said it was a young hoodlum.'

'His name is Tommy Lemberg. Tommy and his brother Roy are supposed to be hiding out in Ontario—'

'Hamburg, did you say?'

'They may be using that name. Do you know Roy and Tommy?'

'I hope to tell you. They been renting the downstairs room for the last two weeks. They told me their name was Hamburg. How was I to know they were hiding out?'

CHAPTER TWENTY-SIX

I waited for the Lembergs on the dark porch. They came home after midnight, walking a bit unsteadily down the street. My parked car attracted their attention, and they crossed the street to look it over. I went down the front steps and across the street after them.

They turned, so close together that they resembled a single amorphous body with two white startled faces. Tommy started toward me, a wide lopsided shape. His arm was still in a white sling under his jacket.

Roy lifted his head with a kind of hopeless alertness. 'Come back here, kid.'

'The hell. It's old man trouble himself.' He walked up to me busily, and spat in the dust at my feet.

'Take it easy, Tommy.' Roy came up behind him. 'Talk to him.'

'Sure I'll talk to him.' He said to me: 'Didn't you get enough from Mr. Schwartz? You came all this way looking for more?'

Without giving the matter any advance thought, I set myself on my heels and hit him with all my force on the point of the jaw. He went down and stayed. His brother knelt beside him, making small shocked noises which resolved themselves into words:

'You had no right to hit him. He wanted to talk to you.'

'I heard him.'

'He's been drinking, and he was scared. He was just putting on a big bluff.'

'Put away the violin. It doesn't go with a knifing rap.'

'Tommy never knifed anybody.'

'That's right, he was framed. Culligan framed him by falling down and stabbing himself. Tommy was just an innocent bystander.'

'I don't claim he was innocent. Schwartz sent him there to throw his weight around. But nobody figured he was going to run into Culligan, let alone Culligan with a knife and a gun. He got shot taking the gun away from Culligan. Then he knocked Culligan out, and that's the whole thing as far as Tommy's concerned.'

'At which point the Apaches came out of the hills.'

'I thought maybe you'd be interested in the truth,' Roy said in a shaking voice. 'But your thinking is the same as all the others. Once a fellow takes a fall, he's got no human rights.'

'Sure, I'm unfair to organized crime.'

The wisecrack sounded faintly tinny even to me. Roy made a disgusted sound in his throat. Tommy groaned as if in response. His eyes were still turned up, veined white between half-closed lids. Roy inserted one arm under his brother's head and lifted it.

Peering down at the dim face, unconscious and innocent-looking, I had a pang of doubt. I knew my bitterness wasn't all for Tommy Lemberg. When I hit him I was lashing out at the other boy, too, reacting to a world of treacherous little hustlers that wouldn't let a man believe in it.

I scraped together a nickel's worth of something, faith or gullibility, and invested it:

'Lemberg, do you believe this yarn your brother told you?'

'Yes.'

'Are you willing to put it to the test?'

'I don't understand you.' But his white face slanted up fearfully. 'If you're talking about him going back to California, no. They'd put him in the gas chamber.'

'Not if his story is true. He could do a lot to back it up by coming back with me voluntarily.'

'He can't. He's been in jail. He has a record.'

'That record of his means a lot to you, doesn't it? More than it does to other people, maybe.'

'I don't dig you.'

'Why don't you dissolve the brother act? Commit yourself where there's some future. Your wife could do with a piece of you. She's in a bad way, Lemberg.'

He didn't answer me. He held his brother's head possessively against his shoulder. In the light of the stars they seemed like twins, mirror images of each other. Roy looked at Tommy in a puzzled way, as if he couldn't tell which was the real man and which was the reflection. Or which was the possessor and which was the possessed.

Footfalls thudded in the dust behind me. It was Mrs. Fredericks, wearing a bathrobe and carrying a pan of water.

'Here,' was all she said.

She handed me the pan and went back into the house. She wanted no part of the trouble in the street. Her house was well supplied with trouble.

I sprinkled some water on Tommy's face. He snorted and sat up blinking. 'Who hit me?' Then he saw me, and remembered: 'You sucker-punched me. You sucker-punched a cripple.'

He tried to get up. Roy held him down with both hands on his shoulders:

'You had it coming, you know that. I've been talking to Mr. Archer. He'll listen to what you have to say.'

'I'm willing to listen to the truth,' I said. 'Anything else is a waste of time.'

With his brother's help, Tommy got on to his feet. 'Go ahead,' Roy prompted him. 'Tell him. And no more kid stuff.'

'The whole truth, remember,' I said, 'including the Schwartz angle.'

'Yeah. Yeah.' Tommy was still dazed. 'Schwartz was the one hired me in the first place. He sent one of his boys to look me up, promised me a hundred bucks to put a fear into this certain party.'

'A little death, you mean?'

He shook his head violently. 'Nothing like that, just a little working over.'

'What did Schwartz have against Culligan?'

'Culligan wasn't the one. He wasn't supposed to be there, see. He got in the picture by mistake.'

'I told you that,' Roy said.

'Be quiet. Let Tommy do the talking.'

'Yeah, sure,' Tommy said. 'It was this beast that I was supposed to put on a little show for. I wasn't supposed to hurt her, nothing like that, just put the fear of God in her so she'd cough up what she owed Schwartz. It was like a collection agency, y'unnerstan'? Legit.'

'What was her name?'

'Alice Sable. They sent me because I knew what she looked like. Last summer in Reno she used to run around with Pete Culligan. But he wasn't supposed to be there at her house, for God's sake. The way they told it to me, she was alone by herself out there all day. When Culligan came marching out, armed up to the teeth, you could of knocked me over with a 'dozer.

'I moved in on him, very fast, very fast reflexes I got, talking all the time. Got hold of the gun but it went off, the slug ploughed up my arm, same time he dropped the gun. I picked it up. By that time he had his knife out. What could I do? He was going to gut me. I slammed him on the noggin with the gun and chilled him. Then I beat it.'

'Did you see Alice Sable?'

'Yeah, she came surging out and yelled at me. I was starting the Jag, and I couldn't hear what she said over the engine. I didn't stop or turn around. Hell, I didn't want to rough up no beast, anyway.'

'Did you pick up Culligan's knife before you left, and cut him with it?'

'No sir. What would I do that for? Man, I was hurt. I wanted out.'

'What was Culligan doing when you left?'

'Laying there.' He glanced at his brother. 'Lying there.'

'Who coached you to say that?'

'Nobody did.'

'That's true,' Roy said. 'It's just the way he told it to me. You've got to believe him.'

'I'm not the important one. The man he has to convince is

Sheriff Trask of Santa Teresa County. And planes are taking off for there all the time.'

'Aw, no.' Tommy's gaze swivelled frantically from me to Roy. 'They'll throw the book at me if I go back.'

'Sooner or later you have to go back. You can come along peaceably now, or you can force extradition proceedings and make the trip in handcuffs and leg-chains. Which way do you want it, hard or easy?'

For once in his young life, Tommy Lemberg did something the easy way.

CHAPTER TWENTY-SEVEN

I phoned Sheriff Trask long distance. He agreed to wire me transportation authorization for the Lemberg brothers. I picked it up at Willow Run, and the three of us got aboard an early plane. Trask had an official car waiting to meet the connecting plane when it landed in Santa Teresa.

Before noon we were in the interrogation room in the Santa Teresa courthouse. Roy and Tommy made statements, which were recorded by a court reporter on steno and tape-machine. Tommy seemed to be awed by the big room with its barred windows, the Sheriff's quiet power, the weight of the law which both man and building represented. There were no discrepancies in the part of his statement I heard.

Trask motioned me out before Tommy was finished. I followed him down the corridor to his office. He took off his coat and opened the neck of his shirt. Blotches of sweat spread from his armpits. He filled a paper cup with water from a cooler, drained the cup, and crushed it in his fist.

'If we buy this,' he said at last, 'it puts us back at the beginning. You buy it, don't you, Archer?'

'I've taken an option on it. Naturally I think it should be investigated. But that can wait. Have you questioned Theo Fredericks about the Culligan killing?'

'No.'

'Is Fredericks doing any talking at all?'

'Not to me he isn't.'

'But you picked him up last night?'

Trask's face had a raw red look. I thought at first that he

162

was on the verge of a heart attack. Then I realized that he was painfully embarrassed. He turned his back on me, walked over to the wall, and stood looking at a photograph of himself shaking hands with the Governor.

'Somebody tipped him off,' he said. 'He flew the coop five minutes before I got there.' He turned to face me: 'The worst part of it is, he took Sheila Howell with him.'

'By force?'

'You kidding? She was probably the one who tipped him off. I made the mistake of phoning Dr. Howell before I moved on the little rat. In any case, she went along with him willingly —walked out of her father's house and drove away with him in the middle of the night. Howell's been on my back ever since.'

'Howell's very fond of his daughter.'

'Yeah, I know how he feels, I have a daughter of my own. I was afraid for a while that he was going to take off after her with a shotgun, and I mean literally. Howell's a trap-shooter, one of the best in the county. But I got him calmed down. He's in the communications room, waiting to hear some word of them.'

'They're travelling by car?'

'The one Mrs. Galton bought for him.'

'A red Thunderbird should be easy to spot.'

'You'd think so. But they've been gone over eight hours without a trace. They may be in Mexico by now. Or they may be cuddled up in an L.A. motel under one of his aliases.' Trask scowled at the image. 'Why do so many nice young girls go for the dangerous ones?'

The question didn't expect an answer, and that was just as well. I hadn't any.

Trask sat down heavily behind his desk. 'Just how dangerous is he? When we talked on the telephone last night, you mentioned a knifing he did before he left Canada.'

'He stabbed his father. Apparently he meant to kill him. The old man is no saint, either. In fact, the Fredericks' boarding-house is a regular thieves' kitchen. Peter Culligan was staying there at the time of the knifing. The boy ran away with him.'

Trask took up a pencil and broke it in half, abstractedly, dropping the pieces on his blotter. 'How do we know the Fredericks boy didn't murder Culligan? He had a motive: Culligan was in a position to call his bluff and tell the world who he really was. And M.O. figures, with his knifing record.'

'We've been thinking the same thing, Sheriff. There's even a strong likelihood that Culligan was his partner in the conspiracy. That would give him a powerful motive to silence Culligan. We've been assuming that Fredericks was in Luna Bay that day. But has his alibi ever been checked?'

'There's no time like the present.'

Trask picked up his phone and asked the switchboard to put through a call to the San Mateo County sheriff's office in Redwood City.

'I can think of one other possibility,' I said. 'Alice Sable was involved with Culligan last year in Reno, and maybe since. Remember how she reacted to his death. We put it down to nervous shock, but it could have been something worse.'

'You're not suggesting that she killed him?'

'As a hypothesis.'

Trask shook his head impatiently. 'Even putting it hypothetically, it's pretty hard to swallow about a lady like her.'

'What kind of a lady is she? Do you know her?'

'I've met her, that's about all. But hell, Gordon Sable's one of the top lawyers in the city.'

The politician latent in every elected official was rising to the surface and blurring Trask's hard, clear attitudes. I said:

'That doesn't put his wife above suspicion. Have you questioned her?'

'No.' Trask became explanatory, as though he felt that he had missed a move: 'I haven't been able to get to her. Sable was opposed, and the head-shrinkers backed him up. They say she shouldn't be questioned on painful subjects. She's been borderline psychotic since the killing, and any more pressure might push her over the edge.'

'Howell's her personal doctor, isn't he?'

'He is. As a matter of fact, I tried to get to her through Howell. He was dead set against it, and as long as it looked like an open-and-shut case, I didn't press the point.'

'Howell should be ready to change his mind. Did you say he's somewhere around the courthouse?'

'Yeah, he's down in Communications. But wait a minute, Archer.' Trask rose and came around the desk. 'This is a touchy business, and you don't want to hang too much weight on the Lemberg brothers' story. They're not disinterested witnesses.'

'They don't know enough to invent the story, either.'

'Schwartz and his lawyers do.'

'Are we back on the Schwartz kick again?'

'You were the one that got me on it in the first place. You were convinced that the Culligan killing was a gang killing.'

'I was wrong.'

'Maybe. We'll let the facts decide when they all come out. But if you were wrong, you could be wrong again.' Trask punched me in the stomach in a friendly way. 'How about that, Archer?'

His telephone chirped, and he lifted the receiver. I couldn't make out the words that came scratchily over the wire, but I saw their effect on Trask. His body stiffened, and his face seemed to grow larger.

'I'll use my Aero Squadron,' he said finally, 'and I ought to be there in two hours. But don't sit around waiting for me.' He slammed down the receiver and reached for the coat draped over the back of his chair.

'They made the red Thunderbird,' he said. 'Fredericks abandoned it in San Mateo. They were just going to put the word on the teletype when they got my call.'

'Where in San Mateo?'

'Parking-lot of the S.P. station. Fredericks and the girl probably took a train into San Francisco.'

'Are you flying up?'

'Yeah, I've had a volunteer pilot standing by all morning. Ride along with us if you want. He has a four-passenger Beechcraft.'

'Thanks, I've had enough flying to last me for a while. You didn't ask them to check Fredericks's alibi.'

'I forgot,' Trask said lightly. 'I'll take it up with Fredericks personally.'

He seemed glad to be leaving Alice Sable in my lap.

CHAPTER TWENTY-EIGHT

The communications centre of the courthouse was a windowless room on the basement level, full of the chatter and whine of short-wave radio signals. Dr. Howell was sitting with his head down in front of a quiet teletype machine. He raised his head abruptly when I spoke to him. His face was grey in the white overhead light:

'So here you are. While you've been junketing around the country at my expense, she's gone away with him. Do you understand what that means?'

His voice rose out of control. The two deputies monitoring the radios looked at him and then at each other. One of them said: 'If you two gentlemen want to talk in private, this is no place to do it.'

'Come outside,' I said to Howell: 'You're not accomplishing anything here. They'll be picked up soon, don't worry.'

He sat in inert silence. I wanted to get him away from the teletype machine before the message from San Mateo hit it. It would send him off to the Bay area, and I had a use for him here:

'Doctor, is Alice Sable still under your care?'

He looked up questioningly. 'Yes.'

'Is she still in the nursing home?'

'Yes. I should try to get there today.' He brushed his forehead with his fingertips. 'I've been neglecting my patients, I'm afraid.'

'Come out there with me now.'

'What on earth for?'

'Mrs. Sable may be able to help us terminate this case, and help us reach your daughter.'

He rose, but stood irresolute beside the teletype machine. Sheila's defection had robbed him of his force. I took hold of his elbow and steered him out into the basement corridor. Once moving, he went ahead of me up the iron stairs into the hot white noon.

His Chevrolet was in the county parking-lot. He turned to me as he started the engine:

'How can Mrs. Sable help us to find Sheila?'

'I'm not certain she can. But she was involved with Culligan, the Fredericks boy's probable partner in the conspiracy. She may know more about Theo Fredericks than anyone else does.'

'She never said a word about him to me.'

'Has she been talking to you about the case?'

He said after some hesitation 'Not being a practising psychiatrist, I haven't encouraged that line of discussion with her. The matter has come up, however. Unavoidably so, since it's part and parcel of her mental condition.'

'Can you be more specific?'

'I prefer not to. You know the ethics of my profession. The

doctor-patient relationship is sacrosanct.'

'So is human life. Don't forget a man was murdered. We have evidence that Mrs. Sable knew Culligan before he came to Santa Teresa. She was also a witness to his death. Anything she has to say about it may be very significant.'

'Not if her memory of the event is delusional.'

'Does she have delusions on the subject?'

'She has indeed. Her account doesn't agree with the actual events as we know it. I've gone into this with Trask, and there's no doubt whatever that a thug named Lemberg stabbed the man.'

'There's a good deal of doubt,' I said. 'The Sheriff just took a statement from Lemberg. A Reno gambler sent Lemberg to collect money from Alice Sable, and maybe rough her up a bit. Culligan got in the way. Lemberg knocked him out, was shot in the process, left him unconscious on the ground. He claims that somebody else did the knifing after he left.'

Howell's face underwent a curious change. His eyes became harder and brighter. He wasn't looking at me, or at anything external. The lines around his eyes and at the corners of his mouth curved and deepened, as if he was being forced to look against his will at something horrible.

'But Trask said Lemberg was undeniably guilty.'

'Trask was wrong. We all were.'

'Do you honestly mean to say that Alice Sable has been speaking the truth all along?'

'I don't know what she's been saying, Doctor. You do.'

'But Trenchard and the other psychiatrists were convinced that her self-accusations were fantasies. They had me convinced.'

'What does she accuse herself of? Does she blame herself for Culligan's death?'

Howell sat over the wheel in silence. He had been shaken, and wide open, for a few minutes. Now his personality closed up again:

'You have no right to cross-examine me about the intimate affairs of one of my patients.'

'I'm afraid I have to, Doctor. If Alice Sable murdered Culligan, there's no way you can cover up for her. I'm surprised you want to. You're not only breaking the law, you're violating the ethics you set such store by.'

'I'll be the judge of my own ethics,' he said in a strained voice.

He sat and wrestled with his unstated problem. His gaze was inward and glaring. Sweat-drops studded his forehead. I got some sense of the empathy he felt for his patient. Even his daughter was forgotten.

'She has confessed the murder to you, Doctor?'

Slowly his eyes remembered me again. 'What did you say?'

'Has Mrs. Sable confessed Culligan's murder?'

'I'm going to ask you not to question me further.'

Abruptly he released the emergency brake. I kept quiet all the way to the nursing home, hoping my patience might earn me an interview with Alice Sable herself.

A grey-haired nurse unlocked the front door, and smiled with special intensity at Howell. 'Good morning, Doctor. We're a little late this morning.'

'I'm having to skip my regular calls today. I do want to see Mrs. Sable.'

'I'm sorry, Doctor, she's already gone.'

'Gone where, for heaven's sake?'

'Mr. Sable took her home this morning, didn't you know? He said it was all right with you.'

'It certainly is not. You don't release disturbed patients without specific orders from a doctor. Haven't you learned that yet, nurse?'

Before she could answer, Howell turned on his heel and started back to his car. I had to run to catch him.

'The man's a fool!' he cried above the roar of the engine. 'He can't be permitted to take a chance like this with his wife's safety. She's dangerous to herself and other people.'

I said when we were underway: 'Was she dangerous to Culligan, Doctor?'

His answer was a sigh which seemed to rise from the centre of his body. The outskirts of Santa Teresa gave place to open country. The hills of Arroyo Park rose ahead of us. With his eyes on the green hills, Howell said:

'The poor wretch of a woman told me that she killed him. And I didn't have sense enough to believe her. Somehow her story didn't ring true to me. I was convinced that it was fantasy masking the actual event.'

'Is that why you wouldn't let Trask talk to her?'

'Yes. The present state of the law being what it is, a doctor has a duty to protect his patients, especially the semi-psychotic ones. We can't run off to the police with every sick delusion they come up with. But in this case,' he added reluctantly, 'it

168

seems I was mistaken.'

'You're not sure.'

'I'm no longer sure about anything.'

'Exactly what did she say to you?'

'She heard the sounds of a struggle, two men fighting and calling each other names. A gun went off. She was terrified, of course, but she forced herself to go to the front door. Culligan was lying on the lawn. The other man was just driving away in the Jaguar. When he was out of sight, she went out to Culligan. Her intention was to help him, she said, but she saw his knife in the grass. She picked it up and—used it.'

We had reached the foot of Sable's hill. Howell wrestled his car up the climbing curves. The tyres shuddered and screeched like lost souls under punishment.

CHAPTER TWENTY-NINE

Sable must have heard the car, and been waiting behind the door for Howell's knock. He opened the door at once. His bloodshot eyes began to water in the strong sunlight, and he sneezed.

'Where is your wife?' Howell said.

'In her own room, where she belongs. There was so much noise and confusion in the nursing home—'

'I want to see her.'

'I don't think so, Doctor. I understand you've been grilling her about the unfortunate crime that occurred on our premises. It's been most disturbing to Alice. You told me yourself that she shouldn't be forced to talk about it.'

'She brought up the subject of her own accord. I demand to be allowed to see her.'

'Demand, Doctor? How can you do that? I should make it clear, I suppose, that I'm terminating your services as of now. I intend to hire a new crew of doctors, and find a place where Alice can rest in peace.'

The phrase set up whispering echoes which Howell's voice cut through:

'You don't hire doctors, Sable, and you don't fire them.'

'Your law is rusty. Perhaps you should hire a lawyer. You're certainly going to need one if you try to force your way into my house.' Sable's voice was controlled, but queerly atonal.

'I have a duty to my patient. You had no right to remove her from nursing care.'

'From your third-degree methods, you mean? Let me remind you, if you need reminding, that anything Alice has said to you is privileged. I employed you and the others in my capacity as her lawyer in order to have your assistance in determining certain facts. Is that clear? If you communicate these facts or alleged facts to anyone, official or unofficial, I'll sue you for criminal libel.'

'You're talking doubletalk,' I said. 'You won't be suing anybody.'

'Won't I, though? You're in roughly the same position as Dr. Howell. I employed you to make a certain investigation, and ordered you to communicate the results orally to me. Any further communication is a breach of contract. Try it out, and by God I'll have your licence.'

I didn't know if he was legally right. I didn't care. When he started to swing the door shut, I set my foot against it:

'We're coming in, Sable.'

'I think not,' his queer new voice said.

He reached behind the door and stepped back with a gun in his hands. It was a long, heavy gun, a deer rifle with a telescopic sight. He raised it deliberately. I looked directly into the muzzle, at the clean, glinting spiral of the rifling.

Sable curled his finger on the trigger, and cuddled the polished stock against his cheek. His face had a fine glaze on it, like porcelain. I realized that he was ready to kill me.

'Put it down,' Howell said.

He moved ahead of me into the doorway, taking my place in the line of fire:

'Put it down, Gordon. You're not yourself, you're feeling upset, you're terribly worried about Alice. But we're your friends, we're Alice's friends, too. We want to help you both.'

'I have no friends,' Sable said. 'I know why you're here, why you want to talk to Alice. And I'm not going to let you.'

'Don't be silly, Gordon. You can't look after a sick woman by yourself. I know you don't care about your personal safety, but you have to consider Alice's safety. She needs looking after, Gordon. So put it down now, let me in to see her.'

'Get back. I'll shoot.'

Sable's voice was a high sharp yell. His wife must have heard it. From deep inside the house, she cried out in answer:

'No!'

Sable blinked against the light. He looked like a sleepwalker waking up on the verge of a precipice. Behind him his wife's crying went on, punctuated by resounding blows and then a crash of glass.

Caught between impossible pressures, Sable half-turned toward the noise. The rifle swung sideways with his movement. I went in past Howell and got one hand on the gun-barrel and the other on the knot of Sable's tie. I heaved. Man and rifle came apart.

Sable thudded against the wall and almost fell. He was breathing hard. His hair was in his eyes. He bore a strange resemblance to an old woman peering out through the fringes of a matted white wig.

I opened the breech of the rifle. While I was unloading it, running feet slapped the pavement of the inner court. Alice Sable appeared at the end of the hallway. Her light hair was ruffled, and her nightgown was twisted around her slender body. Blood ran down over her naked foot from a cut in her leg.

'I hurt myself on the window,' she said in a small voice. 'I cut myself on the glass.'

'Did you have to break it?' Sable made an abrupt, threatening movement toward her. Then he remembered us, and sweetened his tone: 'Go back to your room, dear. You don't want to run around half-dressed in front of visitors.'

'Dr. Howell isn't a visitor. You came to fix it where I hurt myself, didn't you?'

She moved uncertainly toward the doctor. He went to meet her with his hands out. 'Of course I did. Come back to your room with me and we'll fix it now.'

'But I don't want to go back in there. I hate it in there, it depresses me. Peter used to visit me in there.'

'Be quiet!' Sable said.

She moved behind the doctor, making her body small as if to claim a child's irresponsibility. From the protection of Howell's shoulder, she peered sadly at her husband:

'Be quiet is all you say to me. Be quiet, hush it up. But what's the use, Gordon? Everybody knows about me and Peter. Dr. Howell knows. I made a clean breast of it to him.' Her hand went to her breast, and fingered the rosebuds embroidered on her nightgown. Her heavy gaze swung to me. 'This man knows about me, too, I can see it in his face.'

'Did you kill him, Mrs. Sable?'

'Don't answer,' Sable said.

'But I want to confess. I'll feel better then, won't I?' Her smile was bright and agonized. It faded, leaving its lines on her face and her teeth bare: 'I did kill him. The fellow in the black car knocked him out, and I went out and stabbed him.'

Her hand jerked downward from her breast, clenched on an imaginary knife. Her husband watched her like a poker-player.

'Why did you do it?' I said.

'I don't know. I guess I just got sick of him. Now it's time for me to take my punishment. I killed, and I deserve to die.'

The tragic words had an unreal quality. She spoke them like a life-size puppet activated by strings and used by a voice that didn't belong to her. Only her eyes were her own, and they contained a persistent stunned innocence.

'I deserve to die,' she repeated. 'Don't I, Gordon?'

He flushed up darkly. 'Leave me out of this.'

'But you said—'

'I said nothing of the sort.'

'You're lying, Gordon,' she chided him. Perhaps there was an undertone of malice in her voice. 'You told me after all my crimes that I deserved to die. And you were right. I lost your good money gambling and went with another man and now on top of it all I'm a murderer.'

Sable appealed to Howell: 'Can't we put an end to this? My wife is ill and hurt. It's inconceivable that you should let her be questioned. This man isn't even a policeman—'

'I'll take the responsibility for what I do,' I said. 'Mrs. Sable, do you remember stabbing Peter Culligan?'

She raised one hand to her forehead, pushing back her hair as if it got in the way of her thoughts. 'I don't remember exactly, but I must have.'

'Why do you say you must have, if you don't remember?'

'Gordon saw me.'

I looked at Sable. He wouldn't look at me. He stood against the wall, trying to merge with the wall.

'Gordon wasn't here,' I said. 'He was at Mrs. Galton's house when you telephoned.'

'But he came. He came right over. Peter was lying there on the grass for a long time. He was making a funny noise, it sounded like snoring. I unbuttoned the top of his shirt to help him breathe.'

'You remember all this, but you don't remember stabbing him?'

'I must have blanked out on that part. I'm always blanking out on things, ask Gordon.'

'I'm asking you, Mrs. Sable.'

'Let me think. I remember, I slid my hand down under his shirt, to see if his heart was beating properly. I could feel it there thumping and jumping. You'd think it was a little animal trying to get out. The hair on his chest was scratchy, like wire.'

Sable made a noise in his throat.

'What did you do then?' I said.

'I—nothing. I just sat for a while and looked at him and his poor old beatup face. I put my arms around him and tried to coax him awake. But he went on snoring at me. He was still snoring when Gordon got there. Gordon was angry, catching me with him like that. I ran into the house. But I watched from the window.'

Suddenly her face was incandescent. 'I didn't kill him. It wasn't me out there. It was Gordon, and I watched him from the window. He picked up Peter's knife and pushed it into his stomach.' Her clenched hand repeated its downward gesture, striking her own soft abdomen. 'The blood spurted out and ran red on the grass. It was all red and green.'

Sable thrust his head forward. The rest of his body, even his arms and hands, remained stuck to the wall:

'You can't believe her. She's hallucinating again.'

His wife seemed not to hear him. Perhaps she was tuned to a higher frequency, singing like salvation in her head. Tears streamed from her eyes:

'I didn't kill him.'

'Hush now.' Howell quieted her face against his shoulder.

'This is the truth, isn't it?' I said.

'It must be. I'm certain of it. Those self-accusations of hers were fantasy after all. This account is much more circumstantial. I'd say she's taken a long step toward reality.'

'She's crazier than she ever was,' Sable said. 'If you think you can use this against me, you're crazier than she is. Don't forget I'm a lawyer—'

'Is that what you are—a lawyer?' Howell turned his back on Sable and spoke to his wife: 'Come on, Alice, we'll put a bandage on that cut and you can get some clothes on. Then we'll take a little ride, back to the nice place with the other ladies.'

'It isn't a nice place,' she said.

Howell smiled down at her. 'That's the spirit. Keep saying what you really think and know, and we'll get you out of there to stay. But not for a while yet, eh?'

'Not for a while yet.'

Holding her with one arm, Howell stretched out his other hand to Sable. 'The key to your wife's room. You won't be needing it.'

Sable produced a flat brass key which Howell accepted from him, without a word. The doctor walked Alice Sable down the hallway toward the court.

CHAPTER THIRTY

Gordon Sable watched them go with something approaching relief. The bright expectancy had left his eyes. He had done it.

'I wouldn't have done it,' he said, 'if I'd known what I know now. There are factors you don't foresee—the factor of human change, for example. You think you can handle anything, that you can go on for ever. But your strength wears away under pressure. A few days, or a few weeks, and everything looks different. Nothing seems worth struggling for. It all goes blah.' He made a loose bumbling sound with his lips: 'All gone to bloody blah. So here we are.'

'Why did you kill him?'

'You heard her. When I got back here she was crying and moaning over him, trying to wake him up with kisses. It made me sick to death.'

'Don't tell me it was a sudden crime of passion. You must have known about them long before.'

'I don't deny that.' Sable shifted his stance, as if to prepare himself for a shift in his story. 'Culligan picked her up in Reno last summer. She went there to divorce me, but she ended up on a gambling spree with Culligan egging her on. No doubt he collected commissions on the money she lost. She lost a great deal, all the ready money I could raise. When it was gone, and her credit was exhausted, he let her share his apartment for a while. I had to go there and beg her to come home with me. She didn't want to come. I had to pay him to send her away.'

I didn't doubt the truth of what he was saying. No man would invent such a story against himself. It was Sable who didn't seem to believe his own words. They fell weightlessly from his mouth, like a memorized report of an accident he didn't understand, which had happened to people in a foreign country:

'I never felt quite the same about myself after that. Neither of us did. We lived in this house I'd built for her as if there were always a glass partition between us. We could see each other, but we couldn't really speak. We had to act out our feelings like clowns, or apes in separate cages. Alice's gestures became queerer, and no doubt mine did, too. The things we acted out got uglier. She would throw herself on the floor and strike herself with her fist until her face was bruised and swollen. And I would laugh at her and call her names.

'We did such things to each other,' he said. 'I think we were both glad, in a strange way, when Culligan turned up here in the course of the winter. Anthony Galton's bones had been unearthed and Culligan had read about it in the papers. He knew who they belonged to, and came to me with the information.'

'How did he happen to pick you?'

'It's a good question. I've often asked myself that good question. Alice had told him that I was Mrs. Galton's lawyer, of course. It may have been the source of his interest in her. He knew that her gambling losses had put me in financial straits. He needed expert help with the plan he had; he wasn't clever enough to execute it alone. He was just clever enough to realize that I was infinitely cleverer.'

And he knew other things about you, I thought. You were a loveless man who could be bent and finally twisted.

'How did Schwartz get in on the deal?'

'Otto Schwartz? He wasn't in on it.' Sable seemed offended by the notion. 'His only connection with it was the fact that Alice owed him sixty thousand dollars. Schwartz had been pressing for payment, and it finally reached the point where he was threatening both of us with a beating. I had to raise money somehow. I was desperate. I didn't know which way to turn.'

'Leave out the drama, Sable. You didn't go into this conspiracy on the spur of the moment. You've been working on it for months.'

'I'm not denying that. There was a lot of work to be done. Culligan's idea didn't look too promising at first. He'd been carrying it around ever since he ran into the Fredericks boy in Canada five or six years ago. He'd known Anthony Galton in Luna Bay, and was struck by the boy's resemblance to him. He even brought Fredericks into the States in the hope of cashing in on the resemblance in some way. But he ran into trouble with the law, and lost track of the boy. He believed that if I'd stake him, he could find him again.

'Culligan did find him, as you know, going to school in Ann Arbor. I went east myself in February, and saw him in one of the student plays. He was a fairly good actor, with a nice air of sincerity about him. I decided when I talked to him that he could carry the thing off if anyone could. I introduced myself as a Hollywood producer interested in his talent. Once he was hooked on that, and had taken money from me, he wasn't too hard to talk around to the other.

'I prepared his story for him, of course. It required considerable thought. The most difficult problem was how to lead investigation of his actual Canadian background into a blind alley. The Crystal Springs orphanage was my inspiration. But I realized that the success of the imposture depended primarily on him. If he did succeed in bringing it off, he would be entitled to the lion's share. I was modest in my own demands. He simply gave me an option to buy, at a nominal price, a certain amount of producing oil property.'

I watched him, trying to understand how a man with so much foresight could have ended where Sable was. Something had cut off the use of his mind from constructive purposes. Perhaps it was the shallow pride which he seemed to take in his schemes, even at this late date.

'They talk about the crime of the century,' he said. 'This would have been the greatest of all—a multi-million-dollar enterprise with no actual harm done to anyone. The boy was simply to let himself be discovered, and let the facts speak for themselves.'

'The facts?' I said sharply.

'The apparent facts, if you like. I'm not a philosopher. We lawyers don't deal in ultimate realities. Who knows what they are? We deal in appearances. There was very little manipulation of the facts in this case, no actual falsification of documents. True, the boy had to tell one or two little lies about his childhood and his parents. What did a few little lies matter? They made Mrs. Galton just as happy as if he was her real grandson. And if she chose to leave him her money, that was her affair.'

'Has she made a new will?'

'I believe so. I had no part in it. I advised her to get another lawyer.'

'Wasn't that taking a chance?'

'Not if you know Maria Galton as I know her. Her reactions are so consistently contrary that you can depend on them. I got her to make a new will by urging her not to. I got her interested in looking for Tony by telling her it was hopeless. I persuaded her to hire you by opposing the whole idea of a detective.'

'Why me?'

'Schwartz was prodding me, and I had to get the ball rolling. I couldn't take the chance of finding the boy for myself. I had to have someone to do it for me, someone I could trust. I thought, too, if we could get past you, we could get past anyone. And if we failed to get past you, I thought you'd be—more flexible, shall we say?'

'Crooked, shall we say?'

Sable winced at the word. Words meant more to him than the facts they stood for.

A door opened at the end of the corridor, and Alice Sable and Dr. Howell came toward us. She hung on the doctor's arm, depressed and freshly groomed and empty-faced under her makeup. He was carrying a white leather suitcase in his free hand.

'Sable has made a full confession,' I said to Howell. 'Phone the Sheriff's office, will you?'

'I already have. They ought to be here shortly. I'm taking Mrs. Sable back where she'll be properly attended to.' He added in an undertone: 'I hope this will be a turning-point for her.'

'I hope so, too,' Sable said. 'Honestly I do.'

Howell made no response. Sable tried again:

'Good-bye, Alice. I really do wish you well, you know.'

Her neck stiffened, but she didn't look at him. She went out leaning on Howell. Her brushed hair shone like gold in the sunlight. Fool's gold. I felt a twinge of sympathy for Sable. He hadn't been able to carry her weight. In the stretching gap between his weakness and her need, Culligan had driven a wedge, and the whole structure had fallen.

Sable was a subtle man, and he must have noticed some change in my expression:

'You surprise me, Lew. I didn't expect you to bear down so hard. You have a reputation for tempering the wind to the shorn lamb.'

'Stabbing Culligan to death wasn't exactly a lamblike gesture.'

'I had to kill him. You don't seem to understand.'

'On account of your wife?'

'My wife was only the beginning. He kept moving in on me. He wasn't content to share my wife and my house. He was very hungry, always wanting more. I finally saw that he wanted it all to himself. Everything.' His voice trembled with indignation. 'After all my contributions, all my risks, he was planning to shut me out.'

'How could he?'

'Through the boy. He had something on Theo Fredericks. I never learned what it was, I couldn't get it out of either of them. But Culligan said that it was enough to ruin my whole plan. It was his plan, too, of course, but he was irresponsible enough to wreck it unless he got his way.'

'So you killed him.'

'The chance offered itself, and I took it. It wasn't premeditated.'

'No jury will believe that, after what you did to your wife. It looks as premeditated as hell. You waited for your chance to knock off a defenceless man, and then tried to push the guilt on to a sick woman.'

'She asked for it,' he said coldly. 'She wanted to believe that she killed him. She was half-convinced before I talked to her, she felt so guilty about her affair with him. I only did what any man would do under the circumstances. She'd seen me stab him. I had to do something to purge her mind of the memory.'

'Is that what you've been doing on your long visits, pounding guilt into her mind?'

He struck the wall with the flat of his hand. 'She was the cause of the trouble. She brought him into our life. She deserved to suffer for it. Why should I do all the suffering?'

'You don't have to. Spread it around a little. Tell me how to get to the Fredericks boy.'

He glanced at me from the corners of his eyes. 'I'd want a

quid pro quo.' The legal phrase seemed to encourage him. He went on in quickening tempo until he was almost chattering: 'As a matter of fact, he should take the blame for most of this frightful mess. If it will help to clear up the matter, I'm willing to turn state's evidence. Alice can't be made to testify against me. You don't even know that what she said was true. How do you know her story is true? I may be simply covering up for her.' His voice was rising like a maniac hope.

'How do you know you're alive, Sable? I want your partner. He was in San Mateo this morning. Where is he headed for?'

'I haven't the faintest idea.'

'When did you see him last?'

'I don't know why I should co-operate with you if you won't co-operate with me.'

I still had his empty rifle in my hands. I reversed it and raised it like a club. I was angry enough to use it if I had to.

'This is why.'

He pulled his head back so sharply it rapped the wall. 'You can't use third-degree methods on me. It isn't legal.'

'Stop blowing bubbles, Sable. Was Fredericks here last night?'

'Yes. He wanted me to cash a cheque for him. I gave him all the cash I had in the house. It amounted to over two hundred dollars.'

'What did he want it for?'

'He didn't tell me. Actually, he wasn't making too much sense. He talked as if the strain had been too much for him.'

'What did he say?'

'I can't reproduce it verbatim. I was upset myself. He asked me a lot of questions, which I wasn't able to answer, about Anthony Galton and what happened to him. The imposture must have gone to his head; he seemed to have himself convinced that he actually was Galton's son.'

'Was Sheila Howell with him?'

'Yes, she was present, and I see what you mean. He may have been talking for her benefit. If it was an act, she was certainly taken in by it. But as I said, he seemed to be taken in by it himself. He became very excited, and threatened me with force unless I told him who murdered Galton. I didn't know what to tell him. I finally thought of the name of that woman in Redwood City—the Galtons' former nurse.'

'Mrs. Matheson?'

'Yes. I had to tell him something, get rid of him some-how.'

A patrol car whined up the hill and stopped in front of the house. Conger and another deputy climbed out. Sable was going to have a hard time getting rid of them.

CHAPTER THIRTY-ONE

They dropped me at the airport, and I got aboard a plane. It was the same two-engine bucket, on the same flight, that had taken me north three weeks ago. Even the stewardess was the same. Somehow she looked younger and more innocent. Time had stood still for her while it had been rushing me along into premature middle age.

She comforted me with Chiclets and coffee in paper cups. And there was the blessed Bay again, and the salt flats.

The Matheson house was closed up tight, with the drapes pulled over the windows, as if there was sickness inside. I asked my cab-driver to wait and knocked on the front door. Marian Matheson answered it herself.

She had been living on my time-schedule, and growing old rapidly. There was more grey in her hair, more bone in her face. But the process of change had softened her. Even her voice was gentler:

'I've been sort of expecting you. I had another visitor this morning.'

'John Galton?'

'Yes. John Galton—the little boy I looked after in Luna Bay. It was quite an experience meeting him after all these years. And his girl, too. He brought his girl along.' She hesi-tated, then opened the door wider. 'Come in if you want.'

She took me into the darkened living-room and placed me in a chair.

'What did they come to you for, Mrs. Matheson?'

'The same thing you did. Information.'

'What about?'

'That night. I thought he had a right to know the truth, so I told him all I told you, about Culligan and Shoulders.' Her answer was vague; perhaps she was trying to keep the memory vague in her mind.

180

'What was his reaction?'

'He was very interested. Naturally. He really pricked up his ears when I told him about the rubies.'

'Did he explain his interest in the rubies?'

'He didn't explain anything. He got up and left in a hurry, and they rocketed off in that little red car of his. They didn't even wait to drink the coffee I was brewing.'

'Were they friendly?'

'To me, you mean? Very friendly. The girl was lovely to me. She confided they were going to get married as soon as her young man worked his way out of the darkness.'

'What did she mean by the darkness?'

'I don't know, that was just the phrase she used.' But she squinted at the sunlight filtering through the drapes, like someone who understood what darkness meant. 'He seemed to be very concerned about his father's death.'

'Did he say what he was going to do next, or where he was going?'

'No. He did ask me how to get to the airport—if there were buses running. It seemed kind of funny, him asking about buses when he had a brand-new sports car standing out front.'

'He's evading arrest, Mrs. Matheson. He knew his car would be spotted right away if he parked it at the airport.'

'Who wants to arrest him?'

'I do, for one. He isn't Galton's son, or Brown's son. He's an impostor.'

'How can that be? Why, he's the spitting image of his father.'

'Appearances can be deceiving, and you're not the first one to be taken in by his appearance. His real name is Theo Fredericks. He's a small-time crook from Canada with a record of violence.'

Her hand went to her mouth. 'From Canada, did you say?'

'Yes. His parents run a boardinghouse in Pitt, Ontario.'

'But that's where they're going, Ontario. I heard him say to her, when I was out in the kitchen, that there were no direct flights to Ontario. That was just before they took off from here.'

'What time were they here?'

'It was early in the morning, just past eight. They were waiting out front when I got back from driving Ron to the station.'

I looked at my watch. It was nearly five. They had had almost nine hours. With the right connections, they could be in Canada by now.

And with the right connections. I could be there in another eight or nine hours.

Mrs. Matheson followed me to the door. 'Is this trouble going to go on for ever?'

'We're coming to the end of it,' I said. 'I'm sorry I couldn't keep you out of it after all.'

'It's all right. I've talked it out with Ron. Whatever comes up—if I have to testify in court or anything—we can handle it together. My husband is a very good man.'

'He has a good wife.'

'No.' She shook the compliment off her fingers. 'But I love him and the boy, and that's something. I'm glad it all came out between me and Ron. It's a big load off my heart.' She smiled gravely. 'I hope it works out some way for that young girl. It's hard to believe that her boy is a criminal. But I know how these things can be in life.'

She looked up at the sun.

On the way to International Airport my taxi passed the Redwood City courthouse. I thought of stopping and getting in touch with Trask. Then I decided not to. It was my case, and I wanted to end it.

Perhaps I had a glimmering of the truth.

CHAPTER THIRTY-TWO

I drove my rented car into Pitt at three o'clock, the darkest hour of the night. But there were lights in the red house on the riverbank. Mrs. Fredericks came to the door fully dressed in rusty black. Her heavy face set stubbornly when she saw me.

'You got no call coming here again. What do you think you're after? I didn't know those Hamburg fellows were wanted by the police.'

'They're not the only ones. Has your son been here?'

'Theo?' Her eyes and mouth sought obtusely for an answer. 'He hasn't come near me for years.'

A husky whisper rose from the shadows behind her. 'Don't believe her, mister.' Her husband came forward, supporting himself with one hand against the wall. He looked and sounded very drunk: 'She'd lie her false heart out for him.'

'Hold your tongue, old man.'

Dark anger filled her eyes like a seepage of ink: I'd seen the same thing happen to her son. She turned on Fredericks, and he backed away. His face looked porous and moist like a deliquescent substance. His clothes were covered with dust.

.'Have you seen him, Mr. Fredericks?'

'No. Lucky for him I was out, or I'd of shown him what's what.' His hatchet profile chopped the air. 'She saw him, though.'

'Where is he, Mrs. Fredericks?'

Her husband answered for her: 'She told me they went to check in at the hotel, him and the girl both.'

Some obscure feeling, guilt or resentment, made the woman say: 'They didn't have to go to the hotel. I offered them the use of my house. I guess it isn't good enough for mucky-mucks like her.'

'Is the girl all right?'

'I guess so. Theo's the one that's got me worried. What did he want to come here for, after all these years? I can't figure him out.'

'He always did have crazy ideas,' Fredericks said. 'But he's crazy like a fox, see. Watch him close when you go to nab him. He talks smooth, but he's a real snake-in-the-grass.'

'Where is this hotel?'

'Downtown. The Pitt Hotel—you can't miss it. Just keep us out of it, eh? He'll try to drag us into his trouble, but I'm a respectable man—'

His wife cried: 'Shut up, you. I want to see him again if you don't.'

I left them locked in the combat which seemed the normal condition of their nights.

The hotel was a three-story red brick building with one lighted window on the second floor corner. One other light was burning in the lobby. I punched the handbell on the desk. A middle-aged little man in a green eyeshade came yawning out of a dark room behind it.

'You're up early,' he said.

'I'm up late. Can you rent me a room?'

'Sure can. I got more vacancies than you can shake a stick at. With or without bath?'

'With.'

'That will be three dollars.' He opened the heavy leather-cornered register, and pushed it across the desk. 'Sign on the line.'

I signed. The registration above my signature was: Mr. and Mrs. John Galton, Detroit, Michigan.

'I see you have some other Americans staying here.'

'Yeah. Nice young couple, checked in late last night. I believe they're honeymooners, probably on their way to Niagara Falls. Anyway, I put them in the bridal chamber.'

'Corner room on the second floor?'

He gave me a sharp dry look. 'You wouldn't want to disturb them, mister.'

'No, I thought I'd say hello to them in the morning.'

'Better make it late in the morning.' He took a key from a hook and dropped it on the desk. 'I'm putting you in two-ten, at the other end. I'll show you up if you want.'

'Thanks, I can find it by myself.'

I climbed the stairs that rose from the rear of the lobby. My legs were heavy. In the room, I took my .32 automatic out of my overnight bag and inserted one of the clips I had brought for it. The carpet in the dim corridor was threadbare, but it was thick enough to silence my footsteps.

There was still light in the corner room, spilling over through the open transom. A sleeper's heavy breathing came over, too, a long sighing choked off and then repeated. I tried the door. It was locked.

Sheila Howell spoke clearly from the darkness: 'Who is that?'

I waited. She spoke again:

'John. Wake up.'

'What is it?' His voice sounded nearer than hers.

'Somebody's trying to get in.'

I heard the creak of bed springs, the pad of his feet. The brass doorknob rotated.

He jerked the door open, stepped out with his right fist cocked, saw me and started to swing, saw the gun and froze. He was naked to the waist. His muscles stood out under his pale skin.

'Easy, boy. Raise your hands.'

'This nonsense isn't necessary. Put the gun down.'

'I'm giving the orders. Clasp your hands and turn around, walk slowly into the room.'

He moved reluctantly, like stone forced into motion. When he turned, I saw the white scars down his back, hundreds of

184

them, like fading cuneiform cuts.

Sheila was standing beside the rumpled bed. She had on a man's shirt which was too big for her. The shirt and the lipstick smudged on her mouth gave her a dissolute air.

'When did you two have time to get married?'

'We didn't. Not yet.' A blush mounted like fire from her neck to her cheekbones. 'This isn't what you think. John shared my room because I asked him to. I was frightened. And he slept across the foot of the bed, so there.'

He made a quelling gesture with his raised hands. 'Don't tell him anything. He's on your father's side. Anything we say he'll twist against us.'

'I'm not the twister, Theo.'

He turned on me, so suddenly I almost shot him. 'Don't call me by that name.'

'It belongs to you, doesn't it?'

'My name is John Galton.'

'Come off it. Your partner, Sable, made a full confession to me yesterday afternoon.'

'Sable is not my partner. He never was.'

'Sable tells a different story, and he tells it very well. Don't get the idea that he's covering up for you. He'll be turning state's witness on the conspiracy charge to help him with the murder charge.'

'Are you trying to tell me that Sable murdered Culligan?'

'It's hardly news to you, is it? You sat on the information while we were wasting weeks on a bum lead.'

The girl stepped between us. 'Please. You don't understand the situation. John had his suspicions of Mr. Sable, it's true, but he wasn't in any position to go to the police with them. He was under suspicion himself. Won't you put that awful gun away, Mr. Archer? Give John a chance to explain?'

Her blind faith in him made me angry. 'His name isn't John. He's Theo Fredericks, a local boy who left Pitt some years ago after knifing his father.'

'The Fredericks person is not his father.'

'I have his mother's word for it.'

'She's lying,' the boy said.

'Everybody's lying but you, eh? Sable says you're a phony, and he ought to know.'

'I let him think it. The fact is, when Sable first approached me I didn't know who I was. I went into the deal he offered me partly in the hope of finding out.'

'Money had nothing to do with it?'

'There's more than money to a man's inheritance. Above everything else, I wanted to be sure of my identity.'

'And now you are?'

'Now I am. I'm Anthony Galton's son.'

'When did this fortunate revelation strike you?'

'You don't want a serious answer, but I'll give you one anyway. It grew on me gradually. I think it began when Gabe Lindsay saw something in me I didn't know was there. And then Dr. Dineen recognized me as my father's son. When my grandmother accepted me, too, I thought it must be true. I didn't know it was true until these last few days.'

'What happened in the last few days?'

'Sheila believed me. I told her everything, my whole life, and she believed me.'

He glanced at her, almost shyly. She reached for his hand. I began to feel like an intruder in their room. Perhaps he sensed this shift in the moral balance, because he began to talk about himself in a deeper, quieter tone:

'Actually, it goes back much further. I suspected the truth about myself, or part of it, when I was a little kid. Nelson Fredericks never treated me as if I belonged to him. He used to beat me with a belt-buckle. He never gave me a kind word. I knew he couldn't possibly be my father.'

'A lot of boys feel like that about their real fathers.'

Sheila moved closer to him, in a tender protective movement, pressing his hand unconsciously to her breast. 'Please let him tell his story. I know it sounds wild, but it's only as wild as life. John's telling you the honest truth, so far as he knows it.'

'Assuming that he is, how far does he know it? Some very earnest people have fantastic ideas about who they are and what they've got coming to them.'

I expected him to flare up again. He surprised me by saying: 'I know, it's what I was scared of, that I was hipped on the subject. I really used to be hipped when I was a boy. I imagined I was the prince in the poorhouse, and so on. My mother encouraged me. She used to dress me up in velvet suits and tell me I was different from the other kids.

'Even before that, though, long before, she had a story that she used to tell me. She was a young woman then. I remember her face was thin, and her hair hadn't turned grey. I was only a toddler, and I used to think it was a fairy-tale. I realize now it was a story about myself. She wanted me to know about myself, but she was afraid to come right out with it.

'She said that I was a king's son, and we used to live in a palace in the sun. But the young king died and the bogeyman stole us away to the caves of ice where nothing was nice. She made a sort of rhyme of it. And she showed me a gold ring with a little red stone set in it that the king had left her for a remembrance.'

He gave me a curious questioning look. Our eyes met solidly for the first time. I think the reality formed between us then.

'A ruby?' I said.

'It must have been. I talked to a woman named Matheson yesterday in Redwood City. You know her, don't you, and you've heard her story? It made sense of some of the things that had puzzled me, and it confirmed what Culligan told me long before. He said that my stepfather was an ex-convict whose real name was Fred Nelson. He had taken my mother out of a place called the Red Horse Inn and made her his— lover. She married my father after Nelson was sent to prison. But he escaped, and found them, and murdered my father.' His voice had sunk almost out of hearing.

'When did Culligan tell you this?'

'The day I ran away with him. He'd just had a fight with Fredericks about his board bill. I listened to it from the cellar stairs. They were always fighting. Fredericks was older than Culligan, but he gave him an awful lacing, worse than usual, and left him unconscious on the kitchen floor. I poured water on Culligan's face and brought him to. It was then he told me that Fredericks killed my father. I got a butcher knife out of the drawer, and hid it upstairs in my room. When Fredericks tried to lock me in, I stabbed him in the guts.

'I thought I'd killed him. By the time I saw a newspaper and found out that I hadn't, I was across the border. I rode through Detroit tunnel under the burlaps in an empty truck-trailer. The border police didn't find me, but they caught Culligan. I didn't see him again until last winter. Then he claimed that he'd been lying to me. He said that Fredericks had nothing to do with my father's death, that he'd simply blamed Fredericks to get back at him, through me.

'You can see why I decided to play along with Culligan and his scheme. I didn't know which of his stories was true, or if the truth was something else again. I even suspected that Culligan had killed my father himself. How else would he know about the murder?'

'He was involved in it,' I said. 'It's why he changed his story when he wanted to use you again. It's also the reason he couldn't admit to other people, even Sable, that he knew who you were.'

'How was he involved?'

How wasn't he? I thought. His life ran through the case like a dirty piece of cord. He had marked Anthony Galton for the axe and Anthony Galton's murderer for the knife. He had helped a half-sane woman to lose her money, then sold her husband a half-sane dream of wealth. Which brought him to the ironic day when his half-realities came together in a final reality, and Gordon Sable killed him to preserve a lie.

'I don't understand,' John said. 'What did Culligan have to do with my father's death?'

'Apparently he was the finger man. Have you talked to your mother about the circumstances of the killing? She was probably a witness.'

'She was more than that.' The words almost strangled him.

Sheila turned to him anxiously. 'John?' she said. 'Johnny?'

He made no response to her. His gaze was dark and inward:

'Even last night she was lying to me, trying to pretend that I was Fredericks's son, that I never had another father. She's stolen half my life away already. Isn't she satisfied?'

'You haven't seen Fredericks?'

'Fredericks has gone away, she wouldn't tell me where. But I'll find him.'

'He can't be far. He was at home an hour ago.'

'Damn you! Why didn't you say so?'

'I just did. I'm wondering now if I made a mistake.'

John got the message. He didn't speak again until we were a few blocks from his mother's house. Then he turned in the seat and said across Sheila:

'Don't worry about me. There's been enough death and violence. I don't want any more of it.'

Along the riverside street the rooftops thrust their dark angles up against a whitening sky. I watched the boy as he got out of the car. His face was pinched and pale as a revenant's. Sheila held his arm, slowing his abrupt movements.

I knocked on the front door. After a long minute, the door was unlocked from the inside. Mrs. Fredericks peered out at us.

'Yes? What now?'

John brushed past me, and faced her on the threshold:

'Where is he?'

'He went away.'

'You're a liar. You've lied to me all your life.' His voice broke, and then resumed on a different, higher note. 'You knew he killed my father, you probably helped him. I know you helped him to hush it up. You left the country with him, changed your name when he did.'

'I'm not denying that much,' she said levelly.

His whole body heaved as if in nausea. He called her an ugly name. In spite of his promise to me, he was on the thin edge of violence. I laid one hand on his shoulder, heavily:

'Don't be too hard on your mother. Even the law admits mitigation, when a woman is dominated or threatened by a man.'

'But that isn't the case. She's still trying to protect him.'

'Am I?' the woman said. 'Protect him from what?'

'From punishment for murder.'

She shook her head solemnly. 'It's too late for that, son. Fredericks has took his punishment. He said he would rather have digger get him than go back behind walls. Fredericks hung himself, and I didn't try to argue him out of doing it.'

We found him in a back room on the second floor. He was on an old brass bed, in a half-sitting position. A piece of heavy electrical cord was tied to the head of the bed and wrapped several times around his neck. The free end of the cord was clenched in his right hand. There was no doubt that he had been his own executioner.

'Get Sheila out of here,' I said to John.

She stood close to him. 'I'm all right. I'm not afraid.'

Mrs. Fredericks came into the doorway, heavy and panting. She looked at her son with her head up:

'This is the end of it. I told him it was him or you, and which it was going to be. I couldn't go on lying for him, and let you get arrested instead of him.'

He faced her, still the accuser. 'Why did you lie for so long? You stayed with him after he killed my father.'

'You got no call to judge me for doing that. It was to save your life that I married him. I saw him cut off your daddy's head with an axe, fill it with stones, and chuck it in the sea. He said that if I ever told a living soul, that he would kill you, too. You were just a tiny baby, but that wouldn't of stopped him. He held up the bloody axe over your crib and made me swear to marry him and keep my lips shut for ever. Which

I have done until now.'

'Did you have to spend the rest of your life with him?'

'That was my choice,' she said. 'For sixteen years I stood between you and him. Then you ran away and left me alone with him. I had nobody else left in my life excepting him. Do you understand what it's like to have nobody at all, son?'

He tried to speak, to rise to the word, but the gorgon past held him frozen.

'All I ever wanted in my life,' she said, 'was a husband and a family and a place I could call my own.'

Sheila made an impulsive movement toward her. 'You have us.'

'Aw, no. You don't want me in your life. We might as well be honest about it. The less you see of me, the better you'll like it. Too much water flowed under the bridge. I don't blame my son for hating me.'

'I don't hate you,' John said. 'I'm sorry for you, Mother. And I'm sorry for what I said.'

'You and who else is sorry?' she said roughly. 'You and who else?'

He put his arm around her, awkwardly, trying to comfort her. But she was past comforting, perhaps beyond sorrow, too. Whatever she felt was masked by unfeeling layers of flesh. The stiff black silk she was wearing curved over her breast like armour.

'Don't bother about me. Just take good care of your girl.'

Somewhere outside, a single bird raised its voice for a few notes, then fell into abashed silence. I went to the window. The river was white. The trees and buildings on its banks were resuming their colours and shapes. A light went on in one of the other houses. As if at this human signal, the bird raised its voice again.

Sheila said: 'Listen.'

John turned his head to listen. Even the dead man seemed to be listening.

Ross Macdonald

'Classify him how you will, he is one of the best American novelists now operating . . . all he does is keep on getting better.' *New York Times Book Review*. 'Ross Macdonald must be ranked high among American thriller-writers. His evocations of scenes and people are as sharp as those of Raymond Chandler.' *Times Literary Supplement*. 'Lew Archer is, by a long chalk, the best private eye in the business.' *Sunday Times*

The Instant Enemy

The Moving Target

The Underground Man

The Way Some People Die

The Doomsters

The Ivory Grin

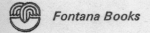 *Fontana Books*

Fontana Books

Fontana is best known as one of the leading paperback publishers of popular fiction and non-fiction. It also includes an outstanding, and expanding, section of books on history, natural history, religion and social sciences.

Most of the fiction authors need no introduction. They include Agatha Christie, Hammond Innes, Alistair MacLean, Catherine Gaskin, Victoria Holt and Lucy Walker. Desmond Bagley and Maureen Peters are among the relative newcomers.

The non-fiction list features a superb collection of animal books by such favourites as Gerald Durrell and Joy Adamson.

All Fontana books are available at your bookshop or newsagent; or can be ordered direct. Just fill in the form below and list the titles you want.

FONTANA BOOKS, Cash Sales Department, G.P.O. Box 29, Douglas, Isle of Man, British Isles. Please send purchase price, plus 6p per book. Customers outside the U.K. send purchase price, plus 7p per book. Cheque, postal or money order. No currency.

NAME (Block letters) _____

ADDRESS _____

_____

_____